A Stranger's Presence

It was very still in the hollow, the pond like a sheet of glass. I could even see the racing clouds above in the water's reflection. But as lovely as the setting was, I was much more conscious of this stranger than any scenery.

"I worry for your safety, Kate," he said as he joined me. "I believe you may be in some danger at Bryce House."

"Oh, I should think the ghosts would bear no grudge against me, my lord," I said, feigning courage as I tried to ignore how close to me he stood.

"Did I mention any ghosts?" he asked, mildly. "But I suppose they could be a source of danger. Certainly I cannot remember a time when they have been so active."

The Scent of Lilacs

Barbara Hazard

A SIGNET BOOK

SIGNET
Published by New American Library, a division of
Penguin Putnam Inc., 375 Hudson Street,
New York, New York 10014, U.S.A.
Penguin Books Ltd, 27 Wrights Lane,
London W8 5TZ, England
Penguin Books Australia Ltd, Ringwood,
Victoria, Australia
Penguin Books Canada Ltd, 10 Alcorn Avenue,
Toronto, Ontario, Canada M4V 3B2
Penguin Books (N.Z.) Ltd, 182–190 Wairau Road,
Auckland 10, New Zealand

Penguin Books Ltd, Registered Offices:
Harmondsworth, Middlesex, England

First published by Signet, an imprint of New American Library,
a division of Penguin Putnam Inc.

First Printing, August 2001
10 9 8 7 6 5 4 3 2 1

Chapter One

I should have known there was something wrong the day we arrived at Bryce House and all the servants left the premises at dusk.

I was in a small parlor on the ground floor at the time, investigating its possibilities as a retreat. My brother had already commandeered the library for his own; indeed, before he even began to see to the disposition of his trunks, he set to work unpacking his books and papers.

We had arrived later than anticipated, slowed by a sudden violent thunderstorm. But by the time we turned into the gates that marked the entrance, the storm had rumbled off to the east and the sun shone warmly again, as if to welcome us to the place that was to be our new home.

Now I held back the curtains and counted the servants trudging past outside. The four maids, the footman, and the gardener and his helper. Bemused, I turned to the butler, a Mr. Harper, and inquired where they were going.

"They do not sleep at Bryce House, miss," the elderly man explained in solemn tones. "They always leave at dusk and return shortly after dawn, winter or summer."

"How unusual," I managed to say. "I am glad that at least you and your wife remain with us."

He coughed behind his gloved hand. "As to that, miss, we will be leaving too, as soon as Mrs. Harper lays out supper for you and Mr. Whittingham. We live in the gatehouse you passed when you entered the grounds."

"I have never heard of such arrangements," I said sharply, sure the servants thought to take advantage of our youth and inexperience. "Why do none of you live in, as is customary?"

Harper looked at some point over my left shoulder. "It has always been the custom here, miss, for the servants to return to their homes in the village at night."

"Well, I do not care for such a custom," I said, not even trying to hide my frown. I was tired from three days of traveling and did not need any vexations to set me off. "What are we to do if we require something at night?"

"Mr. Whittingham never did, miss. Very self-sufficient the master was, miss," Harper informed me.

"Indeed. I am sorry we do not have his fortitude. You may tell the others when they return tomorrow that from now on it will be necessary for them to sleep in the house. Otherwise we will have to engage new help."

"They'll not stay, not a one of them, miss," Harper said. His words were insolent but his tone was not. Instead, he sounded almost sorry about it, as if he hated to disappoint me.

I dropped the curtain and leaned against a heavy mahogany table that was set in the bay window. "And why is that, pray?" I asked, trying to keep any distress from showing in my voice. "Never tell me the house has a ghost."

"If it were only the one, miss," Harper replied mournfully. "But unfortunately there are two of them."

My brows rose. "And that is why everyone leaves at dusk? These spirits must be horrible indeed. And, I assume, very active?"

"They can be, er, tiresome," Harper admitted. "It seems to set them off when there are a great many people in the house, so the master took to sending everyone away at dusk. Quieted them down wonderful, or so he told me. And, of course, it was the only way he could staff the house."

"I wonder how they will take my brother's and my appearance here," I said lightly, sure my great-uncle must have been an eccentric to make up such a tale. And what do you suppose he was up to, all by himself here at night?

"It might take them a while to grow accustomed, miss," the butler admitted. "But at least you have been warned."

I took a seat feeling slightly uneasy in spite of my disbelief. Harper seemed so matter-of-fact about these spirits, almost as if they were old family members who had to be accommodated, their difficult little ways tolerated.

"Who are these ghosts?" I asked next. "Does anyone know? Are they male or female, or perhaps one each? And do they haunt alone or as a pair?"

"It is nothing to laugh at, miss, if I may be so bold as to say so," Harper said with dignity, and I composed myself. "There is a lady. She's a proper terror, she is. She wears white and cries all the time—shrieks, too, if she gets upset. The other one, he generally stays in the large blue bedroom, although he's been seen on the stairs. He's tall and he wears a mask and carries a dagger. That's all I remember. I haven't spent the night here myself for fifteen years."

"They are only seen at night?" I asked.

He nodded. "At least so far," he amended.

Mr. Harper's wife, my uncle's cook and housekeeper, appeared in the doorway and dropped me a curtsey. "Supper is laid out in the dining room, Miss Whittingham," she said. She sounded nervous. I wondered if that was because the shadows were lengthening outside the windows. A cloud must have covered the sun then, for it grew quite dark. "Are you ready to leave, Mr. Harper?" she said breathlessly.

He turned and bowed to me. "We shall return at

dawn, miss. I wish you and your brother a good night."

I barely had time to nod before they were gone. For a moment I listened to the sound of their feet hurrying down the hall, the slam of the side door. A moment later, I saw them hurry past the parlor window, Mrs. Harper clutching her shawl close with one hand while she gestured with the other. She was talking to her husband, and I saw him shake his head, looking grim. Then they were gone, disappearing behind some rhododendron bushes.

The house was very quiet now. All I could hear was the casement clock in the hall, ticking away in its steady rhythm. It was such a homey, ordinary sound, I smiled. Ghosts, indeed, I told myself as I went to find my brother. Still, remembering the conditions of my great-uncle's will, I wondered.

We had not known Mr. Daniel Whittingham; in fact, we had barely been aware of his existence when the letter came from his solicitor telling us of his death and saying he had left his entire estate to my brother Edwin. It had been a wondrous thing for both of us. I remembered how buoyed up Edwin had been when he posted down from London to tell me of it. I had been living with my aunt Sadie for the five years since our parents' deaths. Edwin spent most of his time in London, intent on his own business. I loved my aunt and her large, boisterous family, but still I must admit I was not at all sorry to leave them. Edwin's inheritance seemed a gift from heaven.

The will had one strange condition, although I paid little heed to it at the time, which was that in order to inherit, my brother had to spend one entire month at Bryce House. He could leave the grounds but only during the daytime. And if he missed a single night in residence, his inheritance was forfeit. I did ask who would benefit instead, but Edwin said he did not know.

Dazed by his good fortune—for our parents had left us little besides a good name—my brother agreed to the condition and, when I begged to accompany him, welcomed me to the adventure.

And so we had packed up our belongings, taken an emotional and teary farewell of our aunt and her brood, and set off to make our fortune in what had seemed the easiest way possible.

Or so we had thought.

As I crossed the hall, I paused for a moment, sure I had heard a step behind me. But when I whipped around, there was nothing there. I cursed myself for my fast-beating heart, telling myself I must not be such a gullible ninny. I did not believe in ghosts; I was positive my brother did not either. And even if it turned out there were such things, and they did wander about and rap the walls and wail, or whatever they got up to, they could not hurt us. And, I told myself stoutly as I knocked on the library door, a month is not that long a time. We would manage.

I discovered Edwin sitting crosslegged on the floor, bent over a large book on his lap. It was growing dim in the library, and I scolded him as I lit a branch of candles from a spill I got at the fireplace.

"You'll ruin your eyesight, my dear," I said. "Not that you'll heed a thing I say. But do put that book down and pay attention. I have the most diverting thing to tell you."

"Certainly," he said, looking up but keeping his finger at the place he was reading. "I found this among Great-Uncle's books, Kate. It is the finest thing! One of Kerrmeister's earlier works, full of his drawings and studies of moths and butterflies. Why, I have not seen—"

"Later," I interrupted, well accustomed to Edwin's tiresome habit of ignoring everything but his own consuming interests. "I daresay you have not noticed, but all the servants, including the butler and housekeeper, have left the house. They will not be back until dawn, or so Mr. Harper tells me."

"They prefer to return to their homes in the village?" he asked, his eye straying to his book again. "Well, I daresay we will manage, eh, Kate?"

"Oh, indeed we will—if we don't have to fight off the ghosts that Bryce House is famous for."

He looked up at me, that endearing smile of his curving his mobile mouth and lighting his handsome hazel eyes. "Ghosts?" he drawled. "But how exciting. I shall look forward to meeting them. Did Harper describe them?"

I told him about the shrieking lady and the stair-walking gentleman, and he laughed. He was interested enough to put his book aside and get up to pour us both a glass of sherry. Sitting across from each other before the cozy fireplace, which I saw had a full hod of coal beside it, and with the candles cheering the room and chasing away any lingering shadows, I had to admit the very idea of restless spirits seemed ridiculous.

"Do you suppose that is why Great-Uncle made the condition he did?" I asked idly, admiring the golden color of the sherry before I took a sip. "That you must remain here for an entire month? If that is the case, it is a shame we did not choose February. It only has twenty-eight days."

"You forget that Uncle Daniel stipulated our visit must be in October. It is the first of the month tomorrow. Perhaps we shall be delighted when All Hallow's arrives. Well, Kate, are you still game? There is still time to flee."

"Ha!" I said scornfully. "I suggest we forget such silly tales. They were probably started by some impressionable little housemaid given to hysterics, and then embellished by other servants over the years until all it takes to send everyone into a frenzy is the ordinary sounds any house makes as it settles. Why, I remember how the third step from the top always creaked horribly at Aunt Sadie's."

"But not, I would wager, until someone stepped on it," my brother said. "Still, it is true that houses creak, and this is an especially elderly one. Remember that as the days grow colder. Let me have no complaints from you about ghostly apparitions and groaning walls."

I smiled and nodded, but still I felt vaguely uneasy. Bryce House was, as my brother had pointed out, a very old house. Built in the 1600's of gray stone, it had three stories, odd corners, and wandering corridors with two steps up and the three down, seemingly at random. It was set in thirty acres of grounds enclosed by a high stone wall and very near the village of Lechton, a pretty place from what I had been able to discern through the rain-streaked carriage windows when we arrived.

Not large enough to be a market town, still Lechton sported a mill, a handsome Norman church, and a small inn as well as the usual cottages surrounding the commons and duck pond. I remembered it had been a welcome sight, for we had passed few villages or farms after we left Winchester that morning. Perhaps it was the desolate heathland we drove through, the forests, that made it seem so isolated. But I knew the Solent was near, and the Channel, and I was looking forward to seeing that. I had never been to the sea in my life.

"What are we to do about dinner?" Edwin inquired idly, surprising me, for he cared little for food, eating only when hunger demanded it, and then at irregular hours.

"Mrs. Harper has left a spread for us in the dining room," I reported. "It is not quite what we are used to. Do you think I should engage new servants? Ones more agreeable to staying in the house, as indeed they should?"

Edwin shrugged. "Let us wait and see how we go on," he said, just as I had expected, for like most men, my brother hated change and bother. "Such a move might be taken for arrogance in the village. Besides, the poor things probably need this employment. I saw little else available on our journey here."

"Very well, although I know you say so only because you hate a fuss," I said. "Men!"

He laughed with me, but as our laughter died away, I heard a noise. It was not the house creaking, nor a branch tapping against a windowpane. It was a noise I associated with human beings, and it was right over our heads. I saw Edwin was looking at the ceiling and frowning as the sounds came again. Footsteps, hasty footsteps walking back and forth across a bare floor. All at once they stopped, and distantly I could hear careful rapping.

"That will be The Gentleman, no doubt," Edwin said in a normal voice. I was glad he had spoken, for I was sure my voice would have quavered terribly and disgraced me if I tried it. "The one you told me carries a dagger?"

I nodded. "You—you did not choose that room, did you, Edwin?" I asked. We had inspected all the family bedrooms. I had selected one that overlooked the garden. Where my brother had decided to sleep, I had no idea.

"No, I took the one across the hall," he said. "It is fortunate I did so. Perhaps, since we have left his favorite haunt unsullied, the dagger wielder will not bother us."

"I hope The Lady did not like the room I chose," I said after a moment spent listening carefully. There was not so much as a creak anywhere, but I could not relax. There was no way the noises we had heard could have been anything but footsteps. Since we were the only two living beings in the house now, the noises we had heard proved Bryce House was indeed haunted. And night was drawing on. Indeed, the sun had gone behind the beech trees at the edge of the grounds just since I had entered the library. I wondered how I would manage to sleep tonight, and, more importantly, whether Edwin would call me coward if I changed my room to one closer to his own.

Chapter Two

Before we repaired to the dining room and our supper, my brother and I went through the house again, candles held high. You may be very sure I kept close to Edwin's back. I had prevailed on him to carry the poker from the library fireplace, and I noticed he did not scoff at my suggestion as might be expected. But we did not find anything, not even in the room over the library where the sound of footsteps had originated. Except, as I pointed out in a breathless voice, that room had a fitted carpet. The footsteps we had heard had been on bare wood. Feeling like the coward I was, I was glad to retreat to the ground floor again.

After we had selected our supper from the array of covered dishes spread for us and kept warm over spirit lamps, we sat down at the polished table. Our meal looked and smelled delicious, and Harper had left a selection of wine for us to choose from. We might not be waited on hand and foot while we dined, but we would not miss any of the amenities a gentleman's table should display. The dining salon, like all the rooms in Bryce House, was handsome if old fashioned. Its furnishings showed careful care, and the plate and crystal gleamed in the bright light of the two large candelabra I had lit.

For a while we ate in silence, each lost in our own thoughts. At last, feeling better for the hot food, I sipped my wine and said, "Edwin, do you believe in ghosts? Or do you think, as I do, that there could be—*must* be—some other explanation for the footsteps we heard?"

He stopped cutting his beefsteak for a moment and considered, his head bent over his plate. In the candlelight, his blond hair shone.

"Two hours ago I would have said there was no such thing as a shade. But now? Well, how can I continue to hold that view? I shall send to London for some books on the subject. Perhaps we will be able to make sense of it all if we understand it better."

It was a typical answer, for my brother was a scholar. He had been one since boyhood, his greatest joy a book concluded and understood, while another mystery stood ready to challenge him.

"Our great-uncle might have some volumes in the library," I suggested. "I know I would, if I had had to spend my life being haunted.

"But I tell you truly, I am not feeling as kindly toward that old man as I did when I learned of your inheritance," I added darkly. "To think he would expect you to stay here with ghosts and not even warn you about them!"

"Perhaps he thought his death might stop them," Edwin said. "Perhaps he knew who they were, and why they lingered . . ."

"But they have not gone away. At least the dagger-holding gentleman has not."

"See if you can get Harper to tell you more about them," Edwin suggested. "I would do it myself, but I want to keep a degree of distance for the time being while I feel my way."

I nodded, knowing exactly what he meant. I was twenty-two, my brother six years older. We were young enough that it might be considered odd for us to live alone in this huge mansion, ordering servants and making decisions. Indeed, in a way I had felt like a child playing house this afternoon when Mrs. Harper took me over the place. The immaculate still room and the cellar with its rows of preserves from the past summer's bounty, its barrels of beer and salted meat and flour, were intimidating.

"Do you think it might be a good idea to invite

some friends to stay with us for the month?" I asked. "There was nothing in Great-Uncle's will that said you had to be alone here after all. And even though Harper did say the ghosts don't like a lot of people, I say too bad for them. I know I would be considerably cheered by people in the rooms around me, wouldn't you?"

Edwin rose to help himself to more pigeon pie. Over his shoulder he said, "Yes, I would. But I don't suppose any of our friends' servants could be expected to stay if our own won't. And I cannot conceive of Aunt Sadie doing without her Mollie."

"Oh, I was not thinking of Aunt Sadie," I hastened to say as he took his seat again. "She would insist on bringing all the children, even the youngest, and I would not like to frighten them. Besides, she would take over. You know how she is."

"I do indeed. As for the children, even though the boys might frighten the ghosts away, instead of the other way around, I do not want them here with all their noise and confusion. But who else can we invite?"

For a long moment there was silence in the room. The people I knew from Oxfordshire, where my late uncle had his estate, did not seem suitable. Dear Uncle Frank, I thought. I wish I could invite him. He'd put the ghosts in their places in short order. Colonel Frank Ingalls had died in battle during the Peninsula War two years ago, throwing us all into mourning and misery. I had loved him so much, for he had become the father I had lost. Strange that. I had never felt that his wife replaced my mother.

"Perhaps Bethany? And her new husband?" I suggested. I admit I did so reluctantly. My cousin Bethany was two years younger than I, and newly married. Her husband, a Mr. Charles Buffington, had been visiting in the neighborhood when she caught his eye. I did not care for Mr. Buffington. I had been sure from his behavior that he preferred me at first. But someone must have told him I was only a poor relation of the rich Ingalls family, for very shortly thereafter, he turned his attentions to my cousin. But perhaps I was wrong. I had scolded myself before for hasty judgements. It was entirely possible my quick temper and high-handed ways had given the man pause, especially when he compared them to Bethany's sunny disposition. And I did tend to brood and have black days of unhappiness. I admit that.

"Yes, they might do," Edwin said, recalling me to Bryce House and our problem. "There are a couple of fellows I know from my Oxford days who might enjoy the lark, if I dangle a ghost or two before them. Brede, for example. Do you remember me mentioning Brede Hawes? And then there is John Langley, or even Freddie Carr. We shall do famously, you'll see."

By the time we rose from the table, I was feeling much better even though I was still debating whether it would be wiser not to mention the ghosts to Bethany in my invitation lest it frighten her off. Still, if I did not, I risked the chance of being called devious when the truth came out. It was a problem.

I did not sleep well that first night at Bryce House. I had not changed my room after all. It seemed such a bother, for there was no fire laid ready nor any bed made up except in the room I had chosen that afternoon. I took a book up with me in case I could not sleep, and a large branch of candles, determined to have at least one burning all night if it should be necessary.

To my surprise, I fell asleep easily, lulled by the warmth of the fire, the soft feather bed and pillows, and my weary body, tired from the jolting drive here.

It must have been very late when I woke suddenly, sure I was not alone anymore. I lay as I customarily did on my right side, frozen into immobility, not daring to move a muscle, although it was doubtful I could have in any case. There was no sound, no moaning or weeping—certainly no wild shrieks. But still I was positive there was someone in the room with me. I kept my eyes closed tightly and willed whoever—*whatever*—it was to go away. Several moments passed—perhaps only a minute or so, although it seemed forever—before I felt the cold. It was a cold that seemed to grow as it came closer, to deepen and spread. I tried to control my shivering under the formerly warm quilts that covered me. I was not sure whether I trembled from that cold I could feel so clearly or from fright. Probably a bit of both.

After what seemed another endless time, the cold began to recede. As it did so, I became aware of the faint scent of lilacs. It was the merest wisp, and it was entirely the wrong time of year for lilacs, but still I was sure I was not mistaken. I lay rigid for long minutes, afraid something more might happen, waiting for the ghost to go away, silently begging it to leave me alone. I had never been more terrified.

Finally I dared open one eye slightly. The room was dark. There was only a little glow from the banked coals in the fireplace, and none at all from the curtained windows. Suddenly, as sure as I had known before that I had company, now I knew I was alone. That did not make it any easier for me to go back to sleep, though, for the night stretched before me, minute after endless minute. As I strained to see and hear, the casement clock in the hall downstairs struck three and I almost cried out in despair. All that time to wait for dawn. Alone.

I did not dare light a candle or even change my position in bed lest I tempt the ghost to reappear. Instead, I lay there waiting for daylight, dozing now and then from sheer exhaustion but always waking myself before I fell into a deep slumber.

At last I heard the faint sound of birds in the beech wood near the boundary wall, and a short time later, a wren began singing in the bushes beneath my window. As light filled the room, I slept at last, and I did not wake until much later, when I heard the maids talking softly in the hall as they went about their morning chores.

*   *   *

I did not tell Edwin what had happened. He had finished breakfast long before I came down, and Harper informed me was shut up in the library writing letters. I ate quickly, with little appetite. When Harper asked if I wanted him to fetch his wife for the daily interview about menus and the staff's activities, I excused myself. I did not care if he thought me a careless mistress, I could not wait to quit the house. I could tell he longed to ask me if the ghosts had made an appearance, for I could feel him studying me from the sideboard, but I did not satisfy his curiosity. Perhaps the time would come when I could speak openly of them. That time was not now.

I did not bother to fetch a hat and gloves or a shawl from my room. Instead, I let myself out the side door and raced down the broad lawn. I was breathless when I reached the safety of the beech woods, and turning, I leaned against a large tree trunk and stared back the way I had come.

Bryce House sat innocently among its lawns and gardens. Its light stone walls and shining windows gave no hint of the dark mysteries within. As I watched, the gardener came around the back of the house from the direction of the stables, trundling a large wheelbarrow. I could hear him whistling some gay tune. Above him, a maid opened one of my bedroom windows to shake a dustcloth. The two exchanged greetings, laughing as they did so. It was all so normal, so *ordinary*.

I could feel a black mood coming over me, and to keep it from overwhelming me, I made a conscious effort to think of other things—which of Edwin's old school chums might visit, of how my aunt Sadie and the children were, and whether Bethany would come. I reminded myself I must write to her without fail today. The sooner we were surrounded by people— ordinary, happy, *living* people, the better.

There were paths running through the woods, and I set off to explore them. I was not afraid of getting lost, for I knew I would eventually reach the wall that enclosed the property. Had it been built to keep intruders out? Or to hide its secrets?

I stopped when I reached a rustic bench in an open glade. It was set beside a small pool, fed by a brook. It was a peaceful spot, quiet and serene, and thankfully I sank down on the bench to enjoy it. I could not see the house from here. I decided the glade would make a fine refuge for those times when Bryce House became too much for me.

For I had no intention of leaving, no, not even after the night I had just passed. Not before November first anyway. Edwin would need me, and I was determined he would gain the inheritance our great-uncle had left to him. Perhaps the old man had considered this month's trial a test of Edwin's fortitude. Or perhaps, become childish as the elderly do sometimes, he had done it only to amuse himself, giggling as he pictured his heir cowering in terror before the ghosts he himself had long since come to terms with. I wondered if he had even known who they were, as Edwin had suggested. They might even be relatives. And that meant they were our relatives as well, I realized, shivering a little and wishing I had not been so impetuous leaving the house. It was cool in the woods despite the bright sunlight, and I rubbed my arms briskly.

Suddenly I heard the sounds of someone approaching, and I moved to the edge of the bench, prepared to flee. My heart was pounding again, my breath coming in short gasps. I had not considered that the ghosts might not confine themselves to the house, that they might wander the grounds at will. Dear God! Was there no place I could be safe from them?

A man stepped from the shadows across the pool and stared at me as hard as I was staring at him. Thankfully, he was not a ghost. Oh, no, I knew that at once. Tall, with dark hair and a frowning, masculine face that looked as if it had been carved from rough stone, his curiously light eyes held mine. At last, he abandoned my face to inspect my figure, those eyes lingering at breast and hip. It was an experience I found insolent beyond anything I had ever experienced and it angered me. I rose to my feet, my hands clenched in the folds of my skirts.

"Who are you?" I managed to ask in a reasonably cool, contained voice. "You are trespassing. This is Bryce House land."

He did not bother to answer. Instead he came around the pool toward me. It was only with the greatest effort that I held my ground. My entire being cried for flight, for I knew he might be dangerous. Did I say "might?" No, I was sure of it. But I was also sure it would not be to my advantage to show him any fear. And I knew that if I did run, he could catch me easily.

"Who are you?" I repeated. "How did you get in? Bryce House is walled."

A corner of his mouth turned up for a brief moment. "Not entirely," he said in a deep, careless voice. "There is a back gate."

"I shall see that it is padlocked from now on," I dared to say.

"That won't do you a bit of good. I come and go as I please. Have you encountered the ghosts yet?"

My hand crept to my throat. I was speechless.

"But of course you have. That is why you are hiding here in the woods, covered with gooseflesh because you ran out without bothering to get a wrap. That is why your eyes are so big. Why you have circles under them from not sleeping. Whom did you see? The man or the girl?"

"I think it was the girl," I managed to say. "I did not see her. I only felt the cold last night in bed. But there was a scent of some perfume . . ."

I fell silent, wondering why I was telling him, a stranger, these things. "How—how do you know about the ghosts?" I demanded.

"Everyone for miles around knows of them. They are Lechton's most illustrious inhabitants. Not that old Daniel ever let anyone inside to investigate."

"Was he—sane?" I asked, not really caring to hear the answer, but determined to find out as much as I could about our benefactor.

"A good question. I have no idea. We did not socialize. In fact, he never saw anyone that I know of. It came as quite a surprise to the neighborhood to discover he had relatives to leave the place to. Do you think you will be able to last the month? You and your brother?"

I made myself stand taller and straighter, my chin lifted in defiance. "Yes," I said coolly. "Yes, I know we will."

I took a deep breath. "I asked earlier who you are. This is private property. You have no right here."

"That is debatable. What is your name?"

"I am Katharine Whittingham. My brother Edwin is master here now," I said, astonished to find myself so readily telling him everything he wanted to know. Who was he to question me, after all? Still, I felt more at ease, for whoever he was, he was obviously a gentleman. He was dressed casually in country clothes, but his boots gave his status away. Both my father and my uncle had been particular about their boots. I could see the stranger's had been made by a master, even worn and scuffed as they were. Hoby no doubt. He was the best bootmaker in London.

"It will be interesting to see if you survive here a week, Miss Katharine Whittingham," he said. He sounded almost bored. As I stared at him, he turned and went back around the pool the way he had come. I watched him go, speechless. It seemed odd he would leave me so abruptly. Was he doing so because he had learned everything he wanted to know?

Standing in the shadows at the edge of the wood, he turned back. Those fascinating eyes inspected me carefully again. They were gray. I knew that, now. Pure gray.

"You asked my name," he said, pitching his deep voice to be heard over the sounds of the brook. "I am Tremaine. The Earl of Bryce."

Chapter Three

I was still staring after him long after the sounds of his passage died away. He was the Earl of Bryce? Could there be another estate here with the same name as my great-uncle's? It did not seem possible, but not once did I consider that he might be lying. I knew he would not bother to lie. Besides, he was every inch an earl. In fact, now I knew he possessed a title I was surprised that he was not a duke, he was that arrogant.

I sat down again, and the sounds of the brook and some insects busy droning in the grass faded away as I reviewed our conversation. Tremaine had certainly emerged the victor of it, and I squirmed a little. I had been so open, never once refusing to answer his questions. I remembered his last comment then, that he doubted I would last a week at Bryce House. I frowned and vowed he would see I was not so easily frightened, although I probably would be, half to death in fact. Still, I was determined to stay the course. Not only for Edwin's sake either. My aunt and uncle had been dear, generous with their love and their home. But even so I was always aware I was the niece, the cousin, the poor relation. I would not let them provide for me; indeed, Edwin had sent me pin money now and then. It never came at regular times though, and sometimes it would be months before another draft arrived. I managed, but the money was never enough so I could order gowns at will, or buy anything I saw in the shops without thinking of the cost, as Bethany did. I was in desperate need of a new habit at the moment. Idly, I wondered if Edwin would let me have one made if I asked him for it.

A cool breeze stirred the leaves of the beech trees to soft sighing and ran through the grass at my feet, returning me to the present. I rose. I must go back. It was cowardly of me to sit here trying to escape what must be faced. I would see the housekeeper about the menus and the hours meals would be served. We would have to have our dinner at four in the afternoon—country hours to be sure. Even my aunt did not serve dinner until six. But it could not be helped, not if all the servants insisted on leaving at dusk. And I could hardly blame them, I thought as I set out. Not now, knowing what I did, I couldn't.

And I must write to Bethany and my aunt as well, I thought, mentally changing the subject. Perhaps I would have enough time to do an inventory of the linen room.

By late afternoon I had accomplished a great deal. I had even stolen time for a nap and slept easily knowing I was protected by the presence of the servants. But when they all marched off again, followed by Mr. and Mrs. Harper, I made haste to join my brother in the library.

I told him then of the past night's adventure.

"I wonder if you would feel easier if I gave you a pistol," he said. He was not smiling now; indeed, he looked grim.

"What good would it do?" I asked. "You can't shoot ghosts, more's the pity. And I might just shoot myself somehow, since I'm not accustomed to weapons. Er . . . do you have a pistol, Edwin?"

"I didn't until I discovered the munitions room today. It is that narrow closet off the hall we could not open last night. Harper had the key, which is now safely in my possession. I asked him about the room over this one. He says it is called The Gentleman's Room, and always has been. The fitted carpet is a new acquisition, if you consider something installed in 1782 recent."

"So the male ghost had to have lived here before that time," I said slowly.

"Do not rush to assumptions, Kate. He might have been a casual visitor who just happened to die here."

"Violently?" I asked. "Somehow I cannot picture a kindly old gent with a white beard to his waist dying peacefully in bed and then deciding to haunt the house endlessly. Can you?"

Edwin shook his head, his eyes twinkling at my description. "I found some volumes dealing with ghosts on the shelves here. Quite a lot of them, actually. And there was a detailed history of the family as well. That came to light just before you joined me. I suppose I shall have to wait until the morrow to study it."

He sounded so rueful, I almost laughed. What he meant was that he would dearly love to begin immediately, but since he was a gentleman, he could not be so rude to me.

"Do feel free to start now, my dear," I said, rising and giving him a kiss on the top of his head. "I shall read as well, and we can discuss our day later at supper."

"An excellent idea," he said as he opened the large journal on the desk before him without further ado. "I think there are some old novels on the far wall. No, halfway down. There you are."

He disappeared behind his book and I was left with a thin book of poetry and a novel set in tiny print on the flimsiest paper I had ever seen. They were both very dusty, proof my great-uncle had scorned them. I did not blame him after I had read a chapter of one and a verse of the other.

Laying the books aside, I thought again of the Earl of Bryce as I stared into the glowing coal fire. I admit I am hardly an experienced woman, but I know enough of the world to realize that this was a very dangerous man. Dangerous because he was so aggressively masculine. So compelling, yet at the same time so forbidding. Even so tempting. Now why did that word come to mind? I wondered. And when might I see him again? I realized I had quite forgotten to tell the gardener to make sure the back gate was pad-locked from now on. Deliberately? I asked myself. It was a question I somehow did not care to think about.

The Earl of Bryce. I would have to tell Edwin about him at supper. Tremaine. I wondered what his given name was and grinned to myself. Surely not Chauncy or Galahad or even Francis. Edwin coughed, and I got up to pour him some wine. He was lost in the journal he held, bent over the pages as if that way he could absorb them better.

At supper I remembered that I had not told my brother about the lilac scent in my account of last night.

"I wonder why lilacs?" he asked slowly. "Why not lavender, or jasmine, or roses? There must be some special significance about the flower, not that we shall ever find out, more's the pity. It is not the kind of information you get from family papers, fascinating though they may be."

"How far back have you gone?" I asked as I served the pudding. Mrs. Harper was an excellent cook. I must remember to tell her so.

"Not far at all," Edwin said as he took his dish. "Ah, bread pudding! My favorite.

"I suppose we must commend our ancestors for being so wordy. So far that is all they are, for there is no mention of ghosts in the journal."

I almost dropped the serving spoon. "No mention? But how can that be? And why? Surely the ghosts did not originate with Great-Uncle Daniel. Just consider the fitted rug. How stupid!"

We both gave the ceiling a fleeting glance. The Gen-tleman had not paced over our heads in the library this evening. Maybe The Lady would follow his exam-ple and leave me in peace in my new room?

"It is possible they considered it unseemly to have ghosts," Edwin said mildly, amused at my indignation. "You know, the type of thing you hide, like a son's indiscretions or mad old Granny Bess locked in the attic and never discussed in company. All families have their secrets."

I shrugged, wishing ours had not been so private.

"I met a man in the beech wood this morning when I was out for a walk," I told him. "He said his name was Tremaine, and he was the Earl of Bryce. I could not question him, for that was the last thing he said before he left me. How can that be if this is Bryce House? Is he a relative, too?"

"I have no idea, but it is fascinating news," my brother said as he scraped the last bit of pudding from the sides of his dish. He had done so since childhood. It was endearing to see he had not lost the habit in the years we had been apart.

"Let us repair to the library again, and I will try to find some reference to the Tremaine family. I have not come across any so far, but I have barely begun Great-Uncle's entries."

Once there, Edwin disappeared into his research immediately. I discovered there was an earlier journal as well, and I took it to the large center table to study. It was peaceful in the library, just the two of us, intent on our studies, but in only a short time I found myself yawning. My nap had done little to relieve the tiredness I felt. It was senseless to try to concentrate on anything so dry as the journal tonight. I would have to do it tomorrow.

As I closed it reluctantly, I looked up and saw that Edwin was still lost in his own world, tapping a pencil impatiently, now pausing to make a note to himself. I was glad we were together again, although I wondered what would become of me when he married, as he was sure to do some day. His bride would not want his sister to live with them. I wouldn't. Perhaps I might marry before him. It was not inconceivable now that we were landowners as well as Whittinghams. I might well attract some gentleman. I would have a suitable dowry, if not a handsome one. My grandmother had left me a portion, and perhaps Edwin would add to it.

I wondered if the Earl of Bryce, as he called himself, was married. It seemed to me he must be at least thirty, perhaps even more, although it might be his rugged face that gave the impression of age. He probably had a lovely wife and several eager children at home, wherever home might be. Somehow that was a depressing thought, and I was not sorry when Edwin yawned and suggested we go to bed.

It took me a long time to get to sleep that night, but when I did, I slept undisturbed. And when I woke, I lay happily and peacefully in my warm bed, admiring the handsome furnishings of my new room—the gold silk draperies and bed hangings, and a delicate escritoire in particular. As I studied its graceful lines, I could almost see a young girl seated there before the window, writing quickly and then pausing to bite the end of her quill while she considered her next sentence. A pretty girl, with long chestnut hair held back by a green satin ribbon.

As I rang for my morning chocolate, I frowned. It had certainly been a vivid picture I had conjured up, yet I had never thought myself possessed of any great imagination. Perhaps Bryce House was influencing me?

Dressed at last, assisted by a maid who, although proficient, was so bashful that it was difficult to get her to say anything, I went down to the small sitting room I had chosen to use for breakfasts. The dining room was far too big for the two of us, besides being an uncomfortable distance from the kitchens. I wondered why the man who built the place had been so unconcerned about lukewarm food and the number of times the servants would have to run up and down stairs to serve a meal.

Edwin was just finishing his breakfast, the butler in attendance at the sideboard.

"I wonder when we might have a response to our invitations, Edwin," I said as I selected my breakfast at the sideboard. The muffins looked and smelled delicious. "Next week, do you think?"

"Quite possibly. The groom took them to Southampton as soon as they were ready. Harper tells me the mail coach leaves there regularly.

"If you will excuse me, Kate," he said as he pushed his empty plate aside and rose. "I am anxious to return to the family journal."

I waved him away with a smile. Whenever my brother became involved in the pursuit of the latest knowledge he was after, it was almost impossible to distract him from his course, he was so single-minded.

Alone with Harper, I remembered Edwin's suggestion that I question the man about the family ghosts. As he poured me another cup of coffee, I said, "I am delighted to report I spent a peaceful, uneventful night, Harper. May I take it then that the ghosts do not walk all the time?"

He paused to consider. "I cannot say from personal experience, Miss Katharine, of course, but Mr. Whittingham did tell me there were periods when they were quiet."

"I shall pray this is the beginning of one of them, then," I said fervently.

To my surprise, the butler shook his head. "I am sorry, miss, but I feel I must tell you that the month of October is the worst of the year. It seems to upset them for some reason. I would not count on any peace continuing, if I were you. Now, if you had come in November. . . . It seems then almost as if they are exhausted from all of October's activity."

"What do they do?" I asked, putting down my fork, my breakfast forgotten.

He thought again. I was beginning to realize there was no hurrying Mr. Harper.

"Well, The Gentleman taps the walls constantly, and paces his room. Sometimes he walks the upper halls."

He shivered. He was standing close before me and there was no way I could miss that involuntary quiver.

"You did see him there, didn't you, Harper?" I said softly.

Again that long pause. "Yes, once, miss. I had been delayed going home, for Mr. Whittingham was laid down with a slight fever. I had just delivered a tray to him, and he sent me back for a bottle of brandy even though it was coming on dark. After I brought it, when I was hurrying down the corridor, suddenly, there he was."

Harper stopped. His voice at the end had been little more than a whisper, and caught up in his tale, it was all I could do not to grasp his sleeve and beg him to go on. After a long moment, he continued, "He was at the end of the hall near the servants' stairs. I could see him plainly, and when he lifted the dagger and showed it to me, I fled around the corner to the main flight of stairs. He did not follow me, but I swear I heard him cry out."

"How was he dressed?" I asked, eager to place the ghost in some period of history. It might help us figure out who he had been.

"Like a Cavalier, miss, like the painting in the gold drawing room. A starched pleated ruff, satin small clothes and silk hose, even a sweeping hat with a plume. He was all in white like a bridegroom and he— he *glowed* somehow as he wavered there. It—it was terrible. I hope I never have to see him again."

I could tell from his quavering voice that he was distraught, and I was sorry I had asked him to relive such a terrible memory. He was an elderly man and did not deserve such treatment. I had wanted to ask him about The Lady and what other activities she might get up to, but I swallowed my questions and dismissed him.

After my interview with Mrs. Harper, who beamed when I complimented her on her cooking, I sent the footman to the stables to tell the boy I would require a horse with a lady's saddle brought around to the front.

I had worn my old habit to breakfast with a ride in mind. Not only would it get me out of Bryce House for an hour or so, it would also give me the opportunity to explore the neighborhood. I was not going riding with an eye to meeting the Earl of Bryce, of course. Indeed, I told myself I hoped I would be able to avoid him. But I was eager to discover more about him if I could. I was sure Edwin would appreciate it if I did.

The horse I was to ride would hardly have been a candidate for any prestigious race meets or hunts held here and there in the country. It was an elderly, sway-backed mare. But she was placid, and I am not such an expert rider that I demand a fiery steed. Far from it. As the stable boy positioned the steps for me to mount, I told him I would not require his company and set off down the avenue at a sedate trot. The mare seemed to dislike the gait. Perhaps she preferred a walk.

I reached the village without mishap and paused to admire the busy, ordinary scene, so far removed from ghostly images and behavior. I knew I was being watched—indeed, every eye seemed to be on me. When I smiled at the two women hanging over a fence, their washing forgotten, they curtsied, and a man coming out of the inn's taproom was quick to bow. There was no one near the church or the rectory; I decided to wait for Sunday services to inspect it. As I reached the other side of the common, the miller came out of his cottage and bowed and I pulled up. He was a burly fellow with red cheeks and a grin that revealed two missing teeth, and I smiled back at him and introduced myself.

"Aye, missus, I know who ye be," he said as he doffed his cap and revealed a head as devoid of hair as an egg. He told me he was Jack Purdue at my service, and introduced me to his wife and little boys when curiosity brought them out of the cottage.

When Mrs. Purdue offered me a mug of cider, I was quick to accept and allowed the miller to lift me down. The mare snorted as if glad to be relieved of the burden, and we all laughed.

The cider was cold and refreshing. We drank it seated on a rustic bench set against the cottage wall and watched the little boys playing with a kitten.

"Can you tell me where the Earl of Bryce's estate is?" I asked finally.

I saw my hosts exchange glances before Mrs. Purdue said, "That be beyond Bryce House, miss. The earl owns all the land beyond to the village of Naxley. Owns just about everything hereabouts, even Lechton, all except for Bryce House, he do."

"How does it come about he doesn't own that?" I asked as if only casually interested.

Mrs. Purdue looked helplessly to her husband. "As ter that, who can say, missus?" he told me. "It all happened long ago, and the earl don't exactly talk ter me, he don't. Any grain he wants milled comes by his farmers. I don't think I've ever traded words with the earl, not never."

I left shortly thereafter and resumed my ride, for it was obvious I was going to get no more from either of them.

As I left the village and rode off in the direction I had come, I wondered at the information I had been given. It had been revealed reluctantly, and I wondered why. Was the earl a bad landlord? And did he own the mill as well as "everything else?"

I passed the gate to Bryce House, much to the mare's disgust, and headed down the dusty road. We needed a good rain to lay that dust, I thought as I edged my mount aside to allow a dray headed toward Lechton to go by. The farmer and his helper stared at me, and I smiled at them. I knew the country. Edwin and I would be talked about endlessly for several weeks, perhaps even throughout the winter, for we were new gentry and therefore fascinating.

The land I rode through was flat and barren and visible for miles. On the horizon I could see woods, and once a small herd of wild ponies in the distance. But I did not see anything that could have been home to a shepherd, never mind an earl, and at last, when I saw the mare was tiring, I turned for home.

Home? Well, I suppose I must consider the place my home now, in spite of its resident phantoms.

Chapter Four

When I arrived back at Bryce House, I discovered a strange carriage pulled up before the front door. There was no groom; our stableboy was in happy charge of as handsome a team as I have ever seen. My breath caught in my throat, for I was sure the earl had come to call. To take my brother's measure as he had taken mine? I wondered. Slipping to the ground unaided, I slapped the mare on the rump to send her on her way to the stables. There was no danger she would go anywhere else for she had been longing for her stall the past half hour. As I went up the steps I wished I was wearing a new habit instead of my tired faded blue one.

For a moment, waiting for Harper to admit me, I toyed with the idea of changing, but I had no idea how long the earl had been here, and there were such rigid rules set down for the length of calls, I did not dare delay lest I miss him.

"The Reverend Mr. Beasley has called, Miss Katharine," Harper told me in an undertone as I hurried inside. "With his mother and his sister, Miss Sophia Beasley."

I nodded and took a deep breath, wishing I did not feel quite so disappointed. Only because I was anxious to spar with the earl, and more successfully this time, I told myself as I went to the drawing-room doors, all thoughts of changing gone from my head. Edwin had little patience with the clergy. He would need my assistance.

I need not have worried about him. One glance at

the gentleman who rose from the settee was enough to put my mind at rest. Tall and rangy with a long, narrow face, there before me was the epitome of the sporting parson. He had a number of whip points thrust into his lapel, as well as the wind-burned complexion of a man who spent most of his time on horseback. He even smelled of horses. I knew we should feel complimented that he had taken the time to call on such a splendid riding day.

Reverend Beasley professed to be delighted to meet me, and taking my hand in his arm, he drew me forward to his mother's chair. This lady was so short that her feet dangled above the floor, and she was as round as a ball. I could barely hear her, she spoke so softly, which was quite a change from her son's booming voice. Somehow I was sure he had not acquired it in the pulpit.

Introduced to Miss Beasley next, I saw she was a female version of her brother, with the same loud voice. I concluded she must be just as horse-mad.

"I was quite put out you did not stop at the rectory this morning, Miss Whittingham," she said almost at once. "Our maid told us you was riding through the village and even visited at the miller's. My dear! Perhaps you did not know it is not at all necessary to acknowledge millers?"

She tittered and I decided Miss Beasley and I were never going to be fast friends.

"I daresay you are right," was all I said, however, not daring to look Edwin's way lest his expression cause me to lose control of my own. These people were going to be our neighbors. We must learn to live with them.

"Good of her rather, Sophy, doncha think?" the parson said in reproach. "Christian."

"Thank you," I said. Edwin had not rung for refreshments, and detaching my hand from the parson's arm I went to the door to do so.

I took a seat then near Mrs. Beasley, which seemed

to upset her, for she looked nervously from her son to her daughter as if confused by the attention.

"The church is very beautiful. Is it Norman, sir?" I asked, to give her time to recover.

"As you say. Known hereabouts mainly for its stained glass, a later addition of course. Given by Bryce's father. Now there was a horseman for you, Whittingham! Neck or nothing, my dear sir. Neck or nothing! He died cramming a fence though. Horse refused. Bad show, that. Quite a loss to the local hunt it was."

"You hunt, don't you, Miss Whittingham?" his sister demanded.

When I confessed I did not, she gasped, as if I had uttered blasphemy. "Dear me, I hope you ain't one of those *nice* women, always given to saying this or that ain't suitable," she said, leaning forward to pin me to my chair with a pair of dark, accusing eyes.

Sophia Beasley was tall and slim, and almost too sinewy. She looked as if she were made of wire; even her gloved hands looked powerful.

"You have lived here a long time, ma'am?" I asked, turning to Mrs. Beasley to include her in the conversation.

She stared at me, her mouth falling open and her face turning red. Desperately, she looked to her son for help. He was only too happy to take charge again.

"Yes, we have been here fifteen years now," he said. "This is good hunting country. I could not ask for finer, and never mind what some people say about their own little patch of ground. The heath allows for straight, fast runs—you must come out on opening day, November tenth, Mr. Whittingham. I shall be happy to introduce you to the Hunt Master."

Edwin nodded. I dared to glance at him then and saw that he was staring at our guests with a kind of morbid fascination. Silently I gave thanks that Miss Beasley was well past marriageable age, for I judged her to be close to forty. I wouldn't have put it past her to have tried for Edwin if she had been younger, and I wasn't at all sure my dear brother would have been a match for her determination.

Harper and the footman brought in the tea set and some of Mrs. Harper's delicious confections. Mrs. Beasley looked pleased; her son's mouth turned down. "Tea, is it?" he muttered. "Poor stuff!"

Edwin could hardly help hearing him, and he bestirred himself to offer a bumper of ale, or perhaps a glass of claret, to the Reverend Mr. Beasley's satisfaction.

I thought then of my uncle Frank. He had despised hunting parsons, declaring their livings were a disgrace and their usefulness minimal. Until only recently many of them had not even bothered to live among their flocks or hold services. I was sorry myself to think I would have to sit in that beautiful church and listen to this oaf quote scripture. But perhaps he did not bother? It was possible he employed a poor curate to do his work for him. I hoped so.

Mrs. Beasley appeared to enjoy her tea, although she said not a word as she devoured scones and clotted cream. Even her daughter declared these offerings to be not at all shabby.

"I hope you have brought a better mount for your sister than that slug old Daniel kept in his stables. Horse ought to have been put out of its misery a year ago," Beasley told us, made garrulous by a second large glass of claret.

"I have not had the opportunity to inspect my greatuncle's stables as yet," Edwin confessed mildly. I knew my brother was an excellent rider. I wondered why he pretended to be so disinterested.

"You must do so at once, my boy," the parson instructed him. "Does you no consequence to have your sister seen mounted on such a beast. I'll keep an eye out for you. Squire Higley over Naxley way might have something suitable."

When the Reverend Beasley looked longingly at the decanter for the third time in as many minutes, I rose. I had no idea how long the Beasleys had been sitting in the drawing room boring Edwin before my arrival, but it was definitely time for them to take their leave.

"I do hope you will pardon both my brother and me now," I said, holding out my hand to the parson and smiling. "Although it has been delightful to make your acquaintance, I believe we must not take up any more of your time."

Mr. Beasley looked confused, but since I was standing, he was forced to get to his feet as well. His mother bounced up immediately, but I noticed it took Miss Beasley longer, and as she did so, her eyes were narrowed and her face cold. I made a mental note to keep an eye on Miss Sophia Beasley.

"There is so much to do when you first arrive at a new house, don't you agree, ma'am?" I asked Mrs. Beasley with a confiding smile. Not waiting for an answer I was sure would never come, I turned to her daughter and said, "So nice of you to call, Miss Beasley, when I know how busy you must be this time of year, what with the harvest and everything . . . all that preserving to oversee, the supplies to lay by for the winter . . . women have so much to do, do they not?"

She stared at me as if I had suddenly begun speaking in a strange foreign dialect. Edwin coughed behind his hand, and once again I dared not look at him lest it set us both off.

"We shall hope to see you on Sunday for Holy Services," I said as I ushered them to the drawing-room door. "And to see your beautiful church, sir," I added as Harper came forward to show them out. "Good day to you, and thank you again for coming to welcome us to Bryce House."

Neither Edwin nor I said a word until we heard the front door close behind them, but then one glance at his disgusted face was enough to send me into whoops of laughter.

"How could you, Kate?" he asked indignantly. "How could you prattle on so about the church and the harvest—I was sure I was going to disgrace myself, I wanted to laugh so badly."

"It is one of my minor talents, my dear, being able to go on and on about nothing.

"Weren't they impossible? But it is a shame. I do not know who there is in the neighborhood wc might associate with. We shall have to rely on invited friends to keep boredom at bay."

"If we can get any to come, once the news about the ghosts gets about," he reminded me.

As we went arm in arm to the library, I asked if the Beasleys had mentioned the ghosts before I came in.

"Not a word," Edwin told me. "Strange that. Everyone must know about them."

"That is what the earl claimed. He said they were discussed throughout the entire area. I am surprised you did not mention them yourself. Perhaps the unsuitable Beasleys might have had some inkling of who they were, and how they came to haunt the house."

"It is not likely," he said gloomily. "You heard Farnsworth say they had only been here fifteen years."

"*Farnsworth?*" I said weakly. "Farnsworth *Beasley*?"

But I spoke to the air for Edwin had returned to his reading of the family journal. From the sheaf of paper covered with his fine, precise handwriting, I could see he was making great strides taking notes of it, and I left him to it while I went up to change to something more suitable.

Just before I left the library, he looked up and said, "That is a shabby habit you are wearing, Kate. Why didn't you let me know you were in such dire need of clothes? Order whatever you want to be made up. You are the wealthy Miss Whittingham now. And you may trust me, not the wretched reverend, to find you a horse you will like."

That night was the worst I had ever spent. Perhaps the Beasleys' visit was what stirred our ghosts to a frenzy. I swear I did not sleep all night, and Edwin confessed he had not either when we met, heavy-eyed, at breakfast.

The Gentleman ghost had not been content to pace

his room. Instead, he walked about the corridor outside my bedroom, tapping on the walls and then the
door while I huddled in bed and prayed he would not
come in.

And then there was The Lady. She was not so close,
but she was equally horrifying for her distant shrieks
could easily be heard through solid oak. To distract
myself, I tried to guess where they were coming from.
It did seem they came from the ground floor in the
back of the house somewhere. Sometimes the noises
would die away and I would draw a deep breath, hoping that was the end of them. But then they would
begin again, softly and intermittently, but growing in
volume and tempo. She sounded as if she were being
tortured, and it was unbearable.

"I wonder if exorcism would work," I said to Edwin
as we sat aimlessly at the table, the ruins of a mostly
uneaten breakfast before us. "Do they do exorcisms
in the Protestant faith?"

"I've no idea," Edwin said wearily. "I fear it would
not work. After all, these two have been entrenched
here for at least forty years and probably longer than
that if we go by The Gentleman's outfit Harper mentioned to you."

"Isn't it odd they do not seem to know they are not
alone?" I asked next. "You would think they would
have met somewhere about the place in all these
years. Bryce House is not that large."

"Perhaps they are not visible to each other. Perhaps
they come from different periods of history, although
it seems too much a coincidence to be reasonable, two
different ghosts in the same house."

"Yes, and to think only days ago we scoffed at
ghosts, the two of us. Remember?"

"Kate," my brother said, and I looked up, he
sounded so serious. "There is no need for you to stay
here, you know. Uncle Daniel's will did not require
it, nor do I. In fact, I would feel more at ease if I
knew you were safe somewhere else and not in this
hell-house."

I am ashamed to tell you that for a fleeting moment I thought seriously about this chance he gave me to escape. But then reason returned.

"As if I would leave you to suffer this alone!" I said in mock indignation. "No, I'll not leave you, my dear. We will survive this together, just you wait and see. Besides, what if Bethany and her husband decide to come and discover I have hared off? I would never hear the end of it."

"I will not deny it eases my mind to hear you say so," Edwin admitted. I smiled as calmly as I could, but inside I was still trembling.

An hour later, Harper came to the library to announce a visitor. Hard on his heels was a gentleman about Edwin's age, dressed very fine in driving clothes that had just been over many a dusty road.

"Brede!" Edwin exclaimed before Harper could announce him.

The two met halfway and exchanged those greetings men indulge in—the hearty handshakes, the claps on the shoulder, the wide smiles. I was finally introduced to Mr. Hawes, and after Edwin had poured him a glass of wine, we settled down before the fireplace. Brede Hawes sipped his wine gratefully before he said, "How fortunate I was at the family place near Southampton when your desperate message arrived, old son. Now, what's all this about ghosts? You know there are no such things. I was astounded that you of all people would even mention them. In fact, I thought you must have been half-seas over when you wrote it."

"No chance of that. And there are ghosts," Edwin said seriously. "We have heard them. Indeed, neither of us slept at all last night with the to-do they made."

"I can tell you didn't sleep. You look awful," Mr. Hawes said baldly. "Not you, of course, Miss Whittingham. You are blooming, ma'am, assure you, blooming.

"What did the ghosts do? Tell me everything. Oh, by the way, I made so bold as to instruct your footman to bring my bags in. Following your orders, sir, I gave my man some time off and left my groom at home."

Thus reminded of my duties, I excused myself to see to our guest's comfort. As I told Harper to place him in a bedroom very near Edwin's and my own, I hoped with all my heart he would stay with us and not be frightened off. He seemed brave enough now, almost flippant in fact, but we would see how he behaved when face to face with the supernatural. I wanted him so badly to stay. I could see how much good it was doing Edwin to have his friend here. His eyes were brighter, his face more animated, and his voice had lost its doleful tone. I decided to leave the two alone for a while to catch up on all the news they could not mention in my presence, and made my way down to the housekeeper's room near the kitchens to speak to Mrs. Harper about the additional place that must be set at the dinner table.

As I turned a bend in the corridor, one of the maids came out of the kitchen. She did not see me there in the dimness, and I was startled when she swerved to one side at a particular spot and hugged the opposite wall as she went by. A moment later she was followed by another maid carrying a pile of clean linen. She also avoided the exact same place. When they were gone, I made myself go and investigate. The spot looked innocuous enough. The whole corridor in this section of the cellars had stone walls. It was one of the older, if not the oldest part of the house. But what was there about this particular location that caused the maids to walk around it so gingerly?

I stepped closer to the wall and cried out in dismay. The cold I had felt the first night in the house surged over me, wrapping itself around me, chilling me right down to the marrow in my bones. I felt that if I did not move back, and soon, I would not be able to do so. It took a valiant effort, even as horrified as I was, but I managed it finally, to lean weakly against the wall opposite, gasping as I tried to recover.

The wall here was blessedly normal in temperature,

but I could not help edging along, much as the maids had done, until I was some distance from the spot that I felt had tried to kidnap me. I know, I know. It sounds absurd, does it not? But that is what I felt happening, I swear it is.

As I stared back at the place, I wondered if this was where the screams I had heard last night originated. But why here in the servants' part of the house, if that was true? Perhaps The Lady Ghost was not? A lady, I mean? Perhaps she had even been one of the servants and that was why she stayed down here with them. Most of the time, I reminded myself, remembering how she had come up to my room that first night, trailing the cold and the scent of lilacs.

As I went back up the stairs, forgetting my errand completely, all I could think of was how long a month October was. Thirty-one days long in fact, and this was only the third day of it.

Would we be able to last for twenty-eight more and keep our sanity? It was so important for Edwin to inherit the Whittingham fortune. For me as well, of course. But for the first time I was seriously beginning to doubt we would be able to stay the course.

Chapter Five

As if they were as tired as we were after their extravagant performances, the ghosts did not make a sound that night. Brede Hawes professed his disappointment the next morning as he tucked into a plate heaped with eggs and ham and kippers, eyeing the basket of muffins Harper set before him at the same time.

"Sat up for hours, and what do I get for it?" he complained, his eyes twinkling. "There wasn't a peep out of 'em, and where's the sport in that? I shall think you and your sister have brought me here on a hoax, Edwin, indeed I shall."

My brother had his mouth full and was only able to shrug helplessly. For a moment I toyed with the idea of taking the two men down to the basement and letting them experience the terror I had felt at that icy section of the wall. Then I decided to leave well enough alone. There was little chance Edwin would ever find himself down there; I need not warn him. Men were not known for invading the servants' quarters, not a one of them. I myself had decided nothing would coax me down there ever again.

"What shall we do today?" Mr. Hawes inquired. "I mean, since you tell me the ghosts lie dormant until dark. How about a ride, Edwin? Do you good to get some exercise. There'll be plenty of time for the family journals. It is bound to rain any day now."

I spoke up, urging Edwin to agree. It is amazing what a bright morning following a peaceful night's sleep can do to restore a sense of optimism. Of course

we would make it to November first, I had told myself
as I put up my hair that morning and listened to one
of the maids humming as she swept the corridor. Of
course Edwin would earn the inheritance. And so I
had spoken to Mrs. Harper before breakfast and arranged for the groom to ride to the nearest market
town to ask a seamstress the housekeeper knew, to
call.

"She will not come here, Miss Katharine, no, indeed. She's heard of Bryce House. But I am sure she
will meet you at the inn in Lechton," the good woman
told me.

The seamstress might even come today with her fabric samples and patterns. The habit was the most
important, of course, but I also needed an evening
gown and some gowns for afternoon and visiting. The
ones I had brought with me would do for around the
house. I might even splurge on new sandals, perhaps
a bonnet or two and a new warm cloak. Winter was
not that far away. Edwin had called me the rich Miss
Whittingham. How quickly I had begun to feel that
way.

The two men left shortly after breakfast, Edwin
promising to inquire about a horse for me in Naxley.

Later that morning I was alone in the library studying the journals when the Earl of Bryce sent in his
card.

"I told my lord Mr. Edwin had gone out, Miss Katharine," Harper said, looking indignant. "It not being
suitable for you to receive a single gentleman alone,
miss. But my lord would insist! A very forceful gentleman, the earl."

So the earl was unmarried after all, was he? How
interesting.

I assured the butler it was quite all right to show
Bryce in, my mind in a turmoil. Why had I worn this
horrid old gown this morning? The color had never
flattered me.

And my hair! I knew I should have had one of the

maids wash it for me yesterday. But then Hawes had come and we were thrown into confusion, and . . .

"The Earl of Bryce, Miss Katharine," Harper's disapproving voice proclaimed, and I rose, smoothing down my skirts and hoping I did not look as disconcerted as I felt.

The gentleman I remembered came down the library to where I stood. He was dressed a little more carefully this morning but still with such carelessness that I knew he would never have to worry about being called a dandy. I had forgotten what a big man he was, how rugged. Or was it being inside even as spacious a room as this one that made him seem so?

I held out my hand and smiled slightly, proud of my poise. Behind the earl I could see Harper hesitating at the door.

"Leave us and shut that door behind you," Bryce demanded without even turning to see if he was obeyed. I was not at all astonished when Harper meekly did as he was told.

"Still here, I see. I commend your fortitude," Bryce said, observing me, hands on hips. "Your brother has gone out, I hear. Or has he escaped for good?"

"I assure you he has not," I said quickly. "Won't you be seated, my lord? May I offer you some refreshment?"

"There's no need. This is not a social call."

He sat down in a large wing chair before I could take my own seat again. I was beginning to realize the earl was a law unto himself, but I knew if I taxed him with his discourtesy, he would only scoff at me. Still, I wondered at the rapid beat of my heart, how breathless I felt, and over such a crude man, too.

"Can it be possible the ghosts have remained quiet since I last saw you?" he asked.

"If only they had!" I exclaimed before I told him of the night Edwin and I had spent awake, the two of us. "Of course Edwin's friend has come to stay now, and we are expecting other guests as well.

"There was nothing at all from the ghosts last

night." I sighed. "I do not expect that to last, however."

"Your guests' stay will not be of long duration, you may wager on it," he said easily. "I understand that as October progresses, the spirits grow ever more obstreperous."

"Have they ever—hurt anyone?" I asked, hating the quaver in my voice but not being able to do a thing about it.

"Not to my knowledge. There was a maid a few years ago. She was new here, and young and impressionable. They say she died of fright in a cellar corridor down near the kitchens. There wasn't a mark on her, however, and it was broad daylight. Might not have been a ghost at all."

I gasped at his careless tone even as I wondered if the maid had been standing where I had been yesterday, in that icy, encompassing cold. Thinking a change of subject might be in order, I said, "Tell me, sir, how can it be you are the Earl of Bryce if this is Bryce House? Why don't you, a Tremaine, live here, instead of Whittinghams? I don't understand."

"I see you have been studying family papers," he replied. "Have they nothing to say about the Tremaines?"

"We have not been able to find a word," I replied.

"Typical. The Whittinghams have all of them been stiff and proud and very conscious of their importance, which you may believe has never been all that grand."

For some reason I was not angry. Instead, I felt only amusement. "You insult my ancestors very quickly, my lord," I said. "Won't you tell me the whole story about how they came into possession of Bryce House? Please?"

He crossed one booted leg over the other, and I tried to avoid looking at how the muscles in his thighs moved as he did so.

"Let me see," he said. "I am tempted to begin 'Once upon a time.' Instead, let me just say that a long time ago at the end of the seventeenth century, there were two brothers named Tremaine who lived here in this mansion with the rest of the family. They had several sisters, but because they were girls they aren't part of the story, being so very unimportant."

He paused as if expecting me to comment. When I only tilted my head and looked inquiring, he gave me a mock salute.

"The two brothers had a falling out. Over some woman, I suppose. The quarrel was never mended, and at last their father sent the younger son away. He managed to make a fortune for himself in the service of the Crown and was given the title Earl of Bryce and all the land between Lechton and Naxley as a reward.

"Do not be disturbed. There is no wicked dragon in the story, although I admit it does sound like a fairy tale, does it not?

"At first, the new earl took great satisfaction in ousting his older brother. He took possession of this place and called it Bryce House. But eventually, when the novelty palled, he built a grander house and named it Bryce Court. And he allowed his exiled brother to return here. Out of the goodness of his heart, he deeded him thirty acres to be enclosed in a high wall. I am sure that was the supreme insult, don't you? It had to rankle. It is said they never spoke again.

"The older brother living here was only able to beget a single female child. She inherited, and married a man named Whittingham. The estate has descended in a straight line ever since, probably because the first misguided owner made sure it could pass into female hands even if there was a male heir available. Madness. Pure madness."

"You have a very poor opinion of my sex, my lord," I said evenly.

For the first time in our short acquaintance, Bryce smiled at me to dazzling effect. I cannot describe what a difference it made to his rugged face, how handsome and warm it became.

"On the contrary, Miss Whittingham, I consider women very useful. In some ways," he drawled, looking positively wicked as he did so. "Shall I tell you of them?"

"Please do not," I was quick to say. "Instead tell me, if you would be so good, where the ghosts enter the story?"

He shrugged. "I have no idea. They have been part of Bryce House for a very long time, but the reason for their haunting remains a mystery. It had to be something scandalous, of course. The Whittinghams have always been proud and prim and proper. Are you?"

"What?" I asked, startled. "I—I suppose I am. Proper, at least."

"Too bad. And your brother? Has he ever been wild, feckless? Or is he a sober, pious man keeping carefully to the straight and narrow and boring everyone he comes in contact with in true Whittingham fashion?"

"I do not know what he gets up to in London, sir, for we have not lived together for five years, since my parents died. But he is not a prig, I can assure you, he is not a prig."

"I shall judge that for myself when we finally meet," came the swift reply. "I do not trust a fond sister's report."

"Why did you come here today?" I dared to ask. "You said it was not a social call."

"I heard you might be interested in a new mount. You look amazed. There are no secrets in the country, Miss Whittingham. Gossip is meat and drink here.

"Now, I have a number of suitable horses, and I might be induced to part with one for the right price. You will find nothing superior unless you travel out of Hampshire. I am known for my horseflesh."

"It is kind of you to offer, my lord . . ."

"Isn't it? And I am so seldom kind."

He rose and came toward me to take my hands and pull me up close to him. "Why do you suppose I am doing it?" he asked, his eyes searching mine.

I could feel my knees begin to tremble, and I prayed

it was not noticeable. "I have no idea, sir," I managed
to say. "Why are you?"

He shrugged again and dropped one of my hands
to run a careless finger down my cheek to cup my
chin. "Because you are lovely? And I am bored? Or
do you think it could be a combination of both?" he
asked in a soft growl.

He released me then, and I grasped the back of the
chair I had just quit to steady myself. That made him
grin, his eyes knowing, and I told myself he was impossible. And as for being a gentleman, that was
questionable.

"Tell your brother to come to the Court tomorrow
if he cares to inspect my animals. He can bring that
coxcombe Hawes with him," the earl threw over his
shoulder, for he was striding to the door now. I stood
where he had left me, wondering if he intended to
leave without even saying good-bye.

But of course he did. The library door closed deci-
sively behind him only moments later, and I was left
to sink into the chair I was holding to make what I
could out of a truly astonishing interview.

A short time later, word came that the seamstress
Mrs. Harper had recommended had arrived at the inn
in Lechton. I spent an intent two hours having my
measurements taken and approving patterns and
choosing fabrics. I especially liked the habit I chose—
a dark green merino with gold braid. And then there
was a silk gown, the color of spring leaves, for evening.
I felt quite giddy when I left Miss Sharples, for besides
the gowns and a new warm cloak for winter, I had
ordered sandals, a reticule and a bonnet or two to be
brought on approval when she came back the following week for a fitting.

Edwin and Mr. Hawes did not return until almost
dinnertime. I was delighted to see how much better
Edwin looked, for the exercise had brought color to
his pale face and he was much happier in spirit. Perhaps if we both left Bryce House during the day it
would make the nights easier to bear? It would cer-

tainly be healthier for Edwin than being closeted in the library poring over dusty old papers.

After Harper and the footman had served the last course and I had excused them, I told my companions of the earl's visit.

My brother frowned, and even Hawes looked perturbed when his name was mentioned.

"You should not have seen the man alone, Kate," Edwin scolded me. "I will have to speak to Harper. What was he thinking of to admit him when I was out of the house?"

"He did not want to, but there was no denying Bryce. Please, Edwin, do not say anything to Harper. He is an old man, and he would be mortified. Besides, where would we find a butler and cook as good and faithful as the Harpers?"

"I say, she's right," Hawes said, patting his stomach and looking happily at his empty trifle dish. "Those veal scallops were superb, old son. And the duck—mmm."

"What did he want here?" Edwin demanded, still looking stern. He was obviously not to be distracted by a discussion of cuisine.

I told him about the offer of a good horse, but still my brother did not seem appeased.

"Best horseflesh between here and Tattersall's, I do assure you," Brede Hawes said, nodding as Edwin poured them both a glass of port. "Be a fool if you didn't take advantage of the offer. You know we didn't find anything today."

"I suppose you are right," Edwin said almost grudgingly. I wondered why he had taken such a dislike to a man he had not even met. "At least it will keep the parson and his bustling ways from the door."

"Old Beasley? Pay him no heed, no heed at all. No one does except his fellow fanatics."

"Do you suppose I could come too, tomorrow?" I asked. "It is to be my horse, after all. And I promise faithfully I will not be in the way."

The two men exchanged glances. I was beginning to

feel not only uneasy but surprised when Edwin spoke up to say I might visit Bryce Court with them if I behaved myself.

I was delighted, although I pretended it was no such thing. I did not want Edwin and Mr. Hawes to tease me about thinking I might acquire the earl as a beau. I had no such intentions. Of course not. I was merely interested in seeing the Court.

Besides, it wouldn't have done any good if I had wanted it. I knew that. Bryce might not be a graceful Adonis, but when he smiled he could take your breath away. And somehow I knew, if he put his mind to it, he would have no trouble charming any woman he wanted.

If only my new habit was ready, I thought, as we adjourned to the library and I went apart to read one of the newspapers Edwin had arranged to have sent from London.

That evening, after the servants left at dusk, we spent some quiet hours. I worked on my needlepoint and the two men played cards, wagering large, imaginary sums on the outcome of each game. Thank heavens they were only imaginary, for Edwin lost a considerable sum that would have made the amount I had spent on clothes that afternoon seem like a pittance.

When the casement clock in the hall struck eleven, Edwin suggested we retire. He had been yawning for the past half hour, and I was quick to agree. It was strange that although Edwin played the masterful older brother, giving me orders and watching my behavior, I myself felt almost motherly toward him. I suppose I felt he needed someone to look after him, and there was no sign he had even begun to consider acquiring a wife.

Together, the three of us took up our candles and went out to the hall. I was not looking forward to my lonely room, but I was not nervous for we had not heard The Gentleman pacing over our heads this evening, and there had not been a sound from The Lady either. Brede Hawes told us he thought the whole thing was a hoax, and we should be ashamed of ourselves, telling tall tales to intrigue him into visiting.

We were still denying any such strategy and laughing when suddenly Hawes gasped. I followed his gaze to the stairs before us, moving unconsciously behind Edwin as I did so. For standing at the top of the flight was The Gentleman. It was completely dark up there, but there was no mistaking who it was in the plumed hat and mask, holding a dagger before him. He was all in white and he seemed to glow strangely. I wanted to look away, but I could not take my eyes from him.

He did not make a sound, and thankfully did not start down the stairs toward us. We three stood frozen below him for what seemed an endless time. I do not know about Edwin and Mr. Hawes, but I know I did not even dare to breathe lest I disturb some delicate equilibrium and set The Gentleman off on a rampage.

At last he began to fade away. It was the most frightening thing to watch I had ever seen, and I held tight to the back of Edwin's coat. I knew, if I had been alone there, I would have fainted.

" 'Pon my soul," Hawes said reverently when there was no sign of the ghost left and all was dark above us. "You were not telling tall tales after all, were you?"

Chapter Six

We set off for Bryce Court immediately after breakfast the next morning, and a strangely subdued little band we were, each lost in our own thoughts. There had been nothing more to be seen or heard of The Gentleman last night, for which I, for one, was very grateful. After finally falling asleep, I had a nightmare that he had floated through my solid oak door and come up to the bed, his dagger raised as if to stab me. In the dream, the mask he wore hid a grinning skull. I woke then, my heart pounding so hard I was afraid it would burst, and I slept very little for the rest of the night.

It was a lovely morning now, however, still warm for October, but with a crisp bite to the air, and I told myself to forget the ghosts of Bryce House. I was going to another Bryce establishment today, and I knew I would see the earl, for Edwin had sent the groom over very early to inform him of our arrival.

When we reached the Court gates, I stared in awe at the delicate tracery of the ironworks, the decorative brass eagles with wings spread wide, the sheer soaring height of those gates that towered over us.

"Does himself proud, doesn't he?" Edwin muttered as the gatekeeper admitted us.

"I believe it was an ancestor of his who put up the gates, old son," Hawes said in a mild voice. Since his family estate was fairly close, he knew more of Bryce than either my brother or I did.

"Not that he's not proud as Lucifer. No one has ever accused him of being too humble," Hawes added

with a smile. I smiled back. Brede Hawes was a like-
able man, easy-going and even-tempered, which is
more than could be said for either Edwin or me. I
saw my brother make an effort to throw off his black
mood, and I smiled again at Hawes to thank him.

The Court itself, reached by a long, winding avenue
stretching for over a mile, was more than a handsome
building, it was magnificent. Built of the honey-
colored stone found in the Mendip Hills near Bath, it
glowed in the sunlight. The massive front was adorned
with a colonnade four stories high. In the center of it
as we rode up was the earl, waiting for us. I thought
him a worthy owner of such grandeur.

He came down the flight of marble steps at a leisurely pace and, after nodding to me, inspected my
escorts with a keen eye. It seemed to intimidate both
of them, for Edwin stammered slightly as he introduced himself and his friend.

"I know Mr. Hawes," Bryce said, flicking a cool
gaze in that man's direction. He did not smile and I
wondered what there was about Brede Hawes he
could not like.

"Shall we go on to the paddocks?" he inquired as
a groom ran forward with his horse. It was a large,
powerful-looking gelding, and it ducked its head to
nuzzle the earl when he patted its neck. They were
obviously old friends.

We spent an hour inspecting several paddocks. I
especially enjoyed the foals born that spring and as
gawky as any adolescent. They were curious about us,
too, and several of them kept pace with us on the
other side of the rail as we trotted past.

Edwin soon lost his diffidence admiring the horses.
He was especially taken with a chestnut gelding and
declared it the perfect mount for me.

I was not at all sure. The horse seemed nervous,
and I could not like the way it tossed its head and
pawed the ground.

"The chestnut is not for sale," Bryce informed my

brother. "Besides, it is too unstable an animal for your sister, sir. What can you be thinking to suggest it?"

I saw Edwin redden and wanted to go to his rescue, but I knew better than to do that. He would not thank me if I embarrassed him before the earl.

"Kate is an excellent rider with a superior seat," he said haughtily. "I am not afraid she would come to grief on any horse in your stables, sir."

I stared at him, for it was no such thing.

Fortunately, Bryce only shook his head, his mouth twisting wryly for a moment. "I have had some of the more likely mares brought up to the stables," he said. "Shall we look them over now?"

He waited for me to ride beside him. I could hear Edwin and Hawes exchanging a few quiet words I could not catch behind us.

"Do not worry. I won't let him purchase anything you wouldn't like, Kate," the earl said for my ears alone.

"Thank you," I said, ignoring his use of my first name. "Edwin gives me credit I do not deserve."

"When you are better mounted, you will see what a difference it will make. What a peculiar gait that horse of yours has. And where had you that ancient sidesaddle?"

"It was the only one in my great-uncle's stable," I said. "I will admit it has seen better days."

"Possibly around the middle of the last century," he said.

"As for my poor mare, it is not her fault she is old," I told him.

"Or swaybacked, either," he agreed. "But she is lazy to boot. See how she shuffles along, to let you know how miserable she is to be exerting herself this way."

I laughed. I couldn't help myself, for the mare was not being at all agreeable.

"Perhaps she is jealous, sir," I pointed out. "It cannot be easy for her to see all these splendid creatures in their prime. If I were a horse I know it would give me the megrims."

"I am glad you are not," he replied. "A horse, that is. It would be such a waste. Of course there aren't any horses with tails and manes like the pure gold of your hair."

I could hardly like having my hair compared to a horse's tail. How did one respond to such a dubious compliment? Instead, I told him I thought the Court was outstanding.

"Yes, I am glad my ancestor decided to leave Bryce House."

"I will be glad when we can," I said before I thought. "We saw The Gentleman last night just before we were about to go up to bed," I said in explanation. "I have never been so frightened."

He stared at me, his eyes intent. "You were all there at the time?" he asked.

"Yes. I did not make it up," I said, suddenly indignant. "Edwin and Mr. Hawes saw it, too."

"I beg your pardon. What did it do?"

"Nothing. It just stood there at the top of the flight and stared down at us, and then it—it just went away."

"I do not recall hearing that anyone else has ever seen it," he said slowly.

"Mr. Harper, our butler, saw it some time ago," I told him. "He described it to me perfectly."

We were not able to continue our private conversation, for we had reached the stableyard again. There were three mares for us to admire, a black and two grays. The black had four white stockings and a white blaze and to my eyes was quite the handsomest of the three. I did not comment as grooms put them through their paces, although both Edwin and Hawes had a great deal to say. At last, as if impatient with their discourse, Bryce turned to me.

"And what do you think, Miss Whittingham?" he asked formally once again. I rather missed the "Kate."

"It is to be your mount after all, so there is no point in all this masculine discussion. I will tell you before you decide, there is little to choose from among them. They are all out of Lucifer, the black stallion I keep at stud.''

I knew that horse breeding was not a subject generally discussed between ladies and gentlemen, and I sensed Edwin was offended. To forestall any hasty words, I spoke up quickly. "Since you leave it to me, my lord, I choose the black. She is splendid with those white markings, and she looks even-tempered.''

"She can travel like the wind when you want her to. I suppose you will name her Blaze, or White Stockings,'' he said, shaking his head and grimacing.

"Actually, I thought I would call her Imp in honor of her sire, sir,'' I said coolly. Edwin frowned, but Hawes laughed and the earl gave me that half salute to acknowledge I had more than held my own.

After the business was concluded, Bryce invited us to join him for some refreshments and to see the Court. I was eager to accept and not best pleased when Edwin said we must be on our way.

A groom led Imp forward for me to mount. There was a new-looking saddle on her back, and I asked where it had come from.

"One of my sisters left it here when she married,'' Bryce told me. "Consider it a gift. I really could not permit that ancient thing you have been using to be placed on one of my horses. I have had the grooms discard it. You may leave your former mount, too. I'll see it is taken care of.''

Edwin bowed to thank him, but I shook my head. "I will trail her home with us,'' I said as I rebuttoned my glove to keep from having to look at him and see his scoffing face. "I cannot like to have her put down. And there is enough pasture at Bryce.''

"Women,'' Bryce said, disgusted. "So tender-hearted and impractical. Give you good day, Miss Whittingham. Gentlemen.''

As before, he turned his back without waiting for a reply, to stride off to the Court. I barely heard Edwin and Hawes discussing him on the ride home, for I was concentrating on Imp. What a lovely horse she was, smooth and good-tempered. I was grateful to my brother for allowing me to purchase her, especially since she had been expensive, and after I was spending so much on new clothes, too. I was sure no one had a better brother in all of England, and I intended to tell him so as soon as we were alone.

When we reached Bryce House, we found a dusty traveling carriage drawn up to the front door. I had barely dismounted and given Imp and my former mare into the stableboy's care before my cousin Bethany ran out of the house to greet us. She flew straight into my arms to hug me tightly, exclaiming her joy in seeing me again and telling me how tiresome the journey from town had been. Behind her, her new husband waited to be introduced to Edwin and Mr. Hawes, a slight smile on his pleasant face. I was surprised and relieved to discover I did not feel the slightest tinge of jealousy, and I was glad to see Bethany. Over her shoulder I caught sight of her old maid directing the footman about the baggage. Agnes had been Bethany's maid for as long as I had lived with the Ingalls. I wondered what she would make of the ghosts. I suspected they would not bother her all that much, for she was a phlegmatic soul; indeed, you could have called her stolid and you would not be far from the mark.

Bethany was another story. Easily stirred to tears or laughter, she was a nervous creature constantly on the move. Uncle Frank had called her "Firefly" because she could never seem to settle in one place. When I had come to stay when she was thirteen, she often broke out in a horrid rash if she were upset, all red, itchy blotches on her face and breasts. Fortunately, she outgrew the tendency before Mr. Buffington appeared on the scene, but I could not help thinking uneasily about how our ghosts would affect her. I had mentioned them in my invitation, but only in passing when I described the age of Bryce House. Certainly I had not revealed how intimidating and frightening they were, nor had I told her and her husband about the servants' habit of leaving the house at dusk.

As Bethany and I drew apart, I looked around. I did not see a valet for Mr. Buffington, only a coachman and a groom. I wondered if there was enough room for them to sleep in the stables with our own servants. I would have to ask Harper.

I made the introductions all around before I led our guests into the house and settled them in the gold drawing salon until their rooms should be ready. Harper had put them in connecting rooms near the rest of us, and as far from The Gentleman's room as possible. I was glad of that. There was a small dressing room for Agnes as well, if Charles Buffington did not object to her sleeping so close to him and his bride. I decided I would handle that problem if it arose later.

Bethany was in high spirits. I could see Mr. Hawes admiring her as she talked and laughed and gave me all the news of home. Her blue eyes sparkled as she did so, and I noticed the handsome sapphire-and-diamond ring she sported, the sophisticated new gown she wore. Obviously Mr. Buffington was treating her well. I was glad for her. As for that gentleman, he had little to say for himself. He did smile at me once when no one was looking, which I ignored. I hoped for my cousin's sake that he was not going to have a roving eye.

"Did Kate tell you about the ghosts, cousin?" Edwin asked when Bethany paused to take a breath. "If she did not, I will warn you now. They are not some old wives' tale fabricated to frighten children— no, indeed. They are very active, especially now, although no one knows why that should be."

"She did say something about them," Bethany said, leaning forward to press his hand. I had forgotten her habit of touching the person she was speaking to.

"Isn't it exciting, though! I do hope Mr. Buffington and I will have a chance to see one of them in their long white sheets, moaning and waving their arms.

Tell me, Edwin, do they make eerie sounds? *Oooooooo?* Like that?"

I did not feel the least like laughing as Bethany swayed and waved her arms, pretending to be a ghost. I noticed that neither Hawes nor my brother did either.

"From the looks on everyone's faces, my love, I think the ghosts here must be more frightening than you portray," Buffington told her fondly. She turned and gave him a brilliant smile, pursing her lips in a pretend kiss. I did hope we were not to be treated to a constant stream of honeymoon behavior. I could just imagine how Edwin would enjoy *that*.

"Yes, they are serious phantoms," I said. "We have heard the one called The Gentleman twice now; we even saw him last night at the top of the stairs. It was terrifying. But they do not seem keen to make contact with us . . . no, that is not true. I think The Lady does. I think there is something she is trying to put right. Something that happened to her here that keeps her tied to earth."

"Ooo, how serious you are, Kate," Bethany exclaimed. "You are frightening me!"

Harper came in then to whisper to me that dinner would be served in half an hour. I had forgotten the time, and it was later than I had thought. When I mentioned this, Bethany jumped up, declaring she must do something about all her dust. In a short time everyone had dispersed. I went up to change from my habit myself after conferring with Mrs. Harper. What a treasure the woman was, for not even these unexpected guests arriving so near dinnertime could disconcert her.

We spent a merry time at the table, enjoying all the dishes presented. Edwin was generous with the wine. Harper went around the table several times refilling everyone's glasses. At last, Bethany and I left the gentlemen to their port and adjourned to the drawing room for some serious feminine talk.

"I must say, married life seems to agree with you,

my dear," I said as we settled down near the fire. The day had grown cloudy and colder, and the warmth of the fire was welcome.

"Kate, you have no idea how lovely it is," she told me, her eyes glowing. "And Mr. Buffington takes excellent care of me. Did you remark my ring? Is it not the handsomest thing?" Here she held out her hand and waved it to and fro to catch the light. "He said it could not match the brightness of my eyes. Wasn't that a grand compliment?"

I agreed it was as I took up my needlework. I wanted to turn the conversation to the ghosts, explain them in more detail so Bethany would know what to expect. I had been startled when Edwin introduced them so promptly, but I had come to see he had done the right thing. After several minutes spent listening to my cousin tell of their rooms in London, the new clothes she had acquired, and the sights she had seen, I did manage to turn her thoughts to her stay at Bryce House.

"I must warn you, Bethany, the servants go to the village at dusk and do not return until dawn. Not a one of them will sleep here."

For a moment, Bethany put her head to one side and studied me. Her hand crept to her mouth and she began to worry her thumbnail. All her fingernails were bitten to the quick, a habit she had never been able to break.

"It is serious, then, Kate?" she whispered at last. "It is not just some lark?"

"No, it has never been a lark," I said before I told her some of things that had happened to me, especially the first night when I had been awakened by a cold draft and the scent of lilacs. I did not tell her of the icy spot in the cellars. Like Edwin, she would be most unlikely to go there.

She shivered and frowned. "I shall insist that Mr. Buffington remain with me all night," she said. "I am sure I will manage if he is beside me.

"But Kate, why do you stay here? Why don't you

run away? I would. In fact, I probably will the first time I see a ghost."

"I cannot leave Edwin here to manage alone," I said slowly. "It is so important for him, this inheritance. You know our parents did not leave us wealthy. It has been especially hard on Edwin, a young man without sufficient funds in town."

She nodded, well versed now in the expense of living in London.

"According to the will, Edwin must spend every night here for the entire month of October. Indeed, if he misses even one, the inheritance is forfeit and he will be poorer than he was before. I cannot allow that to happen."

"You are so brave," Bethany whispered, clutching my arm. Her eyes were as big and round as pennies. "I have always thought you the bravest girl."

I smiled. "Not as brave as you might think when I come face to face with one of our phantoms. But I am sure we will manage. The first week is almost over. Only three weeks and three days to go, and Edwin's future will be secure.

"I am so glad you came," I added, reaching out to hug her. "And you came so quickly, too. You must have set out immediately after you received my letter."

"Almost. Mr. Buffington suggested it. He said the change would be good for me, and truly, I was missing you and all the family so. Isn't that strange? I love my husband, but sometimes . . . well, sometimes I want my mother."

"At least Agnes is with you," I reminded her.

"Yes, and she has been a comfort. I am afraid we have had to make other arrangements for her, though. Mr. Buffington does not want her sleeping in the dressing room." She blushed and would not look at me. I did not press her.

"We were going to put her in the servants' quarters in the attic, but Edwin said we must on no account do that. I gather they have not been used in years.

Instead, he found her a room fairly near mine. She will not be able to answer the bell, but I am sure I can manage."

I smiled and nodded, but I was beginning to feel very uneasy about this visit. Perhaps it had not been such a good idea to invite the Buffingtons here. I would never forgive myself if anything unfortunate happened to my cousin. And to be blunt, I did not see how it was to be avoided, the way things were going. There was nothing I could do about the situation now, however, but pray she would be spared.

Chapter Seven

To my relief, nothing happened for the remainder of that day. The servants hurried off as usual, huddled in shawls or coats with the collars turned up, for our spell of good weather had deserted us and it was raining hard. But there was no sign of the mysterious Lady or the ghostly Gentleman. He did not even pace above our heads in the library that evening. By the time we went to our rooms, I was feeling easier. Perhaps we might just scrape through all right, I thought as I brushed my hair. Perhaps the Buffingtons would not stay beyond a week or two, and although I know it was too much to expect for the ghosts to alter their usual patterns, still I had hopes that whatever happened, it would not be too emotionally scarring for Bethany. As for Mr. Buffington, I did not give him a thought.

When I woke the next morning and looked out the window, I saw it was still raining hard. A nasty wind from the northwest was stripping the remaining blossoms from the flowerbeds beneath my room. It appeared we must resign ourselves to a day spent inside. I sighed. I was eager to take my new mare out, but I would have to wait.

As I dressed, it occurred to me that it was Sunday. At least the storm, as well as the arrival of guests, would serve as an excellent excuse to forego church. I wondered what Mr. Beasley, who might well be conducting services since he himself could not get out, would make of our absence.

Brede Hawes was the only one in the breakfast

room when I arrived. He had his usual full plate before him, but he rose when I came in to help me to my seat. Harper watched indulgently from the sideboard before he brought me a bowl of porridge. As I poured cream on, Hawes said, "It is a good thing the ghosts decided to lie low last night, wouldn't you say, ma'am? I could tell you were concerned for your young cousin."

I was amused. "She is only two years younger than I am myself," I told him. "But I know what you mean. She does seem younger. I think it is her mannerisms that deceive one."

"You are very mature for your age then," he said with a smile. "An excellent quality. You are to be commended, ma'am.

"I see you are not dressed for church," he said next with a knowing smile. I was glad I did not have to reply to his compliment. "The rain has been a blessing, has it not?"

I tried to look at him severely over the rim of my coffee cup, but I knew from the twinkle in his eye that I was not fooling him. What a nice man he was, I thought. So much fun.

"Do you expect the Buffingtons to make a long stay?" he asked, his loaded fork halfway to his mouth. I must have looked astonished at the question, for he added, "I am afraid the ghosts might not like more people here, and we do not want to rile them up, do we?"

"Indeed we do not," I said, putting down my spoon, all my appetite gone. "Bethany did not say how long a stay they planned. At least a week, I imagine. Probably two."

"Well, we must hope everything turns out for the best," he said as he wiped his mouth on his napkin. "More coffee, ma'am?"

Edwin came in then, accompanied by Charles Buffington, and I was suddenly afraid.

"Bethany has decided to spend a lazy morning in

bed," her husband announced to my great relief. "She is tired from the traveling we have done."

"I shall have a tray sent up to her," I told him.

"Kate, I have a wager with Brede I trust you will help me win," my brother said, grinning at me. "Tell us, what are you going to do the first thing after breakfast?"

I did not even have to think about it. "Why, I intend to go down to the stables to see how Imp does in her new surroundings," I said. "Why do you ask?"

But both Edwin and Mr. Hawes were laughing, and it was a while before Edwin could tell me he had bet his friend fifty pounds that was precisely what I would say.

I smiled as I rose from the table, even though I could not like Edwin gambling on such a silly thing. Oh, I knew all young men made wagers, some of them losing great sums of money at a sitting in the London clubs. Edwin had told me all about that. I knew he had not been among their number, but now that he was about to come into a great fortune, perhaps he would change? I hoped not—oh, how I hoped not! And then I told myself I was making a great to-do about nothing. Edwin was six years my senior, and even older than that in worldliness. I must stop acting like a mother hen.

The rain continued all day. We read, conversed, played cards and wrote letters. Bethany did not come down until noon, but when she did, she looked better for her long rest.

I spent some time in the stables. I wore a long, oiled coat I found in a hall closet to keep me dry, with a faded old umbrella over my head. By the time I reached the stable, the umbrella was inside out, the struts broken, and my hair soaking.

Imp enjoyed the apple I had brought her and seemed almost to understand my words telling her how beautiful she was. The old mare in the next stall whinnied and I wished I had thought to bring her an apple, too, the poor old thing.

The servants left for the day shortly after dinner, for with the rain it grew dark early. I was standing by one of the library windows staring out and telling myself the storm was easing, when the familiar tapping began over our heads.

Bethany looked up from her book, her eyes searching the room. I knew she was counting. Soon she would know it was the ghost she heard, for we were all here together. I was right. Her face grew still, and her book slipped from suddenly nerveless fingers to land on the floor with a thud.

"Yes, it is The Gentleman," Edwin told her, smiling to reassure her. "In a moment, he will begin to walk about. You'll see. He is a bit of a bore, you know. Always does the same things."

"Agnes is up there in my room, doing some sewing," Bethany said, leaning forward to whisper to me. "What if he—what if he attacks her?"

"He will not do that, cousin. He can't," I said as calmly as I could. Now we could hear footsteps, hurried, impatient. Everyone's eyes followed the sound of them across the ceiling.

The footsteps halted and the tapping began again, moving from left to right along the walls.

"What is he looking for, do you suppose?" Buffington asked in a quiet voice as his wife hid a whimper behind her fist.

"What do you mean?" Edwin asked, frowning.

"He must be tapping because he is trying to locate something," Buffington explained. "Something he thinks is hidden in the wall of that room somewhere. I wonder what it can be?"

"I never thought of that," I said slowly. "I never imagined he might have a purpose. But surely you are right, sir. No one would tap aimlessly, not even a ghost."

"I think we should go up there right now. Perhaps if we invade his territory, he will stop. He is frightening my wife, and I cannot allow that," Buffington said sternly as he took Bethany's hand.

"Why, she is not such a poor creature, sir," I protested, smiling at my cousin to give her heart. I knew that if sympathy was given and suggestions made, it would not be long before Bethany began to believe herself sensitive and fragile.

"I am all right, love," she said, resting her cheek against his sleeve for a moment. "Truly, Kate is right. It is only sounds, and they can't hurt me, or Agnes either."

Her husband frowned. "Still and all, I am going up. Who will go with me?"

"My dear fellow, I should be happy to accompany you if you feel the need for it," Brede Hawes said, rising and stretching. Above us, the footsteps resumed, faster now, as if The Gentleman was running back and forth. I prayed Agnes would stay put. I did not want her to come face to face with The Gentleman in the corridor. Stolid or not, that would be a terrible shock.

Bethany pleaded with her husband to stay with her in the library, but he could not be dissuaded from exploring. But before he and Hawes reached the library door, the footsteps stopped as abruptly as they had begun. Somehow I knew that was the end of the ghost's activities for now. I have no idea how I knew this, I just did.

All the men went up to investigate anyway, and when they returned they reported there was nothing to be seen. Edwin said he had heard Agnes in Bethany's room, and that was reassuring.

The rest of the evening was uneventful, as was the night that followed. When I woke early, I discovered the storm had blown away during the night, and the day promised to be sunny. I decided I would go for a ride before breakfast and dressed in my old habit after I washed in the cold water left over from bedtime. I felt slightly guilty about this decision, for I was my brother's hostess. But I told myself that the Buffingtons could manage breakfast by themselves, and I would not be so long that Bethany would feel neglected. Besides, she had her husband. As I ran down the stairs, I wondered if he was an amusing companion. I did not think he could be, and it was not sour grapes that caused me to believe it. Charles Buffington had always impressed me as a man content with his own worth, one who had but little wit and even less spirit. But I imagined he was just what Bethany needed to make her feel safe and cared for, and I wished them both well. At the same time, I was very glad I was not Mrs. Charles Buffington.

The groom saddled Imp for me and frowned when I announced I wished to ride alone. I ignored him. I wanted to be by myself, as I often had in my aunt's house that was so full of servants and children, dogs and noise.

I paused at the gates to consider which way to go and at last turned right toward Bryce Court. I did not plan to go anywhere near it, I simply wished to avoid Lechton and a chance meeting with one of the Beasleys.

The morning was fresh and the sky full of fat, scudding clouds. Even the road was much improved, for the rain had settled the dust. Eventually, spotting a farm cart coming toward me, I turned off the road and took to the heath. I could see one of the area's herds of wild ponies in the distance, and I headed for them to see how close they would let me approach before they ran off.

A short time later, out of the corner of my eye, I saw a horseman riding diagonally toward me to intercept me. I knew immediately who it was, for he was mounted on the same large gelding I had seen yesterday. I also knew it would be useless to try to outrace him. Instead, I halted Imp and turned to wait for him.

"I am glad you have the sense not to try to avoid me, Miss Whittingham," the earl said in his abrupt way as he came up beside me. "And the sense not to gallop your new mount here. There are many rabbit holes on the heath."

"I gathered as much," I said with composure. "And I am surprised you consider yourself so omnipotent that you can disregard them."

He grinned at me. That white slash in his tanned face was devastating; there is no other word for it. I wanted to applaud.

"Even I have no control over rabbits," he admitted, backing his mount as it tried playfully to force Imp to sidestep.

"But I do have a quarrel with you, Kate," he went on. "It is that you are the one trespassing now. This is all Court land."

"I did not think you would mind. And it is not fenced," I said.

"Shall we walk the horses? I mean to talk to you."

As we set off, he went on, "I understand some guests have arrived at Bryce House. Your cousin and her husband?"

I was exasperated. "For heaven's sake, do you know everything that goes on there?" I demanded.

"Remember what I told you about gossip.

"Are these guests strong, mature people, able to handle the occasional shade wandering through the drawing room?" he asked next.

I smiled at the picture he painted. "So far neither one of our ghosts has done that, for which I am thankful. But to answer you, no, my cousin Bethany is not very brave. She was upset last night when The Gentleman began his eternal pacing over our heads in the library."

"Just as before?"

I thought for a moment. "No. At first it was the same. The careful tapping on the walls, the slow march up and down the room. But toward the end he became quite agitated. By the time the noise stopped, he was almost running. Yet when Mr. Buffington—my cousin's husband—went to investigate, he was nowhere to be seen."

Bryce frowned. We had come to a dip in the ground that hid a pretty pond until you were close to it. Reeds grew at its edges, and one gnarled tree. The earl indicated the tree with his crop, and obediently I followed him down to it.

After he had dismounted and tied the gelding to a branch, he came toward me. I saw he intended to lift me down, and although I had had no intention of leaving Imp's back, now I was quick to slide to the ground on my own. Bryce made me nervous. I did not think it would be at all wise to get that close to him. I could tell by the sardonic look on his dark face that he was well aware of the stratagem I employed to avoid him. No doubt he thought me a silly female, but better safe than sorry.

Bryce did not comment on my cowardice, however, and for that I suppose I must be grateful. Instead, he busied himself tying Imp to a low bush a little distance from his own horse. I went on down to the edge of the pond. It was very still in the hollow, the pond like a sheet of glass. I could even see the reflection of the racing clouds clearly in its still, dark waters. But lovely as the setting was, I was much more conscious of the man with me than any scenery.

"I am worried about you, Kate," he said as he joined me. "I believe you may be in some danger at Bryce House."

"Oh, I do not think the ghosts have anything personal against me, my lord," I said, trying to ignore how close he was to me now. "How could they?"

"Did I mention the ghosts?" he asked, almost mildly. "But I suppose they could be a source of danger. Certainly I cannot remember when they have been so active."

"How could you know that, gossip notwithstanding? I have heard the ghosts only walk at night. No one has ever been at Bryce House then except my great-uncle."

"That is true. But he kept a careful journal of their behavior. I know this for a fact, for at one time not too long ago, one of your maids, who is sister to one of my own, told her so."

"Which maid would that be?" I asked, thinking how excited Edwin would be to learn of the existence of such a journal. It would explain so many things, make it easier for us to understand the ghosts and why they walked.

"I never knew her name. It was unimportant. Besides, she is not there anymore. Married her young man and left the area, or so my mother tells me."

"I do wonder where that journal is," I mused. "We have found nothing like it; indeed, there has been no mention of ghosts in any of the papers we have discovered."

"Or of the Tremaines?" he asked with a sideways glance.

"As you say. Frankly, I begin to agree with you. The Whittinghams do seem a sober group. They never seem to have laughed or played or amused themselves. Their journals are mostly dry accounts of financial transactions, weather reports, and family births and deaths, as well as those of their servants and their stock. Tedious stuff."

"I did warn you they were worthy folk, did I not?"

"I wonder where Edwin and I fit in," I said. "Oh, look," I added softly, reaching out to grasp his arm. Across the pond, eyeing us carefully, was a shaggy wild pony. I could see others, not as daring, a little distance behind him.

"They come here to drink," Bryce murmured.

"They are not pretty, are they?" I asked. "All rough coats and burrs. Scars, too. Just look at the one behind his left ear. I wonder how he got it?"

"Perhaps from some wild creature, but more likely from one of his own," I was told. "The stallions fight for the mares, you know. The strongest and fittest wins. That is how the herd survives."

Once again we were on dangerous ground that I knew my brother would deplore. I did not reply. Instead, I watched the pony pick its way carefully down to the water. As it began to lap, every so often lifting its head to make sure we were not trying to get close, the others approached as well, mares and foals and even a few yearlings.

I was startled when the earl's horse neighed loudly

from behind us. It was a brazen challenge even I recognized. For possession of the territory? I wondered. But the noise broke the spell and the ponies wheeled and fled. The gelding neighed again and I could hear it stamping a foot on the ground to celebrate its victory. It suddenly occurred to me that between males of any persuasion was only a very small step. I had read enough history to know men were not loath to fight for what they considered theirs. It was certainly something I was sure the man beside me was capable of doing, and I could not control a small shiver at the thought.

I wished I were not so everlastingly *aware* of the man, his height and strength, even the shape of his hand with the heavy gold signet ring he wore. How alive he was. How compelling.

I had never felt this way about any man before, and I was not at all sure I cared for it. It seemed to put me at a disadvantage in my dealings with him. I wanted to be cool and sophisticated, able to chuckle at his outrageous remarks without hearing all kinds of inuendoes that he probably did not even intend. For who was a Miss Whittingham to the Earl of Bryce? Certainly someone of no more importance than that maid he had mentioned whose name he had never bothered to learn. Because she was of no account to him. As surely I was. I must remember that.

He lifted me to Imp's back. I was resigned to it, for there was no other way I could mount. But he did so briskly and impersonally. Still, I wondered if he was smiling because I was blushing. I certainly felt warm under my habit, and I'm afraid my farewell was brusque to the point of rudeness, I was so anxious to escape him.

Do you know, I could feel his eyes on my back for what seemed an endless time? The pressure of his big hands on my waist lasted longer, even though they had not lingered there.

Chapter Eight

As soon as I reached Bryce House, I hurried to the breakfast room without bothering to change. My meeting with the earl had made me later than I had intended to be, and I did not want my cousin to feel neglected. But when I came in, only her husband was there, an empty plate before him and one of the London papers Edwin had arranged to have delivered in his hands.

"Bethany is sleeping late again?" I asked lightly after I had greeted him. I was determined to be pleasant even as I wondered where Harper was. I took a serving of baked fish, some coddled eggs, and a muffin. The ride had made me hungry.

"As you say, coz," Buffington agreed as he pulled out my chair for me. I resented him calling me cousin, but I supposed I would have to get used to it.

"I see you have a hearty appetite. Some coffee? If you prefer tea, you must wait. I sent the butler off for a fresh pot."

As he took his seat again, he added, "I wish my dear wife was as ravenous. I can hardly coax her to eat anything these mornings."

A little warning bell rang in my head. "Indeed?" I asked casually as I buttered my muffin. "Would you be so kind as to pass me the jam? Thank you.

"I have been riding for over an hour," I added. "That does make one hungry. It was a glorious morning for it, too."

"Mrs. Buffington will not be riding for some time to come," he announced.

I had been avoiding his eye, but now I looked up at him. Yes, he was smiling in a knowing way, almost preening himself. At his virility, no doubt, now he had gotten Bethany with child. He had not wasted any time about it, had he? I thought. They had only been married three months. Perhaps that was the reason Bethany lingered in bed mornings? I supposed I must be glad for her, although to be truthful, I felt nothing except to wonder if Mr. Buffington wanted a large family and hoping for her sake that he did not.

"I believe I understand you, sir," I said coolly before I asked where my brother and Mr. Hawes were.

Buffington shrugged. "I have no idea. In the library, I daresay. Your brother is scholarly, is he not? He seems to spend most of his time reading. Poor stuff, that. Now I prefer a more active life, more manly occupations. A pity I did not know you intended to ride this morning. I would have liked to accompany you, my dear coz."

I was glad my mouth was full for it prevented me from having to answer him. I had no intention of riding alone with Buffington. Ever.

"I do hope we can get to know each other a great deal better. I have felt a rapport with you since first meeting, my dear Katharine. I am sure you must be aware of my feelings for you," he said. I saw he had abandoned his newspaper completely, and I wondered what could be keeping Harper.

"It will be—er, a trial for me these coming months, without a woman's company. Perhaps you might be coming to London with your brother this winter? How delightful that would be."

"I have no idea of Edwin's plans beyond this month, sir," I said as coldly as I dared.

His brows rose slightly, and I knew I had shown my distaste too obviously.

"Do you plan to take Bethany on a visit to her mother?" I hastened to say, as much to hide that distaste as to introduce a neutral subject. "I expect she would enjoy that, especially now."

"Yes, she has been begging me for the treat. We shall see," was his reply. I was delighted when Harper came in. Until he had poured Buffington another cup of tea and asked if there was anything I required, I felt more at ease, but eventually I found myself alone with my cousin's husband again.

"These ghosts everyone claims are in residence here," he said, more serious now. "They cannot be real. There are no such things as ghosts."

"You heard The Gentleman yourself, sir," I reminded him. "And you can still say that?"

"Of course. It was probably someone walking about up there and tapping the walls, although I have no idea why they would do it, unless it is some kind of prank . . ."

"Who? Why?" I interrupted. "Who would do such a thing? And for all these years, too. Harper tells us the ghost—or thing—has been at this activity for a number of years."

He shrugged. I detested the smug, superior look he sported.

"You believe a servant?" he asked, his voice incredulous. "But there are no more superstitious people than the ignorant lower class. No one more quick to believe in things that cannot be. It is one of the traits that sets them apart and makes them little better than dumb animals. They have an almost childish belief in things like fairies and witches and omens.

"But you are only a woman. I understand how difficult it must be for you to accept this, grasp it even."

I did not reply for a moment for I was trying hard to contain my anger. I could not like anyone talking about servants as if they were hardly human, and I especially disliked being told I was deficient because of my sex. I looked up and saw him regarding me steadily. His hand was moving toward mine on the table, and I was quick to pick up my coffee cup to avoid having him pat it as I was sure he intended. In sympathy for my limited ability to reason, no doubt.

"At one time, before I came here, I would have

agreed with you, sir," I said before I pushed my plate aside, determined to leave him. "But I have been at Bryce House for a week and a day, and things have happened that had no bearing on servants and their superstitions. Furthermore . . ."

"You are susceptible, of course," he interrupted. "All gentlewomen are, poor dears. A failing, but an appealing one for all that."

I rose and looked at him coldly as he got leisurely to his feet. He was smiling still. I was sure he knew I was furious and reveled in his ability to manipulate me. I told myself I would never allow him to best me.

"To the contrary, I am as pragmatic as you yourself," I said. "I am sure, during the course of your visit, you will hear more from the Bryce ghosts. I warn you, The Lady's screams are especially horrible. She sounds almost as if she is being tortured. And it is not impossible that you may see The Gentleman. I have, and so has my brother and Mr. Hawes."

He looked disapproving as he said, "If any such sighting or frightening noise occurs, I am afraid I will have to remove my wife, much as it will pain me to have to deny you her company. However, I am sure a quick investigation will prove the lady's screams, as you call them, no more than the wind in a chimney that needs cleaning. As for seeing the gentleman haunt, perhaps you all overindulged in wine, or some spicy food?

"I shall take it upon myself to investigate. I was surprised your brother and his friend seemed less than eager to accompany me upstairs last evening. If you remember, I went along with the misconception or prank as it well may be, even suggesting the haunt might be looking for something with his tapping. But you mark my words, coz. There is some simple explanation for all this."

I did not argue. Instead I excused myself. As I left the room, I heard him chuckling softly, and I wondered if there were any way I could get him down in that stone corridor near the kitchens, to see how he liked it close to that icy, threatening section of the wall. To listen to his "simple explanation" for that phenomenon.

I found my brother alone in the library. He told me Mr. Hawes had gone riding, not caring to spend such a golden day indoors. Edwin had the usual books spread out before him. I could tell he did not relish my interruption.

"I met the Earl of Bryce this morning while I was out riding," I told him. I noticed the hand reaching for a book stilled for a moment and I wondered why. "He tells me Great-Uncle Daniel did keep a journal specifically for the ghosts and their appearances. I wonder we have not found it. Do you suppose he hid it somewhere because he was ashamed of his resident phantoms?"

"I have no idea," Edwin said slowly, his handsome hazel eyes serious under frowning brows. "How would Bryce know such a thing?"

It was then I realized I had not told Edwin the family history the earl had revealed. He sat quietly for the time it took for me to speak of the two brothers, their argument, how one had become an earl and the property divided.

"Fascinating," Edwin murmured when I fell silent at last. "So that is why there are no mentions of the Tremaines in the journals we have.

"You know, Kate, I do wish you were not becoming quite so friendly with the earl," he went on, to my surprise. "I did not mention it before, but I have heard things about Bryce in London—his unsuitable friends, his questionable activities. I did not tell you of them for they are disgusting and not at all suitable for your ears. You may have noticed how I have held myself aloof. I do not care to become friendly with such a degenerate, and I most certainly do not want my sister left alone with him. You may be sure I have given Harper orders he is not to admit the man if he ever calls here again and I am not to home. And I expect you to avoid him."

"Why, Edwin, how perfectly gothic of you," I said, trying to sound amused. "I am not some little ingenue, you know. I am twenty-two now, and . . ."

"And as ignorant and unschooled in the ways of the world as a hen," he finished for me, his lips thinning.

The comparison drew a laugh from me. In a moment, Edwin was laughing as well.

"What I mean, Kate, is for you to be circumspect," he said when he was able. "Of course we cannot be rude to the man, more's the pity. But do keep in mind his less-than-sterling reputation. Indeed, I hear he is as bad as the royals in many respects, and as you must know, every one of the king's sons is no better than he should be. In Bryce's case, there are even rumors of a rape last winter. I shall say no more. I am sure it is not necessary."

I held my tongue, although I longed to know more. Surely the rumors were wrong. The man I had met had no need to employ force. Far from it.

Still, I did not argue the point lest Edwin think me too interested in Bryce and further restrict my activities, as was well within his rights to do. Instead, I suggested I inspect the bookcases carefully for the journal the earl had mentioned. Edwin agreed, and we settled to our separate activities in companionable silence, he at the desk with his books and papers, and I on the library steps going over every volume beginning with the top shelves. I was not at all sorry an hour later when Bethany came in to find me, for I had discovered nothing of interest and it was dreary work.

I knew her artless prattle would irritate my brother, so I suggested a walk in the gardens and whisked her from the room before she could ask Edwin if he approved of the activity.

It was another fifteen minutes before she was ready to go out, however, for she had to send for Agnes to bring her a shawl and her gloves and a wide-brimmed hat lest the sun ruin her complexion. I watched her, at first amused, and then impatient. It seemed to me Bethany had become very prosaic since her marriage, and I missed the gay girl she had been, always ready for a lark.

As we strolled slowly through the paths between the beds, I tried to keep my mind on her conversation, although I admit I was still trying to come to terms with the description of the earl Edwin had given me. It had certainly occupied my mind to the exclusion of all else during the hour I had spent on the library steps. But even though I had told myself any number of times that my brother must certainly be wrong, I could not quite convince myself. A vision of Bryce's dark, rugged face kept appearing in my mind. It was strange how easily I was able to imagine him involved in orgies, even though I had only the vaguest idea what an orgy entailed. But there was no way I could bring myself to accept his taking a woman against her will. And then I wondered how I could be so sure of such a thing when I really knew little of the man.

"I declare, Kate, I have asked you twice for the name of this flower. Have your wits gone begging?" Bethany asked pertly.

I laughed and hugged her. "I do beg your pardon, coz. I admit to wool-gathering. As for the flower, I have no idea.

"Shall we go down to the beech wood? There is a lovely glade there you might enjoy."

"It is not too far?" Bethany said, shading her eyes the better to judge the distance.

"Have you become so delicate then?" I asked sharply. Surely being with child did not mean a short walk over only slightly sloping ground would be too taxing.

My cousin blushed. "You know what I mean," she said. "Mr. Buffington told me he had spoken to you."

I hugged her again. "Indeed, he did. But the exercise will be good for you. Don't you remember how active your mother was before baby Hal was born?"

I saw Bethany looked thoughtful as we set out for the wood. I wondered if her husband had put the idea of her fragility in her head, and I told myself I must do all I could to make sure she went from Bryce House to visit her mother. I knew my aunt would set her straight as I could not.

Bethany was quick to admire the glade. As she sat down on the rustic bench to rest, she suggested I stock the pool with carp, come springtime. I was delighted to discuss the possibility, for she had spoken of nothing but her condition ever since we left the gardens, and I had found it tedious. And when she paused for breath, I begged her to tell me more of London and the delights to be found there. By the time we started back to the house, I was much more in charity with her.

I excused myself as soon as we reached the terrace, however, claiming I had letters to write, for we found her husband waiting for us and looking concerned. I did not know if Charles Buffington was a hypocrite or not, but I suspected that might be the case. All this anxiety about my cousin's well-being did not jibe with his less-than-subtle attempt to engage me in flirtation. Or perhaps to something more? I could not tell. It only made me want to avoid the man for I could not like him.

The rest of the day was uneventful, although Bethany's maid stopped me as I left my room after dressing for dinner. Of course Agnes had heard about our resident ghosts by now from the other servants, and she told me that if there was a grain of truth to the stories, she would insist on her mistress leaving at once.

"She's not to be distressed right now, Miss Kate," she said firmly. "You've heard about the child, of course. And you of all people must remember how nervous Miss Bethany gets, how easily upset. A nasty ghost would be all we need to set her off like a shot."

I envied Bethany such loyalty as I left Agnes and ran down the stairs—even if I could not envy her her husband. But for better or worse, my cousin was now Mrs. Charles Buffington. As my aunt would say, she had made her bed and now she must lie in it. What a pity Mr. Buffington must lie in it as well, I thought, and I could not help smiling at the mental picture I had of him doing so as I entered the drawing room to find everyone assembled before me.

"Here she is now," that same gentleman said, rising to lead me to a chair. Bethany smiled and nodded at such considerate behavior, but I felt only revulsion for the way his fingers squeezed mine in a secret caress.

The dinner served was excellent as always. I had told Mrs. Harper she might hire another maid to assist her in the kitchen since we were a large company now, and she had beamed at me, well pleased. Course followed course, and there were even three sweets to choose from. Edwin, of course, had his favorite bread pudding. It was always on the menu since Mrs. Harper had discovered my brother was partial to it.

I had placed Mr. Hawes beside me at the table, the newlyweds across. Edwin, as was his right, sat at the head. I looked up at him once as he raised a finger to Harper to serve more wine, and thought how quickly he had become used to being lord of the manor, this brother who so recently had had to struggle just to keep our heads above water. And I thought how delightful it was to be together with him again. I had missed him more than he knew during my years with my aunt Sadie and her family.

"Why do you stare at Edwin so, Kate?" Bethany asked as her husband covered her wineglass so Harper could not pour her any more.

I smiled at them all. "I will admit I was admiring him—thinking how comfortable he looks at the head of the table. As well he should," I added, raising my glass to him in a toast. "Surely no one deserves the position more."

"Here, here," Brede Hawes said gallantly. I had noticed that he and Edwin had exchanged amused glances during my speech. At my devotion? But I did not care who knew I loved my brother and always had. Why, as a child I had toddled after him as soon as I could walk.

*   *   *

Very late that night I had a dream. I was in bed at the time, of course, and it was completely dark. Dark and stuffy, for I had begun to take the precaution of drawing the bed curtains tight around me at night. I knew it was silly. No flimsy curtain could bar a ghost, yet still I persisted.

I dreamed I was awakened, I knew not by what, and I lay perfectly still as the cold I remembered crept over me. I could smell lilacs again, too, and this time I heard music—a sad little air being sung in a girl's sweet voice. The words told of love forever lost.

The music grew louder, and I was sure the singer had come to stand beside me, even though I had not heard the curtain rings rattle as they always did when they were opened. Still, I reminded myself this was a dream and anything was possible. That made it easier for me to open my eyes, for I sensed I could not just cower there tonight. No, I must allow the ghost to reach me. Somehow I was sure that was what she wanted.

Even so, it took several moments before I could make myself do it. I was startled to discover the girl I had pictured earlier at the escritoire in this room was now beside me. She was young, no more than sixteen or seventeen, I judged, with pretty chestnut hair that streamed down her back almost to her waist. She was dressed in a white gown, worn over wide hoops, with a matching fichu crossed at her breast. It was fastened with a small gold circle pin. I recognized the style of the gown from paintings I had seen from the seventeenth century. And it was then I noticed I could see right through her. I wondered, if I put my hand out, whether I would touch her—or air.

She made no threatening moves. The lilac scent was stronger now—the cold deeper. And I saw she was weeping soundlessly, the tears making tracks down her pale, almost translucent cheeks.

I wanted to cry out, scream for help, but I was not able to make a sound, any more than I could move so much as my little finger. And so I was completely at the girl's mercy when she bent over me. I stopped breathing, sure I was about to die, and I had to remind myself I was only dreaming.

And then tears fell on the back of my hands where I had clutched the bed covers close to my breast; I felt my skin crawl with terror.

And just when I did not think I could stand this dream for another moment, she began to slowly fade away. I stared at her until she was gone, leaving behind only a faint wisp of scent.

The curtains hung undisturbed around me. There was no music. No cold. No ghost. There was only that slight scent of lilacs.

Awake now, I struggled to sit up, straining my ears for one last, elusive note of music. But she was truly gone. And it was then I knew it had not been a dream at all. It had been real.

And how did I know? Because my hands were wet—wet with the tears that had fallen on them when she bent over me.

I did not sleep again—no, not even when the dawn came with its gray light and comforting birdsong. What had happened to me had been too shocking to be dismissed so easily.

Chapter Nine

I spent a great deal of time in the days that followed that frightening night wondering why the girl had appeared to me especially. What did she want of me? And what could I possibly do to help someone who had been dead almost two hundred years? I knew now she did not wish me ill, for she had not hurt me, unless you call terrifying someone hurting them. But my hair had not turned white overnight, I had not become a gibbering idiot, and no one noticed anything unusual the next day except the yawns I was not always successful at hiding and my insistence on an early bedtime.

To everyone's great relief, neither ghost made an appearance for an entire week. I do not mean that everything was all sweetness and light at Bryce House. No, indeed. There was still an atmosphere about the place of dark brooding that almost tempted me to succumb to a like state. And there were definite places where no one was tempted to linger—near a certain window in one of the drawing rooms, a particular step on the stairs between the ground and first floors, the munitions room, and the bedroom I had chosen first and so quickly abandoned. Strangely, The Gentleman's room had no disturbing aura. It did not seem menacing or even just oddly still, as if it waited for something unspeakable to happen. It was only— empty.

I wondered sometimes why I did not tell Edwin at least about that disturbing dream and that reminded me I had not told him about the icy spot in the basement corridor either. But I hesitated to bother him, for he was so busy these days, not only with his books and family journals, but with his friend Brede Hawes as well. They were often out most of the day, only occasionally inviting Charles Buffington to go with them. Mr. Buffington had made friends with the hunting parson, however, and did not take offense. He and Farnsworth Beasley spent hours together in the saddle, when Mr. Buffington was not engaged with his wife. Since he felt the need to oblige Bethany for only an hour or so a day, that might have become tedious for me. But my cousin still spent most of the mornings in bed, dozing and trying to overcome a queasy stomach, while her old maid coddled her. And so I was able to ride out as often as I liked, and I had grown adept at avoiding not only Mr. Buffington and his new crony, but Sophia Beasley as well.

The only person I might have wished to see more of had disappeared, or so it seemed to me. I told myself there had been no need for Edwin to warn me away from Bryce, for the earl was nowhere to be seen. I rode the heath unmolested and never saw him, even though I often stopped at the small pond hoping to surprise the wild ponies watering there.

But of course such serendipity could not last. Seven days after I had that experience I thought was a dream, the ghosts became active again.

It began as it had before, with The Gentleman marching back and forth over the library late in the afternoon shortly after the servants had left for the day. I should point out that it was now mid-October and the days were growing shorter. As they did so, the servants' workdays shortened accordingly. Isn't that always the way? On the one hand it was heartening to know we had survived the conditions of Great-Uncle's will for half the term, yet now we faced shorter days and longer and longer nights.

We had adjourned to the library that afternoon because it had been a chilly day and there was a good fire burning there. The drawing room was so large, it was hard to heat unless one kept a fire going all the time, something that I, ever practical, was loath to order. Besides, it seemed to me everyone preferred the library. It was a pleasant room with its walls of books and comfortable old furniture and wide window seats. There was a certain informality about it, quite unlike the starchy propriety of the formal drawing room.

Bethany was sitting at the large center table with her husband, inspecting a book of drawings some long-dead Whittingham had produced on his Grand Tour. Brede Hawes was half hidden behind one of the London papers, and half asleep unless I missed my guess, and Edwin and I were playing chess. We had just had a wonderful dinner and the gentlemen had lingered over their port. Now the whole evening stretched before us to do with as we pleased.

And then those damnable footsteps began their measured pacing, and shortly after paused so the ghost could start banging on the walls again.

Bethany grasped her husband's hand as she stared helplessly at the ceiling. Hawes woke to toss his paper down in disgust. Edwin was the last to notice. Thinking I was taking overlong to decide my next move, he chided me. It was only then that he noticed we were all staring upwards, and why.

"I say," Charles Buffington exclaimed, removing his wife's hand from his own, to her distress. "There that fellow goes again. Come on, you two, let's see if we can give him a surprise this time."

As he spoke he moved towards the door. And as before, the tapping stopped and there was no more pacing to be heard.

"It appears all you have to do is announce your intentions, and off he goes," Hawes drawled. "What an effective ghost deterrent you are, sir."

"I fail to see anything amusing in this, Hawes," Buffington retorted. "You forget my wife is frightened; I daresay Cousin Kate is as well."

Hawes was quick to apologize to us both.

"I expect there is no point in going up, Charles," Edwin said. "I'm sure it will be just as it was before, and the quarry will have vanished."

"Yet you told me you all saw him once," Mr. Buffington insisted.

"Perhaps he only wishes to avoid you," I heard Brede Hawes murmur, as if to himself. Buffington stared at him hard for a moment, only looking away when Hawes coughed behind his hand.

"I don't like this," Bethany said in a high, nervous voice. "I don't like this at all! Where has he gone? I would almost rather he was in the bedroom above us. At least then I would not have to worry about meeting him in a dark hall or just around a corner."

"I am sure there is nothing to worry about, coz," Edwin began. "He seems a fairly benign phantom, wouldn't you—"

But he never got to finish his sentence, for high above us we could hear some violent crashes. It sounded as if someone in a demented rage was throwing furniture about. And as we listened, frozen in place, we heard a new sound—a man's deep roar of fury and frustration. As soon as it died away, we all rose and went to the hall, Bethany and I bringing up the rear. She had grasped my hand so tightly, it hurt.

"Now what on earth is this all about?" Brede Hawes demanded. "Is this some new ghost? We have not heard its like before."

"I have no idea. Harper did not tell me The Gentleman ever acted this way, or called out," Edwin said in some confusion. He had to raise his voice slightly, for the racket had begun again. I saw he had stopped to get the pistol he kept in the desk, and Buffington clutched the fireplace poker. Only Hawes was unarmed.

As the noise stopped for a moment, we heard someone on the stairs, and we all turned to peer upward into the gloom. The hall and foyer were growing darker as the afternoon lengthened; it was difficult to see far. At least The Gentleman was not standing at the top of the flight, dressed all in shimmering white and glowing as he had before. I did not mention this to my cousin. Bethany had turned her back to any danger and was hiding her face in my shoulder.

I began to relax when her maid came in sight, running quickly down the stairs. Agnes was pale and obviously frightened, but she did not hesitate. Marching up to Charles Buffington, she crossed her arms over her large bosom and took a deep breath.

"It is time for us to quit this place, sir," she said in a voice that shook only a little. "I'll not have my little miss frightened, and her in a delicate condition, too. I trust we will be off, back to town, at first light."

"Come now, there's no need for that," Edwin protested.

"I'll not have Miss Bethany sleeping here with heathen ghosts roaming about throwing furniture, Mr. Whittingham, and that's final," Agnes told him. I wondered I had never noticed what a firm jaw she had.

As if to emphasize her remark, the roar came again, and another piece of heavy furniture crashed to the floor. I thought it sounded as if it were coming from the east wing. No one slept there, for it was one of the oldest parts of the house.

"Perhaps you might consider remaining if you could stay at the inn at night?" Brede Hawes suggested. "It's only a short distance away, and you could leave here when the servants do at dusk, come back whenever you like the next day. There's never any ghostly goings-on except after dark."

"So far," Agnes muttered, but I saw she was relieved. I wondered if she thought her new master might insist on remaining. Yet surely Charles Buffington could not be at all loath to leave here. His host had not cared to entertain him, his wife was frightened and sickly, and I had made it plain I was not interested in any dalliance. Why stay? Certainly the company of the Reverend Mr. Beasley could not be that much of an enticement. We had discovered Buffington was hunt-mad, but the opening day of the local hunt was

a good three weeks away. I knew there was no way
he could hope to persuade his bride to endure Bryce
House for that length of time, even if he himself
wished it.

"You are right, Agnes," he said now. "We must
leave. However, let us go to the inn for a few days
and see how that works out. I dislike separating my
wife and her cousin. They are so fond of each other,
and who knows when they will have the chance to see
each other again?"

Bethany had stoppd trying to bury her head in my
collarbone, to my great relief, and now she smiled
tentatively until the sound of another crash came to
our ears. She screamed then and ran to Agnes.

The maid put her arms around her as she said,
"There, there. We'll soon be on our way, Miss
Bethany."

Charles Buffington shook his head in mock reproach. "How often must I remind you, Agnes, your
mistress is a married woman now. You must call her
Mrs. Buffington. I'll thank you to remember that."

He turned away before the maid could comment.
Knowing Agnes, I doubted she would bother. I also
doubted she would ever call my cousin anything but
her girlhood title.

When we were convinced the noises had stopped, at
least for now, Edwin offered to take Agnes and Bethany
up to see to the packing. Brede Hawes volunteered to
play footman and run down to the stables to send the
groom to the inn to make arrangements and to order
the carriage for the short journey.

As the others scattered, I was left to return to the
library with Charles Buffington. I wished he had not
chosen to lead me to a sofa, nor taken his place quite
so close beside me.

"Why do you stay here, Kate?" he asked. "Surely
there is no need for it even if your brother must remain to gain his inheritance. And I know Bethany
would be delighted to have you bear her company at
the inn. You could even come to London with us for

the duration of her confinement. She will not feel like going about much soon, but there is no reason you cannot see the town, enjoy the theaters and concerts in my company. Do say you will come," he added, his arm coming up to rest on the top of the sofa behind me.

"I cannot," I managed to say, getting up and pretending to see to the fire just to escape him. "I am Edwin's hostess, and I cannot like to leave him to his own devices. Besides, how would it look for me to stay at the inn when my home is only minutes away? No, no, I'll not be routed."

I turned to face him then, my hands clasped before me. He was lolling back in his seat, eyeing me with a half smile.

"You have the loveliest hair," he said softly. "In the firelight it glows with a hundred different shades of gold and honey."

"Mr. Buffington! I must remind you, you are a married man," I said stiffly. "These compliments—your suggestions—are not appropriate. And I am unmarried. I cannot think what you are about to speak so freely to me. It is insulting, sir."

"I wish I had spoken freely months ago," he said, getting up and coming toward me. I put the library table between us.

"But I did not know then that you and your brother were about to have such good fortune. It is too bad, that lost opportunity. I wanted you first, you know."

I hated him then for marrying Bethany only for her dowry, and I pitied her the life he would lead her.

Fortunately, Hawes returned before I told Buffington how despicable I thought he was. I knew it would be better for me to hold my tongue, if only for my cousin's sake, but I did not think I had ever met a man I disliked more than Charles Buffington. Nor one more Janus-faced, pretending such love and concern for Bethany when in reality it was no such thing.

The Buffingtons left the house shortly thereafter. Bethany promised to return first thing in the morning, and I shook my head at her, knowing she would do no such thing. For all of her restlessness, she had always been intent first and foremost on her comfort.

As the front door closed behind them, and Hawes and Edwin and I returned to the library, Hawes said pensively, "Now why do you suppose that maid called the ghosts heathens?"

"Because if they were good Christians, they would lie quietly in their graves and stop making all this fuss?" I suggested, and we all laughed and linked arms as we walked.

"The three of us make a good team," Edwin said, smiling down at me and giving me a quick hug before he went back to his desk. He had completely forgotten our chess game. Mr. Hawes took his place and defeated me in short order. I knew I was no match for either man even when I was not distracted by the ghosts, by our circumstances—by the earl's absence, my conscience reminded me. I did not try to deny it. Instead, to give my thoughts a new direction, I took a branch of candles and went to the last section of bookcase I had not inspected. I did not expect it to yield the journal any more than the others had, but it was best to finish what I had begun. High on the steps, I began to take down the books, volume by volume, to shake them before I returned them to their places. So far all I had found were some cards of invitation, a bill of sale for a new bridle, dated 1756, a lady's yellowed handkerchief, and more dried-up beetles than I cared for.

By the time I was finished and announced the journal was not to be found, it was bedtime. I think we were all tired, but we were to have little rest that night, for The Lady Ghost began her wailing again, sobbing and carrying on in the most pitiful way. I do not know how Edwin and Mr. Hawes fared, but I remained awake all night, staring up at the dark canopy over my head and praying as hard as I could that she would be content to remain in the basement and not come visiting as she had before.

There was a storm the following three days, full of wind and heavy rain. Several leaks were discovered, not only in the attics but around some of the older windows. I made a note of their locations as the maids mopped and stuffed rags in place. We would have to hire a carpenter to mend them before winter. If we could get one, I reminded myself. Harper had told me how hard it was to get help at Bryce House, and I believed him. Even my mantua maker had insisted I meet her at the inn for all my fittings. But my new clothes were finished now, and I felt rich indeed with one beautiful gown after another to wear, new matching sandals, even a pretty necklace Edwin had brought me earlier after a visit to Southampton. He had even urged me have a new pair of riding boots made and taken the tracings of my feet himself for the bootmaker.

Bethany and her husband remained at the inn during the storm. I was just as glad. I hoped the respite might make my cousin feel more comfortable here when they came back. There had not been a peep from the ghosts since the night they had been driven away. I was reminded that the same thing had happened before. Perhaps all that activity wearied them? Surely it must be difficult for them to summon the strength to show themselves to the living. Exhausting, even. I wondered if they would ever be able to rest— why they felt compelled to haunt the place when it was obvious they were both miserable. The Lady's wails and tears, The Gentleman's fury and his recent bellowing were proof of that. I wondered what had happened to them here to make them act like that? I wished I knew.

I decided then to begin a systematic search of the entire house. Great-Uncle Daniel's journal had to be somewhere. And I would not tell Edwin what I was up to, either, I decided. No, I would surprise him with it when I found it. I did not fear he would notice my searching. Not he. He was so intent on his own affairs, my brother.

I started on the ground floor. It was unlikely that Daniel Whittingham had hidden his journal in the cellars where the servants held sway. But there were any number of places to conceal it in the upper rooms and closets. And as I went through them, I could make piles of things to be discarded, or mended, or removed to another room. In the very first room I tackled, I found a handsome silver mirror tucked away in an old sewing box, and heartened by the discovery of such a treasure, set to work with a will.

Of course, when the sun came out again, I deserted my chore to ride Imp, but always early in the morning when Mr. Buffington or the Beasleys would not be likely to be abroad.

I rode first to the pond on the heath that first good morning. The storm seemed to have banished summer for good. The day was so brisk, so chilly, the sun could do little to warm it. Still, I had on my new habit with a warm wool shift under it, and my gloves were lined with cashmere, so I did not mind.

I discovered to my delight that I was not the first at the pond that morning when I saw the earl, mounted on his big gelding. Carefully, I guided Imp down to join him.

"Good morning, my lord," I called, smiling at him. "How nice to see you again after such a time."

His brows rose and I cursed myself for being so obvious.

"Did you miss me then?" he drawled. "Why, I was only gone for a few days. Business in Southampton, you know."

"That is none of my affair, my lord," I said stiffly, staring straight ahead and refusing to look at him. "And of course I did not miss you. I have been far too busy myself."

There was silence for a moment, as if he were debating arguing that statement. Then he said, "Have the ghosts been behaving themselves or have they been up to their old tricks?" His horse sidestepped, trying to push Imp aside as it had before, and for a moment, our legs were pressed together.

Flustered, I was careful not to stammer as I told him what they had done.

"I understand some of your guests have retreated to the inn at Lechton," he said after he had moved his mount away.

"Now why am I not surprised you know that, my lord? Indeed, I am sure word of their intention was brought to the Court before they even left Bryce House."

"Perhaps not quite as soon as that. Still, my mother's maid does keep her apprised, and from her ears to mine is only a short step.

"By the way, she is eager to meet you, and your brother and guests, of course. What say you to an expedition to the shore some pleasant day soon?"

"It sounds delightful," I agreed, wondering how I could suddenly feel so happy after being thrown into the dismals earlier when I had shown my joy at seeing him again. "Of course Edwin must return by nightfall. Is it too far a distance for that?"

He assured me it was not. "We will go by carriage. We have to, for my mother is crippled and cannot ride."

"I am sorry. You are sure it will not be too hard for her?"

He laughed. "Not a bit of it. She is a valiant woman. Her injury was incurred years ago when I was still young. She always rode as if the devil were after her, and she came to grief. My father was furious with her, after his initial despair. That was strange, for he died himself in a riding accident years later."

He suggested a time two days hence, and I agreed to discuss it with Edwin. As I did so, I wondered how he would react to the invitation. He had told me to avoid Bryce, never see him alone. But I could not help this chance meeting, I told myself defensively. Perhaps Edwin would agree to the outing. I know I had mentioned how I longed to go to the sea, and we must remain on good terms with our neighbors even if we did deplore their morals.

Not that I was at all sure the earl's morals had to be deplored, I thought as I studied his profile. Surely a man used to debauchery would look more the part. World-weary, his face red and coarsened, his hands shaking from the amount of alcohol he drank. I had seen enough men ravaged by drink to know what they looked like. But Bryce was nothing like that. His eyes were clear and piercing, his complexion healthy. As for . . .

"Why are you staring at me, Kate?" he asked idly. "There is something amiss with my appearance?

"Incidentally, I like your appearance. That new habit fits you admirably."

I prayed I was not blushing as his eyes swept my figure. "Of course I am not staring," I said hastily. "I was only lost in reverie about a household matter and was looking right through you."

"Now I know I have been insulted," he murmured before he smiled. "To think I would take second place to mops and brooms."

I told myself that handsome, devastating grin of his had no effect on me. None at all.

Chapter Ten

That day and the next passed more slowly than any I can ever remember. I had told Edwin of the earl's invitation as soon as I reached home. I could tell he did not care for it, and wanted to refuse. It was Brede Hawes who talked him around, pointing out the advantage of having good relations in the neighborhood, and how pleasant it would be for me, and never mind the opportunity it was for us to meet the Dowager Countess of Bryce. At last, Edwin agreed, but he did not smile. I ran off to write our acceptance before he could change his mind, then took it down to the stable myself for the groom to deliver.

I tried to keep myself busy those two days, working from room to room searching for the journal. When Bethany arrived, I enlisted her help. She gave little of that, of course, but she did get Agnes to help me sift through boxes and chests and cupboards for any hidden treasure we might unearth.

Bethany was also intrigued by the invitation to the shore, and talked about the outfit she would wear until I ceased to listen.

We found a cache of children's ancient toys, some handsome pieces of needlepoint that looked as if they had been done for a set of straight chairs, a man's silver-backed brush and some tortoiseshell combs, and a small gold ring, but we did not find the journal. Still, I was not discouraged. Bryce House was a large establishment. There were a great many rooms left for me to search, although I admit I was not anxious to brave the east wing, even though it had been searched after the clamor and nothing out of the ordinary had been found.

The day of the outing dawned fair. I was the first to know that for I was awake an hour before the sun rose. I dressed in one of my new gowns, a bottle-green merino, tailored with a high neck and tight sleeves suitable for an autumn walking costume. I had a matching bonnet, a gold reticule, and tan gloves, and I was only sorry I must wear my old walking boots. Still, I had had the upstairs maid give them a good polishing, and I hoped they would not be too noticeable.

The carriages arrived promptly at ten. After greetings had been exchanged and introductions made, Bryce ushered me to the first vehicle, where his mother waited in state. He followed me into it as well, to take the seat facing back. That left my brother, Mr. Hawes, and the Buffingtons to occupy the other carriage. I was startled to be singled out and hoped Edwin would not take it amiss. Perhaps another arrangement could be made for the return? Bethany would be sure to pout if she did not have the chance to talk to the countess.

I was instantly drawn to that lady myself. I could tell she was tall and very slim. Her face revealed the great beauty she must have been once. Her hair was pure white now, but her delicate brows were as dark as her son's, and her complexion was so flawless, I vowed to make a habit of always wearing a hat outdoors from now on. The countess was dressed fashionably as well, and as long as she remained seated, showed no sign of her condition.

"I am delighted to finally have the chance to meet you, Miss Whittingham," she said. "But how unfortunate Luke is with us. We shall have to watch what we say."

"I will not listen, if you would prefer it, Mother," her son said mildly.

Luke, I thought. Luke Tremaine. Yes, the name suited him.

"Besides, what can you possibly wish to discuss that I should not hear?" he went on, and I made myself concentrate.

"You would be astonished to know," his mother said wryly, before she glanced at me and smiled.

Now I knew where the earl got that splendid smile of his, the masculine version of it anyway. Looking from one to the other, I realized I had seldom seen such handsome creatures. What a shame the countess had been lamed.

I was questioned about the ghosts, and asked how I liked Bryce House, and told what the countess thought of my great-uncle. She was not at all complimentary; indeed, she had nothing but scorn for the condition he had set.

"To think your brother—and you, too, Miss Whittingham—must bear with those horrid phantoms for an entire month," she said. "You must plan a gala affair for All Hallow's Eve to mark the successful conclusion of it. And it will be an excellent way for you to meet your new neighbors."

"Perhaps that might not be such a good idea," Bryce said. "Isn't All Hallow's the time when ghosts are the most active? The most troublesome?"

"Why, yes, I believe so, but what difference would that make? The Whittinghams are already beset with the creatures. Do you mean there might be more of them lurking about who will appear that night? Good heavens!"

She turned to me then, her eyes twinkling. "I do hope, if you have a party, you will include me. I have never seen a ghost."

"And are probably the only person in the world who would look forward to the experience," her son drawled.

"Not that I would not like to be there as well," he added. "I admit to doubts about these ghosts of yours, Kate."

I did not dare look at his mother, but I wondered what she thought of his use of my given name. It was not at all the thing for a single gentleman to be so free with a woman to whom he was not related. But I only confessed I had no idea what Edwin planned to mark the occasion and said I would suggest the party. "And I suspect we will be more than ready for one by then," I could not help adding.

Somehow I found myself telling them both of the nights The Lady had come to my bedside, how I had thought the last visit a dream, and how I had discovered it was not. And I told them how disturbing her heartfelt cries were to bear.

"I wish there was some way I could help her, but I haven't the faintest idea how that might be accomplished," I finished. "Still, don't you think something dreadful must have happened to her, to make her linger such a long time?"

"It could be a disastrous love affair," the countess said, completely engrossed in the tale. "She might have been separated from the man she loved, and that is why she sang that song and why she weeps. I wonder if he died before they could wed?"

I noticed that the earl did not contribute anything to the conversation. I supposed he thought I was making it all up, and I wished there was some way I could convince him I was not.

When we reached Lymington-on-Sea, I was so astounded by the spectacle before me, all thoughts of the ghosts left my mind. As far as the eye could see there was nothing but water, but not water as I was used to it in lakes and streams. No, this expanse was a gray, green, blue, and aqua mix of shades, constantly in motion, with little fringes of white the earl told me were called, appropriately, whitecaps. And nearer the shore, waves rolled up on the strand and tumbled into froth before they ebbed away. It was so fascinating, I barely noticed the servants who had been sent on before us to prepare a luncheon and a tent, as well as robes and chairs to sit on.

The smell of the sea was intriguing, too, I thought as I took a deep breath. Not only salty but ancient, somehow. The sand under my feet was another color spectrum—beige and gold and gray and brown and white. Near the water's edge there was a line of sea-weed, and mixed up in it were the discarded shells of sea creatures. I was familiar with them, for small items decorated with shells from foreign lands were popular. Even my aunt Sadie had a writing chest she treasured. I looked forward to gathering some shells for a box of my own, and I wished I had thought to bring a bag to collect them in.

But before I could begin, I had to be polite. While the earl carried his mother to a chair placed beneath an umbrella, I followed with her shawl, a large sketch-book, and a box of pastels. When she was settled with her maid fussing around her, the countess asked me to call my cousin over so they might have a chat.

"I understand she is with child," she said for me alone to hear as Bethany came toward us. "It will do her good to talk to an older woman, and to rest, too, I daresay. Besides, I can tell you are itching to explore. No, no, do not deny it, child! Off with you now. We will continue our conversation later."

I needed no further urging. Edwin and Brede Hawes were inspecting some fishing rods the earl was showing them, so I began to walk along the edge of the strand looking for shells. Overhead a few large white birds with a graceful wing span rode the wind. Their cries were nowhere near as handsome as they were; in fact, they sounded as if their throats hurt them. I also saw some strange little brown birds on the thinnest legs I had ever seen playing tag with the waves as they searched the damp sand for food.

I was delighted when Bryce joined me for I had a number of questions about the tides that I couldn't remember from my days in the schoolroom—why there were high and low ones and how the moon af-fected them.

I must say the earl was patient with me. Somehow that surprised me, for he did not seem a man given to lengthy explanations. He even helped me collect shells and took off his hat to carry them in.

By the time we turned to return to the others, they looked like mere specks in the distance. I tried to hurry, sure our absence would be remarked.

"You cannot run well in loose sand, Kate," Bryce said. He picked me up to carry me down to where the sand was firmer near the water for the tide was going out. I put my arm around his neck. Really, I had to. Where else was it to go?

I must admit I felt very strange, being so close to him. His gray eyes had thick lashes for a man, and I could see a tiny scar I had not noticed before at one corner of his mouth.

"Yes, I want to kiss you," he said, his eyes intent on my face. His voice was deep and husky, and I was very conscious of the arm under my thighs, the other around my back. I wanted him to kiss me. I almost moved closer when he sighed and set me on my feet again, holding me for a moment to make sure I had my balance.

"This is not the place for it, unfortunately," he told me. "If I were to start kissing you now, I would not be able to stop at just one."

I realized I was clutching his arm with both hands and I made myself release him. I even managed a step backwards. But I never took my eyes from his, and I had to clasp my hands tightly to keep from reaching for him again.

"Soon," he said. "As soon as I can manage it. Unlike Job, when I want something as badly as I want you in my arms, I am not prepared to wait."

He ran a hand through his dark hair and then looked around. I wondered what he was searching for; at least, I did until I saw him stoop to pick up his hat. The shells we had collected were scattered on the sand. Somehow I had lost all interest in them.

"I suppose we must pick them up. If we do not, we will not have any excuse for our long absence. Damn it," he muttered as he bent to collect as many as he could. I knelt beside him to help, trying not to look at the big hand that just a minute ago had caressed my back. I could feel it there still. I missed it dreadfully.

When we had picked up as many shells as we could find, we set off again. And still I had not said a word. I wondered if I could, and what I could possibly find to discuss if I tried.

"Are you hungry, Kate?" he asked. "The salt air always gives me a tremendous appetite. And I know we are to have lobster. Do you care for it? It is one of my favorites, served with only a little lemon and some melted butter."

I realized he was trying to ease the way for me, and I started to reply, but had to stop and clear my throat before I was able to tell him I did indeed enjoy lobster.

"Oh, look, there is a ship far out on the horizon," I added. "I wonder where it is going, and where it has been."

We managed to converse all the way back to the party, but I could not tell you what about. I was afraid Edwin would be angry at me over my long absence, but to my relief, he had caught a large sea bass and could hardly wait to try his luck again as soon as luncheon was over. I heard him challenge Charles Buffington and Brede Hawes to a contest, and name a large wager to the winner, and I tried not to show my disapproval.

"Your brother enjoys gambling?" Bryce asked. I was startled. I had not been aware he was standing behind me.

"Like most men, yes," I said as carelessly as I could. Then I turned to Bethany to admire the pastel sketch the countess had done of her while I was gone. I was impressed for it showed talent. The countess had caught her winsome expression perfectly, along with the bewildered look that sometimes came to her fine blue eyes.

"You must have this framed, coz," I told her. "It is

just like you! But I do wonder how our Firefly managed to sit still long enough for it to be completed."

I sat for my own portrait after luncheon and watched the men fishing. I noticed Bryce did not join them, although there was a pole for his use.

The countess did not talk much as she worked, and I, of necessity, had to remain silent for the pose. I was glad of that. I wanted to think about Bryce—no, Luke—and how it had felt being held in his arms, what his voice had sounded like when he said he would not be able to give me only a single kiss, how long it might be before we could share a dozen.

When she declared herself satisfied, Lady Bryce handed me the sketchbook. I stared at the girl she had drawn, wondering if that was how I looked to her, to everyone.

"Why, Kate, how solemn you are in your portrait," Bethany exclaimed.

"Do you think so?" the countess asked, pausing as she put her crayons away. "I thought she looked only a little pensive, as if she were contemplating some serious decision. But of course, another artist would see her completely differently."

She held out her hand, and I gave her back the sketch. She did not offer it to me to keep as she had Bethany's, and I wondered what she intended to do with it.

I was distracted then for Edwin gave a loud cry of satisfaction and I looked up to see him pulling in another fish. Neither Hawes nor Charles Buffington had had any luck, and since it was time to leave, they were forced to concede the wager.

I did not ride with the countess and Bryce on the homeward journey. Instead, Edwin and Brede Hawes joined them. Bethany chattered gaily, holding her husband's hand as she did so. Very soon, I put my head back on the squabs and pretended to fall asleep.

It was almost dusk when we reached Bryce House again, and we saw the servants coming down the avenue as we turned into the gates. I knew Mrs. Harper had left a cold supper for us in the dining salon, although I was sure Edwin would be disappointed that he must wait until the morrow to savor his fish.

Bryce handed me from the carriage and turned me slightly away from the others. I did not think anyone noticed. They were all busy saying their good-byes and thanking their hostess for the treat.

"The pond tomorrow, at eight," Bryce said. "If you cannot come, I will wait for you in the glade in the beech wood. Do not fail me."

Once again, I found I could not speak, but I did manage to nod. He pressed my hand and turned away.

The Buffingtons did not join us for supper. It was growing too late for that, and I knew Bethany was on the fret lest they be caught at Bryce House after dark. I was just as glad. I was tired, and I had listened to enough of her artless prattle. I went to bed early, and this night I did not even think for a moment of the weeping girl who haunted us. No, all my thoughts were on Luke Tremaine and what was going to happen between us at eight tomorrow.

To my disappointment, it was raining hard when I woke. Still, I dressed in an old gown and went down to find the oiled coat I had worn to the stables. I could not go to the pond on the heath, but I could go to the glade. Breakfast would be served until ten. There was plenty of time. Of course I knew it unlikely Bryce would come in such weather, for it was not only raining, there was a nasty wind and it was cold. More November weather than October's, I thought as I walked across the lawn, hugging the coat to me with one hand while the other held an umbrella high.

When I reached the glade, I saw at once he was not there. The place looked forlorn in the gray mist, the rain spattering the surface of the pool and the few leaves still clinging to the branches above me. The ground was covered with their fellows in sodden heaps the wind could not stir. I sat down on the rustic bench. The coat and umbrella sheltered me from the worst of the storm, and I decided I would wait a few minutes at least. It was a long ride from the Court, and it was a miserable morning.

For a while I stared idly at the pool, switching the hand that held the umbrella when it grew cold for the other one I was keeping warm in a pocket. At last I sighed and rose. He was not coming. It had been foolish of me to think he would, in this weather. I decided that when he asked me, I would say I had not come either. I struggled with the black mood I could feel waiting to overcome me. But it was not fair when yesterday had been such a golden day. Who would have thought that in only—

The umbrella was wrested from my hand, and I looked up to see Bryce standing there, his gray eyes blazing down at me. I didn't get a chance to say anything for he swept me into his arms and began to kiss me, warm take-your-breath-away kisses, feathery little promises of kisses, long, seductive kisses. The rain pelted us, and when he took his lips from mine, it ran into my open mouth, cold and insistent. I wondered if anyone had ever drowned from rain.

At last I put both hands on the sides of his rugged face and leaned back in his arms to study him. I could barely see for the moisture caught in my lashes and had to blink it away. I caught my breath at the light in his eyes, the hunger there. And then I became aware of the rain pouring down his face, his dripping hair, the coldness of his skin. The only warm, exposed part of both of us was our lips, and I could feel mine beginning to cool rapidly. But it didn't matter. None of it mattered. I was so happy, I felt I might rise and float away if he were to stop anchoring me so firmly to the earth.

"Enough, Luke. What did you do with my umbrella?"

"Hang your umbrella. The damage is done anyway. This damn weather! Impossible to make love in it. I know now why I've never tried it before."

I swallowed the question that sprang to my lips and

broke away to search for the umbrella. I spied it at our feet. As I retrieved it, he said, "We must marry before the snow flies, Kate. I've no liking for winter trysts either."

I did not say anything. I couldn't. Marry Luke Tremaine. *Marry* him.

He cupped my chin and lifted it to stare down at me. "I wish I could take you home with me now, riding double. I wish I could carry you into the Court and up the stairs to my rooms, calling for a hot bath as I did so. I wish I could lock the doors then and undress you, lower you into the tub, join you there. I wish I could dry you off and take you to bed . . ."

"I must get back," I managed to say, afraid that if I listened to another word, I would not ever return to Bryce House. For a moment I was sure he would argue, but finally he let me go, to lift my hand and kiss it in farewell.

"I will call on your brother later today," he told me. "Is early afternoon a good time?"

The dream I was wrapped in dissolved as quickly as a soap bubble. "Oh, no, you must not," I exclaimed. "Not yet."

He looked amazed. "But why not? Do you mean to tell me you can return my kisses as you just did and not demand an almost immediate ceremony? Kate, Kate! I shall think you wanton."

I could tell he was joking, but I did not feel like laughing. Instead I was remembering Edwin telling me of his reputation—the orgies he engaged in, his unsuitable friends, that rape. He had called him "disgusting." I was sure Edwin was wrong, but I knew I must prevent Luke from coming today and demanding my hand. Edwin would not give it to him. But I could not tell him why, so I said, "You must let me prepare him for the visit first. We have been separated for five long years. I cannot leave him so quickly."

"Yes, you can. And you will."

"Well, yes, I suppose I will. But you must give me time to talk to him, to explain how this happened, beg his understanding. It will be all right then, Luke. Give me a week."

"A week? More like a day!"

"No, no. Four days. Please, for me. Four days."

He agreed finally to three, but he was not pleased, and he frowned until I began to kiss him again. Our embrace soon grew so heated, I broke away from him and ran away.

I admit it. I ran as fast as I could. Only when I reached the edge of the glade did I pause and look back. Luke Tremaine stood where I had left him, staring after me. He did not seem to notice how much wetter he was getting with every passing second.

"You are the most seductive, lovely woman I have ever seen, and after my mother, the most gallant," he called. "We will have brave sons and handsome daughters, you and I, Kate Whittingham."

I considered him, head tipped to one side. Then I smiled at him. Slowly. When he started toward me, I turned and ran for Bryce House, and this time I did not stop and look back.

It was only later, when I had bathed and had the maid do up my hair, that I remembered the umbrella. No doubt it still lay abandoned in the glade, the only evidence of the most memorable morning of my life.

Chapter Eleven

I had three days. Three days to convince Edwin that Luke Tremaine was not the man he thought, and if I could not marry him, I would be miserable for the rest of my life. Three days to gain Edwin's consent, no, more than that, his complete approval. I wanted no grudging, hesitant permission.

I knew I did not need it. I was twenty-two, a woman grown. But Edwin was my brother and I loved him. How could I go to Luke leaving behind me an irreparable rift of anger and cold silence? Somehow I must make Edwin understand—and I only had three days to do it.

I did not rush immediately to see him. I had had breakfast in my room, and when I opened my door I heard the two men talking together as they went to the library. It was then I decided it would be better to think of all the advantages my marriage would bring.

I sat down at the escritoire and began to prepare a quill, but I could not seem to concentrate on such a dull thing as a list. Instead, I closed my eyes and remembered Luke and the glade, those mad kisses and how I had felt, like smoke in his arms, although my body had let me know I was all too real. Too hungry. Insatiable, in fact.

I wondered what Luke was doing now. Had he told his mother of our plans? Did she approve? Somehow I was sure she knew. Now I came to think of it, singling me out to ride with her to the shore had been no accident.

Had Luke taken a hot bath? I felt weak just picturing him doing so. Perhaps his valet was shaving him. I touched my face. It was tender all over, proof he had not been shaved before he came to me.

I sat up straighter and forced myself to concentrate. One, I loved Luke. That was the most important thing to put on my list. Two, when I was living at Bryce Court I would still be near Edwin. Three, Luke was wealthy. He would not care that my dowry was no more than adequate. Four, I would be a countess. Strange, that. As a young girl I had considered a title important and longed to be called "my lady" someday. Now it was going to happen and I did not care.

I frowned then. Edwin would bring up Luke's reputation again, I knew he would. And what could I say to refute it? I had never even asked Luke about it, heard his side. But still I was sure, *sure* he was not the man Edwin portrayed. As much as he loved me and wanted me, he had been a gentleman this morning, keeping himself firmly under control. And it had not been simply because it was raining so hard either. I was sure of it.

Suddenly I knew I was not alone in the room. Knew it even before I felt the cold, smelled the familiar lilac scent. I did not turn around. The ghost remained at a distance; I imagined she was somewhere near the door. Why had she come, now, in the morning? Was it because I was sitting at her desk? I wondered, remembering I had pictured her here once.

I put the quill I was holding down carefully and, steeling myself, turned to face her. As always, my heart began to drum in my breast, my breathing grew shallow and hurried, and I had to grip the edge of the desk to steady myself.

She looked even more diaphanous than she had standing beside my bed, almost like a collection of wispy white rags on a body with bloodless hands and face. I could see the panels of the door clearly through her. She was weeping soundlessly again, that pale face distorted with pain, but she was not wringing her hands today. Squinting a little, I saw that she had her arms crossed under her bosom, her hands supporting her elbows. In the gray, rainy-day light, she seemed to waver there, as if her hold on this world was tenuous at best in the daytime.

We stared at each other for I know not how long. It seemed an endless time, but perhaps it was only a minute or so. I lost all sense of time. *What is it?* I asked silently. *What do you want from me?*

I wondered then what would happen if I spoke to her. Until now I had been assuming she could read my mind, but that might not be the case. I cleared my throat, afraid my voice would crack if I did not. Right there and then, before my eyes, she disintegrated; vanished. In a couple of seconds she was gone, the cold and scent gone with her. My cough must have frightened her. I was sorry for that.

For a while, Luke forgotten, I sat and considered my ghost, for I was beginning to think of her as mine. Neither Brede Hawes nor my brother had ever mentioned seeing her. They had only heard her shrieking, as had I, from somewhere in the cellars. I wondered about that. Why would she make such an unholy noise when she was down there, yet be as still as the grave—an unfortunate simile, to be sure—when she was with me? There could not be two female haunts at Bryce House! It stunned the mind even to have to accept the idea of The Gentleman, pacing and tapping the walls in the blue bedroom. No, my girl ghost must make that terrible wailing noise. I wished I knew why. I wished I could find Great-Uncle Daniel's journal.

I glanced down at the list I had made of all the reasons I should marry Luke Tremaine. Perhaps I should add another? To escape the ghosts of Bryce House?

I went out to the hall and halfway down the stairs. There was no one below; the library door was closed. Hawes would not go riding today, more's the pity. I would have to wait to see Edwin. Perhaps I could ask for some time alone with him this afternoon.

In the meantime, to keep busy, I began to search

the last remaining room on this floor in the central part of the house. It did not take me long, for it was almost empty of furniture. When I was done, I sat down on the bare mattress to consider.

I could not picture my great-uncle hiding his journal away. He had lived here alone and most, if not all, of the servants probably could not read or write more than their names. There would be no reason to hide the journal, and that was why I had not bothered to search under furniture or behind it. Besides, he would also want to keep the journal handy for making entries. The ghosts seemed to have no pattern to their appearances. He could not count on The Gentleman tapping and pacing on Sunday evenings, The Lady screaming on Tuesdays and Thursdays. I smiled to myself at the thought and then wondered if I were getting immune to horror, even hardened to it, as surely as my great-uncle must have been after a lifetime spent in their company. Yet somehow I knew, no matter how long I lived here, I would never be able to control the sudden, heart-stopping terror that always came over me when the ghost, or even her scent, was near.

I sighed as I left the room. As I stood in the hall, undecided about what I would do now, I realized Edwin's room was the only one I had not searched. I had not thought it necessary, for surely by now he would have discovered the journal, if it were there. But now I shook my head, sure my wits had gone begging. How could I forget how difficult it had always been for Edwin to find things, even when they were right under his nose? I could remember him as a boy protesting that he could not find his cap, when all the time it had been on a hook under his jacket right behind his door. My mother had told me all men suffered the failing to some degree. I wondered if Luke was among their number.

But I told myself sternly that I could not think of him now. Instead, I let myself in to Edwin's room. I had noticed earlier that this room had a large mahogany chest, the kind used for storing blankets and quilts. It had a chest of drawers and a clothes cupboard as well, and the journal could be in any of them. I knelt before the chest first. I hesitated for a moment, for I disliked pawing through Edwin's belongings, but when I had the lid up, I saw he was not using it. Instead, it was full of old coats and darned hose and stiff, yellowed kid gloves. There were even some ancient patched petticoats. Wrinkling my nose, I took them all out to carry away to be discarded. As I did so, I noticed a large, thick volume at the very bottom of the chest. My heart was beating faster as I picked it up and settled back on my haunches to study it.

You may imagine my delight when I saw it was indeed my great-uncle's private journal, written in a precise, crabbed hand and meticulously dated. It began in 1770, when I knew Daniel Whittingham had been a young man, and the first entry was about The Lady. It described her in detail, right down to the gold circle pin she wore to hold her fichu together. Eagerly, I flipped through the pages. It appeared all the entries were about The Lady. Could it be The Gentleman was not haunting the house then? The cavalier's outfit he wore, the mask, could have been for a masquerade. He might not have been from that period of history at all. It was then I saw an entry detailing a maid's fright on encountering him at the top of the stairs.

I saw the last entry had been written shortly before Daniel's Whittingham's death. I did not stop to read any more. Instead, I ran down the stairs clutching my find to show to Edwin. How pleased he would be, I thought, and how embarrassed to discover the journal had been right at the foot of his bed the whole time. I told myself I must not make too much of that. Men did not care to be ridiculed, or made to feel inadequate.

I found Brede Hawes in the library with Edwin, as I had expected. The two men looked up from their books as I came running in, waving the journal over my head.

"I found it, Edwin," I cried. "I found Great-Uncle's ghost journal!"

My brother stared at me, stunned, and it was Hawes who got up and came to me, saying, "What grand news, Kate! Where on earth was the thing? Tucked away under a bed? Hidden in a closet? Never tell us it was lying on a bedside table in plain sight."

"If you will just give her a moment, I am sure she will be glad to answer you, Brede," Edwin said dryly. I whirled to lay the journal on the desk before him.

"I have been searching for it all over," I admitted. "I didn't tell you because I wanted it to be a surprise. I went through all the rooms in this part of the house, and this morning, I remembered something about you, Edwin. Sometimes you have had trouble finding things, you must admit that. You were always losing a book or a scarf or your gloves when you were a boy. I remember it well.

"Anyway, I found the journal tucked away under a pile of ancient old clothes in that chest at the foot of your bed."

"I don't believe it," Edwin said weakly. "You mean to tell me it has been there all this time and I never even knew it? Kate, you are a wonder, indeed you are. I would never have thought of searching that chest, not in a million years."

As he spoke, he edged the journal closer to open it to the first page and sneak a look at it. I smiled.

"Go ahead," I told him. "I know how eager you have been to read it. Perhaps you will find some clues to the ghosts' identities, some reasons for their haunting. If so, don't you think we might be able to put a stop to it? Persuade them somehow?"

"It is entirely possible," he agreed.

"Do you think I might read it, too?" I asked next. I saw him frown and I hastened to add, "After you are through, I mean. I know you must study it, try and make some sense of it as far as you are able. But later, surely I might have a peek, don't you think?"

"Of course you shall," Edwin said warmly. "Just as

soon as I am finished with it. I warn you, that might take a while though, Kate."

I blew him a kiss. Suddenly I remembered Luke and the serious discussion I must have with my brother. I clasped my hands together before me to steady myself and said, "Could you spare me a few minutes later, Edwin? There is something I wish to talk to you about."

"Here now, Kate, why didn't you say so? I'll take myself off at once," Brede Hawes volunteered.

I had to smile. "No, you will not, sir. I could never get his attention, now it is all given to that journal. Later this afternoon will be fine. Perhaps after dinner, Edwin?"

He nodded, and I left the two alone. As I closed the library door behind me, I saw Edwin bent over the journal, and his eager expression was all the thanks I needed. I went to the sitting room I used in the mornings and rang for Mrs. Harper. There were menus and daily chores to discuss, and I reminded myself the maids must be sent to remove that pile of old clothes from Edwin's bedroom.

Brede Hawes left Edwin and me to our own devices right after dinner. I thought again what a nice man he was, how understanding. And he was so good for Edwin, too. He was not only able to coax my brother from his studies, but to see he got out and rode; he even made him talk of other matters than whatever scholarly research he happened to be engaged in.

We went to the library. I noticed there was no sign of the journal. Edwin must have seen me looking at the desk for he was quick to say, "I have locked it up, Kate. Not the type of thing I want Harper or any of the servants to see. Some of the entries in it are, well, frightening."

"But do you really think they can read?" I asked as I took a seat near the fire. "Most servants can't."

"Harper reads. So does his wife. And that older maid—what's her name, Lizzie? I caught her going through my papers here one morning. She jumped back, claimed she was only straightening them, but I prefer not to take any chances. If anything happened to the journal, we wouldn't have a clue about the ghosts."

"You are right," I said absently, wondering how I was to introduce the subject I had to discuss with him.

"Now, what is the reason for this *tête à tête*? I've been pondering it all day, but I can't think what it might be," he said, smiling at me. His hazel eyes were warm, but I barely noticed.

"Luke Tremaine has asked me to marry him," I said, just like that, right straight out. Inside I cringed. I had meant to lead up to it gradually, prepare Edwin, not fire off a broadside the minute I had his attention. Would I never learn?

"Has he indeed," Edwin said, all good humor gone from his face and voice. "But he should have come to me to ask if he might pay his addresses, as any gentleman would."

"He intended to, but I begged him not to until I spoke to you. I knew how you felt about the earl, but indeed, he is not like that. Those things you heard about him, they are not true."

"And how do you know this? Because he has denied them, as of course he would? A man does not relate his entire sexual history and lack of morals to a girl he hopes to marry. Or give any details of his past, especially if they are as black as Bryce's."

"I have not spoken to him about such things," I admitted. "But I know he is not the kind of man you described to me. I know it!"

My brother shook his head. He did not look angry anymore. Instead, he looked sad, as if he hated to disappoint me. "You are bewitched, Kate. He kissed you, didn't he? I hope that is all he did, or I shall be forced to call him out."

"He did nothing! How can you say such things? He was a perfect gentleman."

Edwin rose and poured himself a glass of brandy.

When he took his seat again, he warmed the glass between his hands before he said, "I want you to remember something, Kate. I love you, and as your older brother, I only want the best for you. Perhaps you do love Luke Tremaine. He's an imposing man, I'll give you that. And he is an earl. Are you tempted to marry to become a countess?"

I would have spoken, but he held up his hand and went on, "But I know the world better than you, dear. And marriage to Bryce will lead to nothing but misery. I cannot bear to think of you being miserable the rest of your life. And so I cannot give you my blessing. I know our father and mother would not want me to in this case."

I had a large lump in my throat, and I could feel the threatening tears. Determined not to weep helplessly, I swallowed hard before I said, "I am of age, Edwin. I do not need your permission. But I did not want it to be this way. I wanted you to approve, be happy for me, see that quite contrary to your prediction, I will be miserable if I do *not* marry Luke. And just think, I will be living near you. You will marry someday yourself, and our children can grow up together. We can see each other as often as we like."

"What makes you think I intend to stay here?" he demanded. "Bring a wife and children into this hellhole to be tormented by ghosts? No, I am only here until Great-Uncle's ridiculous condition has been met, and the fortune is mine. Then I am gone. I will sell the house and land. No doubt Bryce will buy it."

"What will you do then?" I asked, confused.

"Travel, study, buy an estate somewhere else. Perhaps even in the West Indies. I thought we would go together, you and I. You will enjoy traveling, Kate, seeing new things, meeting new people."

He paused, but when I did not say anything, he went on, "There is enough money so you may marry anyone, my dear. Someday. When I can find a man good enough for my beautiful sister. No, don't tell me again how you love Tremaine; how you do not need my permission to marry him. I know that. But I would be derelict in my duty as your brother if I let you go ahead with this madness simply to keep the peace between us.

"No, Kate. I tell you plain. If you persist, and marry him against my wishes, I will never see or speak to you again. It will be the hardest thing I have ever done, but I will do it, and on that you have my word."

I could not speak with those terrible, damning words still echoing in my mind. He would do that? Cast me off?

For a moment I thought of going to him, pleading on my knees for him to reconsider, but something held me back. A vision of Luke's face with its slashing smile perhaps, the memory of his kiss, the love I knew we shared. There was nothing I could do. As I turned to leave the room, Edwin spoke up again behind me. "I cannot forbid you to see him, Kate. I know that. But I do beg you to reconsider, think rationally and unemotionally before you decide. Because a lifetime is a long time to be unhappy."

I could only nod. As I shut the library door softly, I knew I would not change my mind. I loved my brother. Had loved him more than anyone else all my life. But I would give him up for Luke, since he forced me to it. I had to.

Not without regrets, mind you. Regrets for the position *he* had taken, not my own.

Because I knew that if I did not marry Luke Tremaine, the words Edwin had spoken last would come true. A lifetime *is* a long time to be unhappy.

Chapter Twelve

Although I had begged for three days' time, I intended to ride to the pond the next morning in hopes I might find Luke there. But when I came down, dressed in my habit, I discovered Edwin in the breakfast room before me. I greeted him as calmly as I could, afraid he was there to try to talk me out of my decision. I was not surprised when he dismissed Harper with a wave of the hand, but I surely was when he came and took me in his arms and kissed me on the forehead.

"I am sorry, Kate," he began in a sober voice. "Sorry for what I said to you last night. I had no right to forbid you the husband you have chosen. You are a woman grown, not a child to be guided and protected for her own good. I lashed out at you because I was disappointed. You are my sister and I love you, and I have always wanted the best for you. Do say you forgive me . . ."

I cried then. Cried from relief, all the tears I had not been able to shed last evening. "I am so glad . . . you will never know how I felt . . . to think I would never see you again . . . dear Edwin!"

As he handed me a snowy handkerchief, my brother accused me of becoming a watering pot and bade me sit down and compose myself while he selected my breakfast for me. As he did so, he asked me to keep the news of my betrothal a secret until November first, and begged me to delay the wedding until Christmas, to allow him to become more accustomed to the prospect. He also told me he was adamant about not receiving the earl. He was sorry for it, but he could not help it.

I wanted to protest, especially about the delay, which I knew would not please Luke at all, but Edwin had come so far this morning, conceded so much, I made myself agree. It was not that long to Christmas, and never mind those cold wintry trysts Luke had mentioned he did not think he would care for.

With a good appetite now, I began to eat the buttered eggs and the thick slice of country ham. Edwin poured me a cup of coffee before he took his own seat again to read the early post.

"Is there anything from Aunt Sadie?" I asked, for I was still feeling awkward. I could hardly begin to discuss Luke with my brother when his feelings about him had not changed in any way.

He shook his head. I thought he looked tired this morning, as if he had not slept well. When I asked him if the ghosts had bothered him, he stared at me for a moment.

"What?" he asked finally, as if he did not understand. "Oh, the ghosts! No, there wasn't a squeak from either of them, but I did sit up for hours to study the journal. It is fascinating reading, even though it is written in such a dry, matter-of-fact style that belies the sensational things it relates. For example, 'Had poached halibut for my supper and a piece of dried apple pie. Female ghost screamed for sixteen minutes commencing at 5:18PM.' He makes it sound as if the lady's antics were merely another part of his meal, doesn't he?"

I smiled. "I cannot wait to read it for myself," I said, more to keep the conversation going than from any real desire for it. My whole being was anticipating a meeting with Luke. I prayed he might ride to the pond—or should I run down to the glade first, to make sure he had not come there instead?

To my surprise, Edwin was frowning and shaking his head as he said, "I do not think that would be a good idea, Kate. Some of the entries are terrifying, and they are coarse as well."

"Coarse?" I echoed, Luke momentarily forgotten.

He nodded. "Great-Uncle was not a polished man. His language can be disgusting. Furthermore, the ghosts' behavior is not suitable for you to know. Trust me, Kate. I will give you a censored version eventually, but I do not want you to be shocked and suffer nightmares."

I would have protested being wrapped in cotton-wool, but I contented myself with a nod. Edwin had always been stubborn, not easily swayed. And, I was beginning to suspect, he had grown up to be a bit of a prig, at least where I was concerned. I supposed it was not important for me to actually read the journal. Still, when I rose at last to kiss him before I went to the stables, I could not help but wish I had spent more time going over the volume I had found before I put it in his hands.

By no stretch of the imagination could it be called a lovely morning. True, it had stopped raining, but it was chilly and dank with a lingering mist and pockets of fog. I told myself it was a good thing both Imp and I knew the way to the pond. It would be easy to lose one's bearings today. As we set out, I decided all that was needed to make the setting complete was the haunted baying of a giant hound off in the distance.

To my delight, when I reached the pond, I saw Luke's gelding tied to the usual branch, and my impatient suitor throwing pebbles into the pool. I watched him for a moment, admiring his height, those broad shoulders, that proud, dark head. When his horse neighed, Luke turned around, his rugged face lightening when he saw me. In only a moment, he was beside me to lift me down, wrap me in a crushing embrace, and kiss me until I was breathless.

"He has consented? You have talked him around already?" he asked finally. "Oh, my clever Kate, my marvelous, heady, beautiful, *persuasive* Kate!"

As he talked, he dropped little kisses all over my face, and I laughed.

"Tell me about it. When may I call on him? If the banns are posted this coming Sunday, we can wed in less than a month. I know it will be November, not June, but you will not mind the weather, will you?"

I put my hand over his mouth. "Will you let me say something, sir?" I demanded, pretending to look fierce. "I foresee a sorry state of affairs for me if I am never allowed to get a word in edgewise."

He grinned at me then. "You may have as many words as you like, love. I apologize. I am feeling so jubilant, I fear I have become addled. Now. You were saying . . . ?"

I was not saying anything at all. Yet.

"I spoke to Edwin last evening. At first he was adamant that I should not marry you. He even threatened to cast me off and never speak to me again if I persisted. But this morning I discovered he had had a change of heart. He said he could not bear to lose me. What is it? Why do you look that way?"

"Why?" he said, frowning. "Why would he behave like that? Not to boast, but I am the Earl of Bryce, wealthy, well born, sound of limb and sane of mind. What could he possibly find to object to?"

I hesitated. A part of me did not want to tell Luke the things Edwin had said about him. But another part longed to hear him refute them. That part won.

"Edwin says you are not a good man. That you are known in London for your bad reputation, an addiction to orgies and unsuitable companions. He said it was common knowledge last year that you forced a woman against her will . . ."

"What?" Luke demanded, grasping my arms so tightly that I cried out. He let me go at once. "I beg your pardon, Kate," he said. There was a white line around his mouth, and he looked so grim that I was glad Edwin was several miles away.

He paused for a long moment to collect himself. "I have never forced a woman in my life," he said finally.

"As for my friends, they are gentlemen, good men and true, as you will discover. I do not gamble or drink to excess; I do not lie or cheat. As for orgies—well, my love, I must ask your brother to define the word before I admit or deny being a devotee of them. I have had my mistresses. Lord, I am thirty years old. I will not have another, not now."

"I wonder where Edwin heard those things about you then?" I mused, ignoring his report, although I did wonder about those mistresses. How many had he had? Had they been beautiful? Accomplished in ways I knew nothing about? It seemed to me I would have a difficult time being anywhere near as fascinating, I was such a naive babe in the woods, and for a moment, I despaired. As if he knew what I was feeling, Luke put his arms around me again and kissed me, long and tenderly.

"Where he heard them I do not know," he murmured, his mouth only inches from mine. "They are not true, not a word of them. I hope you believe me, Kate."

I leaned back so I could study his face. Of course he could be lying and I would have no way of knowing it. But somehow I did not think he was. I nodded.

His dark expression vanished then. "I am glad," he said. "May I ask what convinced you of my innocence?"

"Well, it was simply that I could not believe there is a woman alive who would not welcome you with open arms. You are entirely too devastating, and that is the last time I will tell you that, for you are already much too proud of yourself."

We did not say anything else for a long time. At last, seated on his coat under the gnarled tree, we spoke again of our wedding.

"There is one thing I must tell you," I began. I was leaning back against his broad chest now, both of us staring out at the pool. "Edwin has asked me to keep our betrothal a secret, at least until the end of the month."

"I cannot imagine why, but I have no quarrel with

him there. How could I? The thirty-first is only six days away."

"Yes, well, he does not wish the ceremony to take place until Christmastime."

"Now just a moment," Luke began, sitting up and turning me to face him. "Why should we delay? What is his reason? Can it be all Whittingham brides are married then and he hates to break custom? I will accept no other explanation."

"I don't know," I admitted. "He didn't tell me."

"Then let us ignore him," Luke said. "We can be married by special license next week, or we can elope. Granted the border is a goodly distance and winter is coming on, but it will be an adventure. And you'll see, Kate. When you are my countess, he will not be able to put these ridiculous blocks in our way, and he will soon become reconciled to our marriage."

"I will not elope. The very idea! Your mother would be horrified, and so am I."

"Women have no sense of adventure," he grumbled. "I assure you, my credit with the *ton* is good enough to weather the storm such an unconventional ceremony would provoke. Assure you, Kate, the Earls of Bryce are a law unto themselves. They always have been."

"But the next Bryce countess is not, and has no desire to be," I retorted. "Come, sir! Surely we can delay for my brother's sake. It is such a little thing, after all."

He cocked a brow at me, and I wondered why he looked as if he was going to laugh. Finally he said, "It is hardly a little thing, woman, as you will see." He paused, then added, "Still, I suppose I must let you have your way. Dear me. I hope I shall not find myself under the cat's foot after we are married. All meek and mild and agreeable."

I chuckled at the mental picture I had of such an impossible turn of events, a chuckle that was soon lost in a kiss.

As we walked to the horses much later, arms around

each other, Luke announced he would not be able to see me for the next couple of days.

"I have business in Southampton, my dear," he said, holding me close before he helped me to the saddle. "I shall be as quick as I can."

"Two days?" I repeated. "I shall miss you."

"Two, certainly no more than three," he said, watching me adjust my right leg and the apron of my habit. "Kate, if you have any problems, anything at all, I want you to ride over to the Court and see my mother. I have told her of our plans and she is delighted. And she would help you, no matter what troubled you."

"I don't foresee any problems," I told him, confused by this concern. "And if one should arise, there is always Edwin, and he is closer to hand."

He nodded, but I noticed he did not smile. He had removed his hat, and now he stood beside Imp holding her bridle. It was the only time I could look down at him, and I admired that dark hair, blown by the wind, his gray eyes and rugged face, that wonderful, warm mouth.

"Take good care of yourself, love," he said. "I wish I did not have to go, but the sooner this business of mine is resolved, the better."

I blew him a kiss from the top of the rise before I turned for home. I could not remember a time in my life when I felt as happy as I had these past two raw, miserable mornings. How little did I suspect that happiness was soon to end.

When I reached home I hurried to change my habit for a morning gown, for once again the Beasleys' carriage was pulled up to the front. I knew Edwin would be waiting for me to rescue him.

The Reverend Mr. Beasley and his sister Sophia had come alone. When I inquired for their mother, I was told she was laid down with the headache, an affliction she often suffered. I was not surprised to hear it.

The parson was quick to change the subject. He

spoke glowingly of the coming hunt season, which courses had always been the most promising, those members who could be counted on to attend Opening Day—an event, I gathered, the equal, in his mind at least, of any royal coronation. Edwin was again admonished not to fail; reminded that his standing in the neighborhood depended on him making a good showing.

"You must be in the forefront, sir, as I shall be," Beasley went on. "Neck or nothing—leading the hunt—if you care anything for your reputation."

I could almost guarantee that Edwin intended to be laid down on his bed that morning with at the least a putrid cold if he did not decide to claim a severe attack of the gout. In fact, I would wager on it.

Miss Beasley tried to persuade me to come out as well, but I refused, knowing well that not many women rode to hounds and there was no stigma attached to those who did not.

"It has come to my ears that you went on an expedition to the Channel a little while ago," she said next. The change of subject was welcome, but I was not sure I was going to enjoy this one, either. I was right.

"To be sure it is a great thing to be taken up by the nobility, but one hopes you will not forget where your true devotion should lie, Miss Whittingham," she said, shaking a stern finger at me. "May I remind you that the Bible tells us, 'Lay up for yourself treasures in Heaven,' and again, 'for where your treasure is, there shall your heart be also'? I have not seen you at Sunday services yet."

I could only stare at her, so stunned that even my professed talent for meaningless small talk had deserted me.

Edwin came to my rescue. "We have been very involved with guests, ma'am, as well as the business of getting settled here. And I must confess, my sister has been much troubled by the ghosts who inhabit Bryce House. Quite unnerved she has been, so much so that

I have almost summoned a doctor to see to her in her weakened mental condition."

"There are no such things as ghosts," Miss Beasley told him.

He smiled at her. I thought it would be a rare woman who would not return that smile. Miss Beasley, I saw as I glanced at her, was not that singular. I stifled my indignant feeling that Edwin had made me out to be such a cowardly ninny when I am sure he and Hawes had been just as frightened by The Gentleman, but I held my tongue. I was not likely to complain about anything that drew Miss Beasley's attention away from me, although to be lectured about my piety by a hunting parson's sister who was horse-mad herself was a bit much. Edwin smiled sweetly at me. For some reason I thought of that old expression, "Butter wouldn't melt in his mouth," and was hard put not to make a face at him.

"Yes, well, I am sure you will both come to church soon," the parson interjected. "As for ghosts, my dear Miss Whittingham, I imagine you are succumbing to the power of suggestion. Rise above it, ma'am, rise above it! Ignore it, in fact.

"Now, sir, about the hunt . . ."

Brede Hawes joined us then, and after introductions had been made was entreated to join the hunt as well. He said, rather vaguely for him, I thought, that he had no idea whether he would still be in residence at the time, and so could not commit himself. He did not add how sorry he was that it must be so.

"Foxes, is it?" he asked the parson, quite the picture of a London fop. "Did you know Mr. Brummell never goes out beyond the first wall? He has such a regard for the white tops to his boots, you know. And if the day should be muddy—well, I daresay you would not see him at all."

I could tell the Reverend Mr. Beasley was becoming incensed at the tepid reception his plans were receiving, and I hastened to order a decanter of burgundy, and some sherry for Miss Beasley and myself.

This move had the effect of calming the parson's indignation, but gained me a disgusted look from my brother. Now I smiled sweetly, for it served him right.

We were all in the hall half an hour later saying our good-byes, when Harper answered the door and came back bearing an armful of flowers. He presented it to me with a low bow.

I could see Miss Beasley was all attention, even craning her neck to try to read the card. I tucked it in my pocket before she could do so.

"How kind of the countess to send this bouquet from her glasshouse to Bethany," I said. "She told me the other day when we went to the shore she thought my cousin was looking blue-deviled. I hope we may see Bethany for dinner; otherwise I must send these on to the inn."

Sophia Beasley offered to deliver them. She was denied.

I could see Edwin approved my subterfuge, and I was glad, although I did not like to give up Luke's flowers. Still, I could keep that fervent card, I thought. And perhaps one rose?

But we three were to have dinner alone. I had not seen Bethany or her husband for four days now. True, the weather had not been pleasant. I hoped this absence of hers meant nothing more than a dislike of going out in the rain. I resolved to ask one of the maids to inquire for her at the inn, and decided it would do no harm to keep the bouquet till morning.

Edwin was absentminded during dinner, lost in some world of his own, and it was left to Brede Hawes and me to carry the conversation. I could tell by that gentleman's knowing look that he had learned of my attachment to the earl. Of course we did not discuss it.

When Hawes came to the library after dinner, he was alone.

"Edwin asks to be excused," he said as he poked the fire. "He is not feeling all the thing and intends to read in bed.

"I realize I am not supposed to know anything any

more than anyone else, but may I wish you every hap-. piness, Kate?" he said next, abandoning the fire to bow to me before he took his seat.

I know I blushed even as I thought again what a pleasant man he was, how kind and even-tempered. I had never seen him out of sorts or at all ruffled the entire three weeks he had been here. Edwin was lucky in his friend.

"Thank you," I said.

"The wedding is to take place at Christmastime?"

"Yes. As I'm sure you know, that is Edwin's wish."

"And the earl is agreeable?"

I only nodded. I did not want to tell him what a task I had had getting him to agree to that date.

"I suppose you will be glad to leave Bryce House. Who could blame you, with the ghosts acting up as they do, so often? You must permit me to applaud your bravery. You have never even cried out in alarm, and I am sure in your situation most females would have swooned if they had not succumbed to hysterics. My compliments, Miss Whittingham."

"Please, sir, you give me too much credit. But since compliments are in order, let me say how glad I am you have been here with us. You are a good friend of Edwin's indeed to endure the ghosts. We must, of necessity, but they are not your family phantoms."

"Never say so! I have enjoyed myself immensely. I've never been entertained by ghosts before. I hope we will have further contact with them, although I probably should not say so. If they are listening, it might encourage them to think up some truly horrible haunting to pay me back. Er, do you think ghosts can hear?"

"I have no idea. It seems unlikely, doesn't it? And they are so wrapped up in their own problems, they are really quite selfish. What I find amazing is that they are still lingering here after all these years."

As if on cue, The Lady's voice could be heard in the distance. It was faint at first, mere moans and sobs, but it grew louder and louder until it was a constant, full-throated wail of agony. I could almost picture waves and waves of sound swelling up the stairs from that cellar, echoing through the halls, to find and torment us here in the library.

Hawes and I exchanged glances. I found I was hugging myself to escape the shivers I could not control. So much for my celebrated "bravery."

We had to listen to the ghost for some time. How could we not? I tried to picture that young girl with the long, chestnut hair held back with a ribbon, whom I had seen so often, making those harsh, tortured sounds. I found it hard to accept, and I wondered why she had never shown me this side of her personality when she was with me.

At last a blessed silence returned, and I accepted our guest's challenge to a game of chess.

Chapter Thirteen

Eventually, thoroughly defeated by Brede Hawes's superior play, I settled down by the fire to read. Hawes excused himself sometime later. I hoped he would look in on Edwin, make sure he was all right. I could just imagine my brother brooding over his decision to let me choose my own husband, but I told myself I would not take the blame for that. All too often I had done so in the past, begun blaming myself for whatever misfortune occurred, even when it had little or nothing to do with me. I could still remember how long I had felt responsible for my parents' death in that boating accident, sure if I had only been a better daughter, loved them more, they would have been spared.

To be truthful, I was feeling low myself this evening and it had nothing to do with Edwin or the ghosts. Two days, I thought as I put my book down to stare into the fire. He would be gone two days, and possibly three. The time stretched endlessly before me. I could tell I was on the verge of a black mood because of it. I rose and began to pace the library, up and down, up and down.

I must not be so—so easily discouraged, so *spineless,* I scolded myself. Two, even three or four days, was nothing. I had plenty to do to keep myself busy here in the house. I could ride mornings, go for long walks, talk to the gardener about the spring planting. . . . But Edwin had said he did not think he would remain here once the inheritance was his. Had he meant that? About traveling and possibly buying an estate in the

West Indies? Or had it merely been a remark tossed out because he was angry with me?

I paused for a moment, so quickly it caught me in the middle of a step. Had I heard a noise just then? Seen something out of the corner of my eye over there in the dark? Straining to hear, to see, I waited for a long, empty moment. There was nothing. I was imagining things. Because it was dark. Because I was alone in this vast room, and both men were far away upstairs.

I made myself go to Edwin's desk, to list all the times I had had contact with the ghosts, where that had been, and when. When I studied it, my eyes widened. It seemed strange I had only seen The Gentleman once, that night at the top of the stairs with Edwin and Brede Hawes beside me. Of course the three of us had heard him several times, pacing over our heads and tapping the walls. And then there had been the time he roared and threw furniture. But I had only seen him once. I did not think the men had seen him more than that either, unless they were keeping it from me. But why would they do that?

But I had seen the girl ghost many times. I had imagined her at the escritoire, at my bedside singing that sad little song, standing in front of the door of my room one morning, and oh, yes, that first terrible night when I had not dared to open my eyes but had sensed her there trailing the cold and that distinctive lilac scent. But as far as I knew, neither Edwin nor Hawes had seen her at all. Did she appear only to women? Or had she chosen me because she wanted me to do something for her? I had no way of knowing what that might be, and I wished I did. I would have liked to help her, poor lost soul that she was.

Perhaps she sensed that another woman might be more sympathetic. I remembered her cold tears on my hands and shivered. Of course I pitied her. I was sure whatever had happened to her had been catastrophic. Otherwise she would not remain here but go quietly to whatever place souls went to after death. It was not something I had pondered before, what happened to the dead. As a child I had been taught about heaven and hell, and I supposed I believed in them. But where I had thought hell with its eternal fire the most dreadful place I could imagine, now I knew there was something worse. Limbo. A spirit forced to spend centuries in nothingness. It was too terrible to contemplate.

I studied the list I had made again, then carefully wrote down all the places I had felt the unusual, numbing cold. That cellar corridor first, for surely that was the most malevolent of all. How strange that I would think of it that way. The other spots had only caused a little shiver up the spine, whereas the spot outside the kitchens had been awful, evil in a way the others were not. Something ghastly must have happened there. If I knew what it was, I might be able to solve the ghosts' mystery.

It was late when I went up to bed. The foyer and the hall looked frightening, a vast, yawning blackness my wavering candle flame could not dispel. I hurried up the stairs, keeping my eyes on the toes of my slippers and humming mindlessly to myself to keep from hearing any unearthly sounds. I had hurried so, I was breathless when I let myself into my room and closed the door tightly behind me. I even wished I had a key until I remembered ghosts were not deterred by locks and chains or stone walls either.

The water the upstairs maid had brought for my use before she left the house at dusk was ice cold, but I was used to that. After I undressed, I washed and cleaned my teeth with it. Hurrying again, I put some coals on the dying fire and climbed into bed. I knew that if I had been a child, I would have pulled the covers over my head and hidden there till morning.

The nights were becoming colder. Soon we would need more quilts on the beds and flannel nightrobes and a heated brick at our feet. Five days to November, I told myself. Just five days. And then I turned on my right side and willed myself to think only of Luke— to remember his face, his eyes, the kisses we had shared, even the way the sun had silhouetted his dark head at the shore when we gathered shells there. His hands, and how they had felt caressing me, his warm breath on my skin. I smiled at the memories. He would return soon, and when he was only a few miles away at the Court, I would stop feeling so bereft.

I woke some time later, dazed and confused. Lying there in my warm nest of covers, I frowned as I tried to figure out what could have brought me out of a deep sleep. And then I knew.

"Katharine." The drawn-out whisper came softly, yet I heard it easily. "Kath—ar—ine."

"What is it? Where are you?" I demanded before I thought. Then I lay frozen with terror, all my senses awake now. I had not been able to tell from the whisper if it were a man or a woman. I said a quick prayer that it was the girl with the chestnut hair. The man was frightening with his dagger, his mask.

"Kath—ar—ine," came the whisper again.

I was afraid it was not the girl. There was no cold air stirring in the room, none of the telltale scent caught in the ancient folds of her white gown.

"Kath—ar—ine," whispered the voice. It sounded as if the speaker was right beside me, and I could not bite back a whimper of pure terror.

There was a long pause, so long that I told myself whoever had spoken my name had gone away. And then the whisper came again. I seemed to feel it wreathing around my head like smoke, hanging there, waiting for me to relax, let it do what it had come for. But I resisted the temptation for I felt that way lay madness.

"Kath—ar—ine."

This time I heard a breathy sigh at the end, the kind of sigh a person might make just before fainting. Or dying, I thought grimly. I loosened my fingers one by one from the covers I was clutching to my throat. They ached from the strain they had been under. Then I began to count. I decided I would time the whispers,

to give myself something to do, see how long it was
between them. Several minutes passed. The whisper
came at irregular intervals, and it did not sound especially urgent or threatening when it did. Finally there
was silence. I waited. And waited. When the whisper
did not come again, I tried to relax, close my eyes,
think of something else.

I must have been just about to go back to sleep
when I heard the whisper again, this time from the
opposite side of the room, and it brought me out of
my doze into full awareness. The voice calling my
name sounded different now. The cadence was
quicker, the whisper harsher, more demanding.

"Katharine . . . Katharine . . . *Katharine,*" it
persisted.

I spent the night with that whisper. Sometimes it
would go away for a bit, but it always came back. And
just when I would decide it was only a whisper and it
could not hurt me, it would come from another part
of the room, or change to a growl

It was almost dawn when whatever it was stopped
calling my name. When I heard what it said, I wished
it was still whispering "Katharine," however. For the
words I heard were enough to frighten the bravest
person, and as I had discovered here at Bryce House,
that person was not me.

"I—am—coming," the voice whispered. "I—am—
coming—for—you."

I slept no more that night. Instead, I cowered in my
bed until I heard the maids outside my door, beginning the morning chores. I did not feel a bit pleasant,
but I made myself smile at the girl who helped me
dress.

When I entered the breakfast room, I found both
Edwin and his friend at the table, discussing a ride
they intended to take that morning. To my eyes they
looked remarkably well-rested and robust, sitting
there with plates filled with steaming-hot food before
them, and I resented it. Obviously no one had called
their names all night.

"You look terrible," Edwin said as he pulled out a chair for me.

"Thank you so much," I replied. "I had a bad night."

"You will feel more the thing after you have eaten," he said calmly, ignoring my sarcasm as he went to the sideboard. "Brede, pour Kate a cup of coffee, there's a good fellow. Kate, my dear, eggs? Sausage? Some finnan haddie?"

I had never understood why people enjoyed smoked haddock at breakfast, and I shook my head. "Did either of you hear anything unusual last night?" I asked as I buttered a piece of toast.

They shook their heads in unison. "Did you?" Edwin asked, suddenly concerned.

"There was a voice whispering my name, over and over. All night, in fact," I told them. I saw Edwin looked shocked, Hawes thoughtful. "And then, just before dawn, the voice threatened me. Whoever it was said it was coming for me. I will not deny I was terrified at that. I am still shaking."

"Have you heard this voice before, or is this something new?" Edwin demanded.

"It is new. I could not even tell if it was The Gentleman or The Lady. Not from a whisper. Somehow I suspect that cavalier dressed all in white we saw at the top of the stairs."

"Why is that?" Hawes asked, pushing the pot of marmalade closer to me.

For some reason, I hesitated to reveal all the times I had been visited by The Lady ghost, and the circumstances. Both Hawes and my brother would think it odd I had not mentioned it before, and I could see why they would. Searching my mind for something to tell them, I shrugged. "I—I suppose because he seems more threatening to me. That mask he wore, the dagger he flourished. Surely he intends to harm someone."

"Whereas The Lady with her ungodly screams does not?" Edwin asked. I saw he was trying not to smile, and it angered me.

"It is not funny, Edwin," I told him with as much dignity as I could muster. "And if you had spent the night trembling, afraid for your life, you would not think so either."

"My dear Kate! I am sorry. I do not mean to make light of your experience," he was quick to say as he reached out to pat my hand. "Why don't you go back to bed and sleep? It will do you good."

I looked out the window at the perfect October day, the sun streaming in the windows to cast broad stripes of light and shadow on the floor, the bright, clear blue of the sky.

"It is too nice a day to sleep it away," I told him. "I may go for a ride later. First I must confer with Mrs. Harper. And I am sure Bethany will be coming, now the rain has stopped."

I wondered at my brother's suddenly serious look, the way he frowned. "She will not be coming, my dear," he said solemnly. "Charles has taken her away—to visit Aunt Sadie, I believe."

"What?" I demanded, so startled that I dropped the piece of toast I was holding. "They have left without even saying good-bye? I cannot believe Bethany would be so rude."

"She did write you a letter," Edwin said, patting his pockets. "Yes, here it is. I gather Buffington was worried about the possibility of more autumn storms. I understand they can be quite fierce here near the coast. And these past days could not have been pleasant for them, cooped up at the inn. You know how noisy and unpleasant inns can be, even the best of them.

"Here, read it. No doubt Bethany explains it all."

The two men excused themselves as I sat staring at my cousin's letter. When Harper came in to ask if there was anything further I required, I waved him away. I could not believe Bethany would just up and go without coming to see me. It was so out of character, for my aunt had been a stickler for propriety. And even if Bryce House had ghosts, she did owe me a thank-you. Somehow I detected the hand of Charles Buffington at work.

The letter was brief and full of apologies for their hasty departure. Charles had felt it best—Charles had thought she should not be frightened by ghosts, *especially now*—Charles was taking her to visit her mother.

There was no mention of the Earl of Bryce and my betrothal to him. It occurred to me that maybe Bethany had been jealous of the match I was making and had written these conventional pleasantries in a pique—until I realized there was no possibility she could have known of it. Edwin wanted the betrothal kept secret until after All Hallows. And surely, feeling about it as he did, he would not have told the Buffingtons.

I went to my sitting room and rang for Mrs. Harper. I did not feel up to riding, and now that Bethany would not be coming, the thought of a good sleep was tempting. Still, I managed to last the morning reading the London papers and the post, and answering some letters. It was early afternoon before I succumbed to temptation and sought my bed to rest until dinnertime.

When I woke, it was dark, and for a moment I did not know where I was, or what I was doing here, and it startled me. As memory came flooding back, I marveled I had slept so long. Just then I heard the casement clock downstairs strike six, and I scrambled out of bed to light a candle. But why hadn't Edwin had me called for dinner, I thought as I splashed cold water on my face and ran a comb through my tousled hair. Not bothering to change my wrinkled gown, I ran down and found my brother and Brede Hawes playing cribbage in the library.

"Edwin, you are very bad," I said first. "Whyever did you let me miss dinner?"

"Because after the way you looked this morning, I thought it better for you to get some sleep," he said calmly. "Fifteen two, four, six, eight and two pair are twelve. My game, sir."

"Well, I thank you. I do feel better," I told him,

although to be truthful I did not. My head was heavy and I had the headache. I wondered if I were getting a cold. Those meetings in the rain and the damp with Luke might be taking their toll.

Edwin said Mrs. Harper had left some supper for me. It was keeping warm over spirit lamps in the dining room. The smell of it, generally so appetizing, did not appeal to me this evening, and I took only a small piece of chicken, some salad, and a helping of Edwin's bread pudding. There was red wine as well, and I filled a glass before I carried it all back to the library on a tray.

"I have been considering this voice you heard, Kate," Edwin said as Hawes laid out a game of patience now the cribbage match had concluded. "Would you feel easier if I sat up in your room tonight, in case the ghost returns?"

I smiled at him. "How good you are to offer! But no, there is no need for both of us to lose sleep."

"Promise me you will come and get me if anything happens, then," he persisted. "And tomorrow, what say you to a change of room?"

I thought for a moment as I ate some salad. "But surely the ghost could find me no matter where I slept. And, do you know, I really don't think he—it—will be back tonight. If you recall, the ghosts never do repeat anything immediately. Even the tapping does not occur every night."

"For which we are truly grateful," Hawes said, as if finishing my sentence as he glanced up at the ceiling. I smiled at him as well.

"More wine, Kate? Join me in a brandy, Brede?"

We both nodded, and as Edwin did the honors, he said, "I was disappointed to learn of this voice of yours, Kate. It did seem the antics of our ghosts were getting fewer and fewer, and further apart as well. I truly hoped they might be fading away forever. But now—well, we are right back where we were the night we arrived."

"Not quite," I said. "After all, there are only five

days left to All Hallow's Eve now, not thirty-one. And that, you must admit, is a big difference. I would not live this past month over again for anything."

Except, I added silently, all the times I spent with Luke. I closed my eyes for a moment, suddenly almost overcome with my need for him. The need to hold him close, feel his hands on my body, his mouth possessing mine. I tried to make myself concentrate on the fact that at least one day of his absence had elapsed. Why, I might even be seeing him again as soon as the day after tomorrow. In the morning. At the pond. Early.

Conscious of the sudden silence, I opened my eyes to see both men staring at me, and I was glad they could not read my mind.

"You do look much better, Kate," Hawes told me. "And I hope you will have some uninterrupted rest tonight. I missed you at dinner, for after spending the day with your esteemed brother, I could have used a respite from all that lecturing about—what was it about this time, Edwin? Moss? Or seabirds? I forget. To be truthful, I was not exactly listening."

"You are not only ignorant, you are an ingrate," he was told severely. "I shall waste no more time trying to educate a philistine.

"Forgive me, Kate. I believe I shall work on Great-Uncle's journal again. If only the man had had better handwriting and had not writ so small, it would be an easier task."

I lit two work candles and took out my embroidery while Hawes went to the bookshelves to find something to read. It was quiet then, and somehow comforting in the large room. There were several branches of candles lit here and there to dispel the gloom, and the fire crackled softly on the hearth, sending out a welcome warmth. Looking around as I pulled my thread through, I marveled that such a homey setting could be home to two very demanding, noisy ghosts. And then I wondered if every old home in England might not have a resident phantom or two. When one considered the generations that had lived in them, the births and deaths they had seen, it became entirely possible.

We went up to bed around eleven. I had provided myself with a book in case I could not sleep after my long nap, and I intended to take a dose of James's Powders for the headache that still lingered. Promising once again to call Edwin if anything strange occurred, I went to my room. And I must admit I leaned back against the door for a moment once I was inside it, to pray I would not be visited by the whispering man again.

Chapter Fourteen

It took me a long time to fall asleep that night. I heard the clock in the hall strike twelve, then one, and still I was awake. Finally, I sat up to light a candle and pummel my pillows into a comfortable backrest before I opened my book. I had purposely chosen a selection of sermons. It was heavy reading, but it did not put me to sleep. Even the faint scent of the bouquet Luke had sent, which I had placed on my dressing table, could not comfort me. I told myself that no matter how tired I was, I must not sleep again during the day, not if it was going to keep me up all night.

At last, I blew out the candle and tried to compose myself for sleep again. I sighed as I slid down in bed and pulled the covers to my chin. It was then I heard it. Not calling my name, not threatening to come and get me, like some large, awkward adult trying to play with a terrified child. No, tonight all I heard was the sound of someone chuckling.

I sat up in bed as softly as I could, trying to decide where the sound was coming from. I could not tell. It seemed to wander the room, circling me again as it had last night, weaving in and out of the bed curtains, now softer, now louder, but always completely amused. I wanted to hurl something at it to stop it, I was so furious, but even though I picked up the book of sermons, I could not decide where to throw it.

The sudden silence when it stopped was as startling as the chuckle had been. I heard a board creak across the room, and I whipped around to stare fixedly into the dark. There was no further sound from that corner.

A little later, the wind came up. Even through the closed windows I could hear it racing through the trees and moaning around the house. My head was throbbing now, and I put the fingers of both hands to my forehead to press harder, trying to ease the pain.

My mind darted from one thing to another, silly, inconsequential things—the apple butter Mrs. Harper intended to make this week, the straggly bushes on this side of the house that I wanted the gardener to uproot, the possibility of Luke visiting an old mistress in Southampton—no! He wouldn't do that! What was I thinking?

Edwin's preoccupation with his studies and his indifference to Bryce House. It was his inheritance. He should have a care for it. My aunt Sadie and her brood. Brede Hawes and his pleasant smile. Even the ship I had seen on the horizon—was it only a few days ago? The ghosts here—no, I would not think of them. Luke, I told myself firmly. Dear, darling Luke. I wished he would come. I missed him terribly. Ached for him, in fact. I do not think I have ever felt so frightened, so alone.

I did not hear the chuckle again, nor anyone calling my name, but it was almost dawn before I slept. This morning I did not bother to get up, and when I finally came down it was almost noon.

I found Edwin in the library. His concern warmed me, for he jumped to his feet as I came in to inquire if I had had a good night. Upon learning of the ghostly chuckle, he frowned.

"But I told you to come and get me if you heard anything, Kate. Why didn't you?" he asked.

"Because—oh, I don't know. I was too fearful to move at first, and when the chuckling stopped I saw no reason to bother you. Please don't be cross with me. I am so tired, I am afraid I will start crying if you are."

"Of course I won't be cross. I am upset for you, not with you."

I sank down into a chair near his desk. I felt strange

to myself, fragile somehow, unsettled and shaky. It was almost as if I had lost some important part of my brain—the part that helped me function as a whole.

"Why do you look that way? What is it?" Edwin demanded.

I knew I could not explain it logically to my brother, and logic was all he could understand. A vague unease in the pit of the stomach, the headache that appeared to be becoming a part of me, the chaotic jumble of thoughts I had spent the night with—no, he would not be able to grasp those. Instead, I told him I was not feeling well.

"Perhaps a cup of tea and some scones would help," he suggested, ringing for Harper. "I am sure some hot tea with plenty of sugar in it will do wonders for you. And may I suggest that a walk might blow the cobwebs from your head?"

I nodded, for the sun was shining. As a pile of leaves swirled by one of the long windows, I saw that the wind was still blowing briskly.

Later I had to commend Edwin for his advice. The cold, fresh air seemed to restore the sense of balance that I had been missing in Bryce House. As I entered the beech wood and made my way down its paths to the glade, I took deep breaths and swung my arms as if I were marching. I even tried skipping. A squirrel chittered at me from high in a tree, and as I pretended to shoot him, I called, "Bang! You are dead, sir!" I had to laugh at such foolishness, and I was glad no one was around to see me acting so childishly.

It was quiet in the glade. I saw someone had been here to clean the fallen leaves from the pool's surface and unclog the brook. But even a I watched, more leaves fell to float on the wind-ruffled water.

Of course I thought of Luke, relived our first meeting here. What an arrogant enigma he had been to me then, but even so he had been able to set my heart to pounding.

As I returned home, I saw the gardener and his helper putting mulch on some of the flower beds and

I stopped to talk to him about the homely bushes beneath my bedroom window.

He frowned, twisting his homespun cap in both big, dirty hands, and peering at me intently. I wondered why he was staring.

"Aye, them be the white lilacs, missus," he said finally. "I'll root 'em up, but they'll be back next spring. They allus come back."

"Lilacs? I did not recognize them, they are so ungainly," I admitted.

"Aye. I used ter try to get rid o' 'em every year till I gave up. Didn't do a whistle a' good, all that work. Them lilacs is just set on growin' there."

"How long have they been there, do you suppose?" I asked, not really wanting to hear the answer.

"Almost as long as Bryce House has been here, missus," he said, leaning on his rake. "You there, Sam! No slackin' now, hear me?

"I did hear tell one of the first Bryces planted 'em fer his daughter. She were named May, the month the lilacs come in bloom, ye ken."

I thanked him and went into the house, thinking hard. Was the girl ghost who visited me this May? And if she were, what had happened to her that kept her haunting here? The gardener was an old man. He must have heard any number of tales about the house, the gardens around it. Still, I did not like to question him too specifically, or show my interest in May Whittingham too openly.

I told Edwin and Brede Hawes the story of the lilac bushes at dinner. Edwin was frankly skeptical that any plant so constantly uprooted could survive for two hundred years.

"Well, we only have the gardener's word it was," I argued. "True, he has been trying to get rid of it, but that is not to say all the gardeners before him were."

"A great many people do not care for lilacs," Brede Hawes spoke up. "They can be difficult bushes. They grow so fast and send out so many shoots. And they do get to looking like stunted trees, all those twisted, naked trunks."

"I have seen them like that," Edwin agreed. "We'll get rid of them, never fear, Kate."

"I have always like the scent of lilacs," I said perversely as I buttered a roll.

"As long as there is not too much of it, it is fine," Hawes said. "My mother finds it cloying, and it makes her sneeze."

Edwin told us of the journal entries he had read that day, and the subject of the lilacs was dropped.

"When I glanced through the journal when I first found it, I was astonished there were so few entries dealing with the masked man," I said. I noticed both men studying me closely, and I wondered the ghost should have captured all our imaginations so completely. "The entries I did read dealt mainly with The Lady and her moaning."

"You may call it moaning, Kate, as much as you please, but I beg to differ," Hawes said, continuing to ignore his plate of veal in a Marsala sauce. "I am sure we could all manage to deal with moaning. It is The Lady's shrieks and screams that have become wearing.

"By the way, did you hear your name whispered last night?"

I remembered he had not been present when I told Edwin about the chuckles, and I explained.

"How maddening for you," he said. "Not to make light of the horror you must have been feeling, but there is nothing more frustrating than having to listen to a person laughing at a joke no one told you."

Edwin was moving his fork on the table in a rapid, nervous pattern. "I wonder what he found so amusing," he mused. Turning to me, he added, "You will forgive me for calling the ghost a 'he', Kate. It just seems easier. And I have never been able to forget they were human once. I feel better giving him that final dignity of not referring to him as 'it.' "

I stayed at the table after dinner while the men enjoyed their port. To tell the truth, I was reluctant to walk alone to the library even though it was not quite five o'clock. And it was still light when the three of us left the table. I told myself I was becoming frightened of my own shadow.

Edwin went immediately to his desk, and I took what was becoming my customary chair near the fire. Brede Hawes paced up and down, his hands clasped behind him and his brow furrowed. I wondered what was making him so uneasy.

"There they go," he said, pausing at the window. "All of them, right down to the Harpers. I swear you could set your clock by them, they are so punctual. It really is ridiculous, the servants deserting us every night at dusk."

"Just be glad they return at dawn, old chap," Edwin said absently. I saw he was not working on Great-Uncle's journal tonight and wondered when I might get a look at it.

Hawes exhaled sharply. "You are right, of course. I never realized how difficult it must be to staff a haunted house. Still, I must admit I am not happy with the cold water I must wash in when I go to bed. It wakes me right up, it does."

"Perhaps we could put a kettle over the fire here," I suggested. "Take the hot water up when we go to bed."

Edwin looked up from his reading. "I do not recommend going down to the kitchen to get one, Kate."

I shivered, thinking of that spot in the cellar corridor. "Never fear! I would rather wash a hundred nights in cold water than do so. But perhaps Mr. Hawes might fetch it?"

He laughed and shook his head as he sat down, London papers in hand. Edwin returned to his studying. I did not feel like sewing this evening. For some reason my hands felt clumsy, and the tips of my fingers tingled. I picked up the book I had been reading but found I could not concentrate after only a page or two.

Instead, I stared at the fire. Two days had passed, and there had been no word from Luke. I wondered he had not sent me a message telling me when he would return. But surely he would be here tomorrow! I recalled he had said it might take three days, but I told myself I would not regard that. He *had* to come tomorrow. I missed him so dreadfully. And I was frightened—frightened in a way I could not understand. It was more than the whispers, that horrid laughing—the sounds no one heard but me. It was a nameless dread of something unknown, and the more I tried to think what it might be, the less I understood of it. And yet, in my frustration, I grew even more alarmed.

I turned to study my companions. Edwin sat with his head propped up on one hand while the other turned a page. What was he studying tonight? It might be anything from that moss Hawes had mentioned to an ancient philosophy. As for Hawes, his face was a study in human emotions. He smiled at some article he was reading, frowned at another, turned a page, and looked astonished.

I sighed and opened my book again. I envied them their calm, ordered lives when mine was in such a shambles. I resented them, too. It hardly seemed fair the ghosts should have decided to haunt me while leaving them alone. Did they sense I was the weak link here? The one more easily frightened and influenced? The one they could get to?

Furious with myself for these stupid speculations, I made myself concentrate on my book.

At ten, Edwin rose to stretch and suggest we all have some brandy and water. I did not want any, but he insisted.

"Do you good, Kate. Help you sleep," he said as he went to pour us each a glass. "And tonight you are to come and fetch me if so much as a mouse squeaks at you, do you understand?"

I nodded and took the glass he held out. He bent to kiss the top of my head and I had to turn away lest he notice the tears that sprang into my eyes. Really,

I was becoming maudlin, and I hated the weakness. Hated it!

The brandy certainly was a help, for I fell asleep almost at once, and for the first time since Luke left, slept deeply. When I woke, I wondered why I felt so cold. Still more than half asleep, I groped for covers that seemed to have disappeared, and as I did so I realized I was not in bed at all, but lying on an uncomfortable stone floor somewhere.

My eyes flew open, but it was pitch dark. I did not dare to move and my breath came in quick, ragged bursts as I tried to figure out where I could be, and how I came to be there. I did not remember waking and leaving my room—in fact, I was sure I had not. Yet I was here. It had happened.

Both hands rested on my stomach. I put the right one down on the stone beside me. It was cold, colder than I thought even stone could get. Shaking now, I moved my hand a little farther away from me and gasped. The icy cold I remembered from that cellar corridor washed over it, surrounded it, and began to spread up my arm. I could feel my hand moving away, as if someone had grasped it and was pulling it toward them. Frantic, I grabbed it with my other hand and yanked it back to cradle it close to my breast while I tried not to whimper.

I was in the cellars, near that place in the wall that the maids avoided so carefully. But how had I arrived here? Had someone—something?—brought me, put me down carefully and then gone away, taking their candle with them? Left me alone with whatever evil lived behind that wall?

I forced back a scream. No one would hear me, for Edwin and Brede Hawes were two flights and several solid oak doors away. There was no one else in the house. Except for the ghosts, I reminded myself.

I lay perfectly still for a long time. Then I slowly and carefully edged to the left, away from danger. It did not seem any warmer, but then, it was no colder either. I paused to take a deep breath and listen.

So far, so good. Nothing moved. Nothing made a sound. I considered what I should do next. I could lie here until morning, of course, whenever that would come. The servants would find me when they returned at dawn. That was the safest way. But I hesitated because I did not want them to discover me here in my nightclothes. What would they think? I knew what I would think—that the lady had lost her mind. No, better not to remain.

The only other option I had was to try to make my way back upstairs. I closed my eyes and tried to reconstruct the route. I knew the corridor ran straight for some distance. There were doors leading from it, and eventually one came to the back stairs the servants used with their mops and brooms and trays. I had used those stairs the day I came down looking for Mrs. Harper. I remembered the housekeeper's room was along here somewhere, around a bend in the corridor. I would be safe if I could reach it. Better still, I could find a candle to light my escape.

Of course, it was entirely possible that I was not in the cellars at all. Possible there was some other place in the house where it was cold and threatening. But I told myself I would not think of that as I moved until I touched a wall. Thankfully, I inched up it until I was standing, both hands spread on the cold stone to support me. Ordinary cold, not an icy menace. There was nothing reaching out for me here.

I stayed there, clinging to the wall, resting. I felt dizzy, sick to my stomach, and my head was throbbing. I prayed I would not vomit, and I took several deep, steadying breaths.

It was terrible there, alone in the dark, but I knew it would be better not to think of it. I was about to move when I felt something press against my leg. I screamed then, screamed and kicked out. There was a terrified yowling and even without being able to see, I knew it was the kitchen cat on its nightly prowl.

It was some time before I could make myself put one foot ahead of the other slowly as I felt my way along the wall. When I came to the first door, I discovered it was locked. I told myself there was no need to be discouraged. It could not be the housekeeper's room. I rested there for a moment. My heart had been beating so fast for so long, I was afraid it would stop just from exhaustion.

There is nothing to worry about now, I told myself. *You are safe. Nothing can hurt you. Dark is only the absence of light, and only children are afraid of the dark.*

At last my heart settled into a more normal rhythm, my breathing as well, and I began to move forward again. I was confused when the wall ended and my hand could feel nothing but empty space. Perhaps one of the doors had been left open? I forced myself to move forward, still holding on to the last of the wall. I could feel a draft now to my right, and I felt around with the toe of one slipper until there was no more floor, nothing but emptiness. *It cannot be a bottomless pit waiting to swallow you, goose,* I scolded myself. It was probably just some steps going down. To what? This is the cellar. I racked my brain trying to picture that tour of the house Mrs. Harper had conducted. I did not remember any subcellar, but then, my inspection of this floor had been cursory.

I made myself take another, grudging step forward, both hands outstretched now I had had to let go of the wall I had been clutching. You may imagine my relief when I felt it again ahead of me. I pressed against it, hands, face, body. The rough stone hurt my cheek, but it was a good hurt and it seemed to cut through the dizziness I felt, the sick stomach, the aching head. Encouraged, I moved forward again. I passed two more doors on my slow journey. I opened the second one. It turned out to be a storage closet filled with sacks and no help to me at all.

I never did find the housekeeper's room. Instead, I found the stairs, and giving up the idea of a candle to light the way, I began to climb the flight, hanging tight to the banister. I wanted to put that icy spot in the wall as far behind me as fast as I possibly could. And if that meant I had to remain in the dark, so be it.

Chapter Fifteen

The servants found me after all.

I had managed to reach the ground floor and make my way to the foot of the main staircase. What happened then, I have no idea. I must have fainted. I do remember being able to see where I was going, so it must have been almost dawn when I escaped the cellars. The first thing I knew there was a maid screaming, then Edwin's and Hawes's feet thundering down the stairs and my brother kneeling beside me to rub my hands and beg me to wake up.

I opened my eyes long enough to see his worried face with Hawes hovering behind him, and then I fainted again.

When I regained consciousness, I was in my own bed with a hot brick at my feet and the covers piled high. And I was warm, blessedly warm.

My throat was dry, and I coughed. I heard the rustle of a maid's apron before I saw her. It was the youngest maid, a plain girl with eyes this morning that were huge in her pale face. I asked her for water, and when she handed me the glass, I wondered why her hand shook. I was not a bit sorry when she left me. I was almost asleep again when Edwin came in.

"Kate, my dear," he said as he came up to the bed to take both my hands in his and squeeze them. "What a fright you gave us, you bad girl! But never mind that. How are you feeling?"

"Thirsty," I said past a still-parched throat. "And my head aches, and my stomach is upset, and I have been scared out of my wits. But at least I am warm."

"I'll order a tray for you."

"I do not think a cup of tea is going to solve this problem, Eddie," I said, using his childhood name.

He sat down on the bed, and I imagined how horrified my aunt Sadie would be if she could see him. "Why did you go downstairs, Kate?" he asked.

"I didn't. I know I didn't," I insisted. "Last night I fell asleep quickly and I didn't wake until much later when I discovered myself lying on the cellar floor near the kitchens."

His brow wrinkled, and his generally warm eyes looked grim. "You were found at the foot of the stairs on the ground floor, my dear," he said gently. "You must be mistaken about the cellars."

I shook my head and then wished I hadn't when the room tilted and whirled. "No, I am not mistaken. Listen, Edwin, please listen! I am frightened and afraid of what is happening to me. It— it doesn't make any sense!"

"All right," he said, taking my hand again and stroking it.

"Something—someone—had to have carried me to the cellars last night and left me there, for I did not go by myself. After I woke up and discovered where I was, I managed to make my way to the servants' stairs. Obviously I got as far as the main stairs. What happened to me then I do not know. I must have fainted. It was near dawn, though, for I could see where I was going as soon as I left the cellars."

I saw he was shaking his head as if in regret, and I wanted to shake him for his disbelief. "It happened that way! I swear it did!" I told him as I struggled to sit up.

He pushed me gently back on the pillows. "But it couldn't have, Kate," he said solemnly. "When we found you, you were wearing your dressing gown over your nightrail, and you had on your slippers. Ghosts don't dress people. They don't carry them places either. And I do assure you, both Brede and I were asleep. We did not hear a thing, either of us. You had to have put on your slippers and robe and gone down there looking for something. Maybe you had a dream about fetching that kettle we were talking about this evening. Or maybe you were sleepwalking. That would explain why you did not have a candle. Have you ever done so before?"

As I shook my head, he added, "I would not be surprised if that was it, and it is certainly understandable after the strain you have been under."

He rose and smiled at me. "Rest, my dear, until the tea arrives." He was halfway to the door when he turned back to say, "Perhaps you should see a doctor. Yes, I will see about that today."

"No, Edwin, don't do that," I said quickly, although I did not understand why I was so adamant that I did not want a physician to examine me. "Please, just let me sleep. I am sure I will be better soon."

I thought his nod reluctant. Through the open door I could see Brede Hawes waiting for him, two maids behind him craning their necks to see into my room. It seemed I had become a raree show, and I did not care for it one bit.

The tray arrived piled high with eggs and muffins and a large pot of tea. I drank cup after cup of it until I felt I could float, but I could only manage a bite of muffin. Mrs. Harper had brought the tray herself, and as I tried to eat, she bustled about my room hanging up my robe, aligning my slippers at the bedside, and arranging the draperies so the sun did not fall on my face. And she talked. About the dinner she planned to cook, the laundry the maids had begun, the disappearance of the gardener's boy.

"Where has he gone to, do you suppose?" I asked finally, more to stop her constant chatter than from any real desire to know.

"Who knows?" she said with a shrug of her massive shoulders. "Took himself off in the night, Jake says. Didn't even wait for his year's wages due at Christmas. Jake says it must be the house, but I can't see that. Sam was never inside it even for a cup of tea. Jake had to take it out to him, no matter the weather, he was so terrified of the ghosts."

I gathered Jake was the gardener I had spoken to. I could not imagine the dignified Mr. Harper with the first name of Jake, or carrying tea to the gardener's boy.

"Jake also said Sam saw something yesterday, but then he stopped talking and Jake couldn't find out what that might have been. Oh, do try to eat more than that, Miss Whittingham! You must regain your strength."

Mrs. Harper finally left, taking the tray with her and admonishing me to rest. I had intended to get up, but somehow I dropped off again and slept most of the morning.

My head felt heavy when I got up, although the headache had eased. My stomach felt better, too.

The maid who usually helped me dress was more reticent than ever this morning, and after attempting some conversation and getting nothing but a breathless "yes, miss," or "no, miss," I gave up and sat quietly while she arranged my hair.

Several memorable things happened to me that day. The first was a note that came from the Countess of Bryce inviting me to join her for a drive at one; the next was a long letter from Luke. You may imagine how I devoured that, read it over and over until I had all but memorized it. He had been delayed in Southampton for what he called "a tiresome, endless time," but he would be home late tonight. He begged me to meet him at the pond at eight tomorrow and plan to spend the day at Bryce Court for he wanted to show me my new home. There was a great deal more, but there is no need to speak of it. It was private.

I changed for my drive with the countess, glad I was feeling better. But the first thing that astute lady said when I joined her in the carriage was, "Whatever has happened to you to make you look so worn, Kate? Oh, I may call you Kate, my dear? Luke told me of his betrothal. I am so pleased! Come here and let me kiss you."

I sank into her scented, warm embrace and immediately began to cry. No one had hugged me like this since my mother died. My aunt was not given to casual caresses, and with the brood she had, an older niece took last place.

I could not manage to hold back a sob, and Lady Bryce's arms tightened. When I sat up at last, I tried to control myself. The countess handed me her handkerchief. It was a mere wisp of linen and lace, and she made a face.

"Isn't it strange? We women cry so much more often than men do, and yet they have the large handkerchiefs and we must make do with these insignificant little scraps. Wipe your eyes, Kate, and then sit back and tell me what is troubling you."

I did as I was told, happy to bow to older authority. But when it came to telling the lady everything that had been happening at Bryce House, I found I could not. Strange, that. Perhaps it was the feeling I had that it would be disloyal to Edwin if I bruited the story about; perhaps I did not want the countess to think me unbalanced, lest she try to persuade her son not to marry me. I am not sure what made me hold my tongue that October day. Instead, I told her a tale of missing Luke and not feeling very well besides, neither of which was a lie.

"I will never forgive myself if I have exposed you to whatever is making me sick, ma'am," I finished. "And I am sorry I cried. I am not generally so weak and insipid. Indeed, I feel much better today."

"You say you have had the headache for two days? A queasy stomach and dizziness? My dear, I beg you to see a doctor without delay. There is no need to suffer these things when a few doses of whatever the doctor prescribes for your condition will help you regain your good health again.

"But I will not tease you about it. Tell me when you and Luke are planning to wed."

I mentioned Christmas. She did not question the short length of time her son and I had been acquainted, and I was grateful for that. No doubt, if she had known how he had implored me to elope, she would have been not only indignant but dismayed.

"A Christmas wedding can be so pretty," she said. "I hope we will have snow by then, but not enough to make travel difficult. You do realize the Tremaine family is huge, don't you? They will all of them descend on the Court for the wedding and the Christmas festivities. I shall hope to see the last of them by the end of January. In fact, I may be traveling by then myself. I have always wanted to see the West Indies. It is warm there, or so I am told, and lately the winter cold makes my bones ache."

I wondered if she was speaking the truth or just planning to move herself so Luke and I could begin our marriage alone. I knew I was lucky such a woman was to be my new mother. Perhaps some day I would be able to speak freely to her. I looked forward to telling her everything.

We drove through Lechton and along the road that bordered the Solent, occasionally stopping at some vantage point so I could get down and admire the view. It was almost dinnertime when I arrived home again, much more knowledgeable about the little boy Luke had been, and the young man, as well as the large family he headed.

Edwin and Hawes both remarked on the color in my cheeks and told me how glad they were the outing had done me so much good. We were at the table and Edwin added, "I understand you did not eat any breakfast. You must be starving. Harper, bring Miss Whittingham more game pie."

"That was not because it was not excellent as always," I said, smiling at the butler. "Mrs. Harper is a wonderful cook."

The butler bowed and looked gratified.

"I understand the earl returns home tonight,"

Hawes remarked. "He has been gone for some time, has he not?"

"Four days," I said, feeling as if I had missed him every minute of every hour of those days "I will be at the Court all day tomorrow, Edwin. Do not expect me for dinner."

"Have you forgotten tomorrow is a special day, Kate?" he asked, his voice tight and controlled. "It is All Hallow's Eve, and I was planning an especially festive meal to celebrate our release from Great-Uncle Daniel's ridiculous stipulation."

"Why, of course, so it is!" I exclaimed. "How splendid you will come into your inheritance at last, Edwin. Please, could we not celebrate on November first? I suppose the lawyers will want to see you regarding the estate? Papers to sign and so forth? No doubt you will want them to come to Bryce House."

My brother frowned. "No," he said, "I feel I have earned a change of scene. I shall go to Southampton for two days and take care of business there, leaving the day after tomorrow. As for the celebration, I suppose we can have it when I come back. You will return with me, I trust, Brede? The party will not be complete if you do not share it, for you have been most faithful through this difficult time."

"Hear, hear," I said, giving him my warmest smile. "You are a true friend indeed, sir.

"Perhaps we might invite the Countess of Bryce and the earl?" I asked tentatively. Ignoring Edwin's frown, I hurried on, "She mentioned she would love to come, that day we went to the shore. And perhaps we should include the Reverend Beasley and his sister as well."

"Not the Beasleys," Edwin said coldly. "I have met one or two other families in the neighborhood on our rambles whom we can include if you are set on the Tremaines."

Mr. Hawes raised his glass to me. I wondered at the small smile he wore as he did so.

We spent the evening in the library. I was tired, but so keen thinking of Luke's return, I knew it would not do to go to bed early. I would not sleep. Instead, I held a book I did not read or stared into the fire, dreaming of him and our reunion.

The two men talked for a while of some scheme Edwin was considering to increase his inheritance. I hoped he would seek good counsel. I did not think my brother an expert on financial matters. But no doubt the lawyer knew a good agent and could suggest various investments.

"Do you realize we have not had The Lady screaming or The Gentleman pacing about and tapping for some time now?" I remarked a little later, glancing up at the ceiling. "Yet when we first arrived, Harper told us the ghosts were more active in October, working themselves into a frenzy by All Hallow's Eve. It has been no such thing. Do you suppose they are fading away at last?"

"Bite your tongue, Kate," Edwin admonished me. "Do you want to summon them up?"

"Surely not," Hawes said. "She is the one who has borne the worst of it, Edwin, and she a woman, too. I told her how brave I thought her to handle this so well, especially after last night's adventure. Women are truly remarkable, and so resilient, too."

His words recalled waking up on the cold floor in the dark, the icy flood that tried to capture me, and I shivered. My drive with the countess, thinking of Luke, had swept the memory of last night from my mind, but now the horror I had felt, the helplessness and the fear I had known, returned. I wished Brede Hawes had not mentioned it.

I did not drink any brandy, although Edwin assured me it would help me sleep. I had to rise early to be at the pond by eight. As usual, we took our candles from the table in the hall where Harper always left them, after the men had seen to the library fire and extinguished all the candles there. "Playing footman," Edwin called it. I was tempted to remind him that growing up as poor as we had, we had never enjoyed the luxury of a footman's services. To be scornful of

chores he had always done was silly. But perhaps he
did it to impress his friend. I had gathered from various conversations I had overheard that Mr. Hawes's
family had not been blessed with an abundance of
worldly goods either.

And then, just as I put my foot on the first tread,
something made me look up. I gasped in horror, for
there in the dim light at the top of the flight stood
The Gentleman. He was masked and holding his dagger high as if to threaten us.

I heard Hawes chuckle at something Edwin had said
to him, heard my brother's answering laugh, and I
turned to face them in astonishment.

"What is it, Kate?" Edwin asked when he noticed
me staring at them.

I opened my mouth, but no words emerged. Instead,
I pointed up the stairs with the hand that held the
candle. Its flame cast wild, weaving shadows on the
walls, for I could not hold it steady.

The Gentleman was still there. His body swayed to
and fro in the darkness as if he were being buffeted
by a strong wind. If he had made a sound, any sound
at all, I would have died of fright, for my heart was
pounding in terror.

"What are you looking at?" Hawes asked in a normal voice.

"The Gentleman," I whispered at last. "See him there,
at the top of the stairs?"

I gestured again, and obediently both men looked
upward. Their expressions did not change and, horrified, I watched the ghost begin to disappear into the
blackness above us. A moment only and he was gone.

"There is no one there, Kate. What can you mean?"
Edwin asked, sounding perturbed. I saw him exchange
a glance with Hawes. It was a look of incomprehen-
sion and concern.

"But he was there! Right where he stood before, at
the head of the flight!" I told them, my voice rising
in my desire to make them understand. "I saw him as
clear as day. He was dressed in those white clothes,

and he wore that mask. And he was holding the dagger high. I saw him, I tell you! I did! How was it possible you missed him?"

"I saw nothing," Edwin said somberly. "Brede?"

Hawes shook his head. Then his expression brightened. "You are jesting with us, aren't you, Kate? Pretending to see the ghost to frighten us? I applaud you. Your acting is superb."

"I am not acting," I insisted. "It is no jest. The ghost was there, I swear, he was there just as I told you."

Hawes nodded now. "Well, if it was not an act to trick us, the game pie must be the culprit," he said. "You had two pieces of it, remember? Perhaps it did not agree with you and is making you see things that don't exist. I thought it rather heavily spiced myself."

Edwin's face cleared. "Of course, that must be it. Come along, old thing," he added, wrapping an arm around me to help me up the steps. "A good night's sleep is what you need to banish these illusions of yours."

I did not say anything. Indeed, I was so shocked I did not think I could. The ghost had been there. The game pie had nothing to do with it. I had seen him plainly with my own eyes, and yet they had not. I did not understand it in the slightest, and I could think of no logical explanation. In fact the only thing that occurred to me was that somehow this evening I had turned a corner and was now in danger of losing my mind.

Chapter Sixteen

It was with a heavy heart that I dressed early the following morning. I had not been able to stop thinking of The Gentleman, so real to me, yet invisible to my brother and Brede Hawes. It was not until I put on my riding hat and picked up my crop that I realized I had just spent a peaceful night. No one had called my name, threatened me, or laughed at me, and I had not gone sleepwalking. Even the girl ghost with the chestnut hair had deserted me. I grimaced as I decided I had something to be thankful for after all.

Downstairs, I could hear the servants busy at their work. The maids were in the breakfast room talking to each other as they arranged the table, lit the spirit lamps, and carried up Mrs. Harper's delectable breakfast. I did not stop, not even for coffee. I was not hungry.

As I passed the library, I heard the footman laying a new fire and spotted the butler opening the draperies in the drawing room.

Outside, I noticed the sharpness of the air. Winter was not far off. There had been no killing frost as yet, but surely that was only a matter of days.

I wanted to scream with frustration in the clear, cold morning. Here I was going to meet Luke as I had been longing to do, and it was all spoiled for me. I felt more than sad, I felt destroyed. Destroyed, because if I was truly losing my mind, I could not in all honesty marry Luke. It would not be fair. The Earl of Bryce deserved someone better than a bride he had to keep locked up at the top of the house, as Edwin had put it once. When had he said that? And why? It seemed an age ago.

All the way across the heath I wondered what I was to do when I saw Luke. I could not pretend that everything was all right, that nothing had changed. Because of course it had. Drastically. There could be no wedding now, even though I wanted it as much as he had written he did, in his letter.

As it turned out, I did not get a chance to say anything for a long time. Luke was waiting for me, and when he lifted me down, my feet had not even touched the ground before he began to kiss me. In only a short time I was lost. Lost again in the power of that kiss, reveling in the taste, the smell, the touch of him. So caught up in dreams I forgot I could never be his wife.

My lips tingled when he raised his head at last to stare down at me. I closed my eyes, afraid of what he might see there, but it was no use.

"My mother said you had not been feeling well, Kate," he murmured, one thumbnail stroking my cheek. "It would be so much more satisfying if your pallor was the result of pining for me night and day."

"I have been," I told him. "Every single minute. Well, almost."

He chuckled. "My honest Kate! I have been longing for you, too. At night I have these wonderful, frustrating dreams.

"Tell me, have you had breakfast? I am starving, for I was here at seven, hoping you would come early."

As he helped me into the saddle again, he added, "We will be more comfortable at the Court. After we eat, I will show you around. I'm sure we can find many places more conducive to making love than this pool, now it is almost November."

We trotted off side by side. "So, your brother has done the thing, has he?" Luke said. "Managed to fulfill the terms of Daniel Whittingham's will, I mean? Imagine, thirty-one days without missing a night in residence. He is to be commended."

"He has indeed. He is off to Southampton tomorrow to see the lawyer. And when he returns we are going to . . ."

"And you are traveling with him?"

"Why, no. Brede Hawes is going."

"Leaving you to spend the nights alone with the Whittingham ghosts?" Luke asked, his voice deceptively even. "I think not. You will come to the Court, at my mother's invitation, of course, so I can take care of you."

I could only nod. I had not considered how I was to manage when Edwin and Hawes left. And just the thought of spending the night alone after the servants went to the village made me begin to tremble. I wondered Edwin had not thought of this himself and insisted I accompany him, before I realized he had forgotten it completely in his satisfaction at finishing the task set for him. And, I must not forget, his glee at inheriting such a tidy fortune. I smiled even though I shook my head at his carelessness. I would roast him for this, I decided.

And how could I be truly angry when his negligence provided me with an opportunity to spend two days with Luke? Two whole, lovely days close beside him, listening to him, watching the expressions that crossed that rugged face that had become so dear to me—two days in his arms being kissed and caressed.

You see, I had begun to search my mind for some way I might still marry Luke. Some honorable way I could avoid telling him of the things that had been happening to me. Perhaps away from Bryce House and its ghosts and secure in Luke's love, I might well throw off these illusions I suffered. Because I was still not positive deep inside that I *was* mad. I had never seen an insane person and hoped I never would, but surely they could not turn their madness on and off at will. Surely if you were insane, you were that way all the time, or so it seemed to me. And since that was the case, it meant I was as sane as the next person.

"What are you thinking, Kate?" Luke asked, the

big gelding held to a sedate trot so we could converse. "You look so serious, so thoughtful. And you still have not told me what is bothering you. Something is, so do not bother to deny it, woman."

For a moment, I stared ahead, wondering what I could possibly tell him. Then inspiration struck and I turned my head slowly to smile at him as I had that morning when I was safely on the other side of the glade. His eyes warmed and he grinned, that wonderful white grin that always made my heart skip.

"That is all very well, and I hope you will always smile at me just that way," he said. "But I will not be distracted. When we reach the Court, you will tell me about the trouble you are in. I insist on it."

Of course, when we did reach the Court and gave our mounts into a groom's care to climb the marble steps to the front door, we were unable to be private. The butler admitted us, bowing low, and a great number of servants seemed to have business in the front of the house. Maids carrying piles of linens or pitchers of water paused to curtsey and those footmen in attendance along the walls bowed. I had not thought Bryce would need such an army to wait on him, but then I had never known an earl and had no idea of their requirements.

The countess joined us for breakfast, sitting regally in a wheeled chair she could manuever herself. She said it had been built for her by the estate carpenter and it was a clever piece of work—narrow enough to get through the doorways and light and easily managed, yet padded with comfortable velvet cushions.

There seemed to be a great many servants in the breakfast room as well, all busy bringing hot toast, another dish of preserves, or a new pot of coffee. I saw the countess looked amused and wondered at it until Luke ordered the room cleared.

As the door closed behind the last of them, he said, "I wondered why the servants were so busy this morning, Mother. At least I did until I saw the scullery maid bringing up another pile of plates we could not possibly need. They have all come to inspect Kate, haven't they?"

Lady Bryce nodded as she buttered her boiled egg. "But of course they have," she said serenely. "The woman who will be your wife is a source of great interest to them. Right now I imagine they are clustered in little groups discussing whether she looks kind or cruel, strict or easy, nice or nasty."

"I hope I pass judgement," I said, putting down my fork as my appetite deserted me.

"Of course you do," Luke said as he poured me a cup of coffee. "Not that it would matter if you didn't. But they will not find a thing wrong. How could they when you are so beautiful and good? Eat your breakfast, Kate."

"He does tend to be autocratic, my dear," the countess murmured as she patted my hand. "Still, there are ways to get around that which I shall be happy to tell you about some time soon."

"Mother," Luke said, glowering at her. "Behave yourself."

"When have I ever?" she asked before she laughed and asked me to pass the toast.

After breakfast, the countess left us to our own devices, claiming she had a number of letters she must write. Luke and I began our inspection of the Court. It was a revelation to me, one handsome, grand room after another. There was even a large ballroom. I thought it looked forlorn, as if it had not been used for some time. When I mentioned this to Luke, he nodded. "Not since my mother's accident, I'm afraid. We must bring the place to life again. Those brocade draperies badly need replacing, they are so faded. And later, we shall have grand house parties—invite twenty or so couples and dance the night away."

He took me in his arms and hummed a waltz as he turned me quickly around and around the floor. I had to cling to him when we finally stopped, I was so dizzy. And that led to a kiss, and then another.

I felt awkward inspecting the bedrooms and suites

on the first floor and had little to say for myself. The prettiest room, which overlooked the avenue, was obviously a woman's. It was decorated in soft shades of cream and gold and light green, and the rosewood furniture was graceful and delicate. The large four-poster bed had a canopy of cream satin embroidered with gold bees that was caught up near the ceiling in an elaborate knot. A green velvet-covered chaise near the windows had pillows in the same fabric, and a handsome Persian rug complemented the color scheme. There was even a writing desk and comfortable chairs near the fireplace. As I admired the striped wallpaper, I wished I did not feel so awkward.

Luke came up behind me to put his arms around me and kiss the back of my neck. His warm breath made me shiver in delight.

"This was my mother's room before she moved to one overlooking the gardens. She claimed she liked it better, but I knew she was leaving the way clear for me to install my wife here. I am right next door, in what was my father's room."

He turned me a little so I faced a pair of double doors. Afraid he would take me in there, I said, "Your mother must be fond of bees," and then felt foolish, inept.

"You shall change it any way you care to, love, although I hope you will not want to replace the bed. I have fond memories of evading my nanny to run down here and jump into it mornings when mother was having her chocolate. I felt so comfortable and safe next to her among the pillows."

I found myself staring at the bed, picturing myself there with a son or daughter of Luke's cuddled close. It was then I decided I would not reveal any of my fears. If that was wrong, I suddenly did not care. I loved Luke Tremaine. I wanted to marry him more than I had ever wanted anything in my life. I would be fine, I told myself. As soon as I was away from Bryce House for good, I would be fine.

"What is it, Kate?" he asked quietly. "Tell me what is troubling you. Let me help you."

"It is difficult for me to say," I said, playing for time.

"Is it Bryce House?" he asked, drawing me over to the bed and sitting down beside me on the edge of it.

"Yes, it is all the ghosts," I admitted, resting my head on his shoulder so I did not have to look into his clear, all-seeing gray eyes. "Things have grown worse during the time you have been gone. I hear voices at night now, voices that call my name over and over, threaten to come for me."

I paused then, afraid I had said too much. I had no intention of telling him about finding myself on the stone floor in the cellars near that icy, menacing spot, nor about seeing The Gentleman when neither my brother nor Mr. Hawes did even though they were standing right beside me. It had happened. I knew it had happened, but telling about it would make me sound—mad.

"I will be so glad to have you out of there," he said in an even voice. "Please reconsider waiting until Christmas, Kate. There is no need for it. We do not even have to wait for the banns to be called if we do not care to. I can have a special license in only a few days."

"At least I will not sleep there tonight, thanks to your invitation. And it is All Hallow's Eve, remember? Does the Court have any ghosts I should know of, sir?" I asked.

Luke shook his head. "Stop trying to divert me, Kate. Tell me instead what else has happened to make you seem so forlorn?"

As he spoke, he held me closer and stroked my hair, and I wanted to weep. Weep because I could not tell him and oh, how I longed to unburden myself, share this frightening turn of events that had me dancing on the edge of sanity. Instead, I said, "I have not been feeling well. I often have the headache and sometimes I feel queasy, both probably due to my loss of sleep.

"But we will not discuss such unromantic things, if you please. I am sure I will be well shortly."

"As you wish," he said, but when I looked up at him, I saw his face was grim. I began to tell him of the party Edwin planned to celebrate coming into his inheritance. "When he returns from Southampton, that is," I concluded. "I do hope you and the countess will come."

"You may rely on us," Luke said. He sounded as if he were thinking of something else, and afraid of his next question, I reached up to kiss him. This did divert him, and only moments later we were stretched out on the wide bed in each other's arms and I was seriously reconsidering a Christmas wedding.

I only left the Court to return to Bryce House to pack some clothes. When I told Edwin of the scheme, he flushed.

"There is no need for this, Kate," he said sternly. "I intended you to stay at the inn in Lechton the nights I am away. Did you think I would permit you to remain here alone, after all your frights? You are my responsibility. Besides, I love you."

He sounded angry and indignant. I was ashamed that I had imagined even for a moment that he had forgotten me in his haste to claim the inheritance. But no matter what he said, he could not dissuade me from returning to the Court. Edwin bade me good-bye stiffly as I climbed into the carriage Luke had sent for me, and he did not smile when I assured him I would be home before him in two days' time.

I admit I fretted about it all the way back to the Court. I loved Edwin so much, it pained me to see him angry. Still, when Luke was there at journey's end, I forgot my brother completely.

And what did we do those two magical, much-too-short days? We rode, we talked, we made a hundred plans and shared a hundred kisses. And I admired the pastel the countess had done of me at the shore, now framed and placed beside Luke's bed. Luke seemed almost afraid I would disappear somehow, for he held my hand so tightly most of the time. The countess watched us with a smile, and when we two were alone, told me many stories about Luke and his father, and Bryce. Most of the time, however, I spent with Luke, and as passionate as he was, he never forgot to treat me with deference. I admit sometimes I wished he would forget himself, for I wanted him so. But there came a time in every encounter when he drew back to straighten my gown, help me pin up my curls, and tell me we must behave ourselves.

"For now," he always added, those clear eyes of his smoldering with suppressed ardor. "Just for now, mind you. When you are my countess, Kate—ah, then, beware! I have no intention of behaving myself then."

We were lying on the bed in the front room that was to be mine at the time, and I smiled up at him lazily where he leaned over me, propped up on one elbow.

"Good," I said happily. "I have had such an urge to misbehave lately myself. My, my. It is most unlike me."

All Hallow's Eve passed without an incident of any kind. I thought then of Bryce House, dark and empty with only the new moon to show its bulk against the sky. And I wondered if that night our ghosts looked for us and were disappointed when they could not find us anywhere. Did The Gentleman call my name to an empty room, and the girl ghost with the long chestnut hair weep and wring her hands alone? And did the icy cold in that stone cellar wall creep out to capture a victim only to discover it was all in vain for there was no one there?

I do not remember when I have ever slept as soundly as I did those two nights I spent at Bryce Court. It was wonderful.

Chapter Seventeen

Of course all good things come to an end, and much sooner than I would have liked, I was on my way back to Bryce House. It was a nasty morning even for early November, cold and windy with low, dark, threatening clouds. Indeed, we had barely traveled a mile before I could hear sleet on the carriage roof. From the shelter of Luke's arms, I spared a thought for the poor grooms and coachman called out in such weather and only to drive me home.

I did not ask Luke to come in when we reached Bryce House, for I remembered Edwin's unreasonable dislike of him, and I was not sure Edwin was still absent. Instead I tried to bid Luke thank his mother for inviting me and was stopped by a passionate kiss. When he lifted his head at last, he muttered, "I invited you. I'll consider that kiss my thanks."

I was very conscious of the array of windows across the front of the house, the carefully indifferent coachman and grooms, even the possibility that the Reverend Mr. Beasley and his sister might pay a call and catch us embracing, and I was quick to escape.

I found my brother and Brede Hawes in the library. I knew at once that Edwin had had a successful trip, for he wore a foolish grin and his eyes were shining.

"There you are at last, Kate," he said. "It is now official, and you are the sister of Mr. Edwin Whittingham of Bryce House, Lechton, Hampshire."

As he spoke, he grabbed my hands and whirled me about in an impromptu jig. Hawes looked on indulgently. "I'm rich, Kate," Edwin crowed. "I'm rich at last! And now I can live as I was always meant to do."

I laughed with him, but I was perturbed. It seemed inappropriate to me for Edwin to celebrate in such a boisterous way. After all, he was only the heir because he was Daniel Whittingham's sole surviving male relative. He had done nothing to earn the bequest.

I remembered something then and I said, "Did you ever recall whom Great-Uncle was going to leave the estate to if you did not last out the month here?"

I thought Edwin stared at me oddly for a moment before he chuckled. "No, but I asked the lawyer about it. It seems all that wealth was to go to a London society devoted to investigating ghostly appearances, if you can believe such a thing. And can't you just picture them crawling around here, tapping the walls, and holding serious meetings trying to summon them . . ."

"Questioning the elderly residents of Lechton, and writing scholarly papers of several hundred pages that no one would read?" Brede Hawes contributed, a twinkle in his eye. "Much better Edwin have the spending of it, right, old chap?"

My brother's smile grew even wider. Then he spotted some papers on his desk, and as he went to arrange them, he said, "I've something for you to sign, Kate. It is a surprise, so I am going to cover the top of the page."

"A surprise? Whatever do you mean?" I asked, looking down at the blank exposed piece of the paper that was all I could see.

Edwin sighed. "I can tell you are going to pry until you find out. Women!" he said. "Very well. I will tell you it is about your dowry. I have always wanted to make it more substantial for you, and now I can."

I felt like crying at his generosity. In fact, I did sniffle a bit and had to take out my handkerchief and blow my nose before I said, "You are too good to me, Edwin. But surely there is no need to give any of your inheritance away. Grandmother Whittingham left me a respectable portion, and besides, Luke is so wealthy, he doesn't care about dowries."

Edwin frowned. "Be that as it may, I do not care to be accused of being paltry, not where my only, beloved sister is concerned. Here now, Kate! No more tears, and no more roundaboutations. Sign the paper and Brede will witness it and I'll send it back to Mr. Gardner today. Then things will be as right and tight for you as they are for me. Besides, even if you do not need the money, you may have a granddaughter someday who will."

I wanted to protest still, but I could tell how important it was for Edwin to do this. Silently, I took the quill he handed me and signed my name at the bottom of the page.

As Hawes witnessed it, Edwin rang for Harper and ordered a bottle of wine. "We must have a celebration," he said. "This is such a momentous day for all of us."

When he handed me a glass, I was happy to raise it high to toast the new owner of Bryce House. I only wished there were some way to banish ghosts who insisted on inhabiting it with us. Life would be perfect then. But of course, when I mentioned this, Edwin waved an expansive hand. "Let 'em have it, Kate!" he said, his face still flushed with excitement. "I can build another, even grander place wherever I like. Yes, perhaps that is what I shall do, after I return from my travels. Brede is going with me, you know. We intend to see the world before we become settled old men."

"Hear, hear," Hawes declared.

I made my excuses shortly thereafter, leaving them to their plans. It seemed they were both in danger of becoming pot-valiant, and at eleven in the morning, too. As I went up the stairs, I could only hope Edwin would not squander his inheritance. Those plans of his sounded very grand. Then I scolded myself mentally. It was Edwin's inheritance, not mine, and I was the younger by six years, hardly the one to urge caution.

I remembered the dowry he had insisted on providing for me so I could go to Luke with my head held high, and I smiled at his generosity and, more important, this very real evidence of his love.

The little upstairs maid who was unpacking my clothes jumped when I entered my room. I wondered the girl was still so nervous, when I had been here for a month.

When I went to confer with Mrs. Harper, I found she had the party well in hand. She had spent the two days we had been away having the maids clean all the main rooms. Even the footman had been pressed into service to wash and shine the crystal prisms of the chandeliers. There was little for me to do but approve the menu and write the cards of invitation. Unfortunately, it would have to be an afternoon party, since the servants would be leaving at their usual hour. The time was set for two, with dinner to be served at three. This was tempting fate a bit, for it would be dark before the meal was over, but Mrs. Harper assured me it would serve.

"The house will be full of people, Miss Whittingham, and that will make a difference," she said. "I am sure the servants will risk it, especially if you offer them a few extra shillings each for their trouble."

And if they did not, I thought as she bustled out, it would certainly be a novel entertainment, watching them all march by the dining-room windows, torches held high to light their way, while the guests sat awaiting the arrival of the next course.

I returned to my room. It was sleeting hard now, an icy mix that frosted the lawns with white. I took a seat near the window so I might read the book of poetry Luke had pressed in my hands as I left him. Love sonnets, I saw with a smile, and for a long time I only sat and stared through the window, reliving those past two days, my happiness, my yearning. It was then I decided I would insist on marrying him long before Christmas. I would not mention it to Edwin just yet, for I did not want to spoil the triumph he was feeling, but certainly after the party I would go to him and tell . . .

"Kaaa-thaa-rinnne . . . Kaaa-thaaa-rinnne . . ."

I spun around in the chair, my hand to my throat as I searched every corner of the room wildly. The ghost was back, calling my name in that hoarse, drawn-out whisper that made chills run up my arms and the back of my neck.

"Sooon . . . Kaaa-thaa-rinnne . . . sooon . . ."

"Stop it!" I shouted. "Stop it this instant!"

There was a long pause, during which all I could hear was the rapid beating of my heart. Had I actually dared to shout that order? I was astounded at my bravery.

The hoarse voice began to call my name again then, and I covered my ears and shook my head. But the voice did not stop, and finally, in a fit half of temper and half of fright, I ran down to the library and ordered Edwin to come to my room at once. As he and Brede Hawes stared at me, I saw they were slightly befuddled for they had broached another bottle of wine.

"You must come, right now," I demanded. "That voice is calling my name again, the one no one else hears. Please, Edwin, come quickly! It has never called in the daylight before."

Still looking dubious, Edwin followed me, trailed by our faithful Hawes. "Kate, are you sure it was a voice you heard?" Edwin asked as we reached the top of the stairs and started down the hall. "The wind has come up. Perhaps it was only the wind you heard."

"Or the sleet tapping on the window," Hawes said helpfully.

I shook my head as I pushed them into my room. Out of the corner of my eye, I saw two of the maids standing close together at the end of the hall, their eyes big with fright.

The three of us stood in the middle of my bedroom. Again there was nothing but silence, such a deep, heavy silence that I knew at once the ghost had gone away. I could have wept with frustration. Why, oh why, was I the only one to hear the thing?

Because it wants *you,* something told me. No one else. *You.*

I shook my head to clear it and looked up to see both my brother and Brede Hawes staring at me.

"There is no voice here, whispering or otherwise, Kate," Edwin said somberly.

"Not now, but there was!" I insisted. I could tell, in my eagerness to make him believe me, my voice had grown higher, more strident than normal. "I did not imagine it, Edwin. It called for me, it did!"

"Of course it did," Hawes said. His voice was so soothing, I wanted to hit him for it was obvious he was only humoring me and did not believe a word I said.

"Perhaps it does not like a crowd," he added, then coughed to hide a wine-induced giggle.

"Never mind," I said more softly, acknowledging defeat. "It was here. I heard it. But it is gone now. Oh, I wish I could leave here, never come back . . ."

"You may always return to Aunt Sadie's," Edwin said stiffly. "No one is forcing you to stay."

Resentfully, for I was sure he knew I would never go since it would remove me so many miles from Luke, I was quick to say, "I cannot leave you. There is the party to see to. It would be a fine state of affairs for the guests to arrive and find Bryce House without its hostess. No, I will not go to Aunt Sadie's."

Edwin looked startled and began to search his pockets. As he drew out a letter sealed with a vivid glob of red wax, he said, "Here is a letter from our aunt for you, Kate. In all the excitement, I forgot to give it to you."

I took it and turned my back as the two men went to the door whispering together. I suppose they think I am mad, I told myself as I sat down in a chair. I would certainly think that myself if someone claimed to hear voices I could not hear, saw ghosts that were not there, went sleepwalking in the middle of the

night. I would consider such a person as mad as a
March hare, so I must not blame Edwin and Hawes
for their very real doubts about my sanity. No, indeed.

As I opened the letter, I realized it was the first one
I had received from my aunt since our arrival here. I
had begged her to write often, but she had not been
able to bring herself to do so. I knew she was not easy
about the recipients of her letters being forced to pay
for the privilege of hearing from her, and I had been
no exception. The letter was written in tiny, cramped
letters on a single sheet, and Aunt had crossed her
lines.

It took me a long time to decipher the contents.
Everyone was fine. Ann had had a summer cold, and
the baby had lost his two front milk teeth. The harvest
had been good. The curate had asked for me. And
Bethany and her husband had come for a visit. Of
course my aunt would not be so indelicate as to mention anything about her daughter's condition, but she
did write it had been thought best for Bethany to remain with her mother through this difficult time. She
added that Mr. Buffington had returned to London.

I am sure he did, I thought sarcastically, and he
would not return until after the blessed event. Instead,
he would have a fine time spending Bethany's money
in town, horrid man!

There was no mention of the ghosts at Bryce House
in the letter, no reference to our troubles, although at
the end of it Aunt Sadie said she would be delighted
to hear from me any time I cared to write. A sad, stiff
little letter, I thought as I crumpled it in my hands.
Very unlike my vibrant aunt. Strange how putting pen
to paper changed some people completely.

A faint aroma teased my nose then, and I closed
my eyes. I really did not think I would be able to face
another ghost this morning, not even the young girl
in white who wept so piteously. But I knew there was
no escape. She would stay until I acknowledged her,
perhaps even come closer and touch me. I shuddered
and opened my eyes. She was standing where she had

before, in front of the door to the hall. She seemed fainter to me somehow, as if she were disintegrating like smoke, or fog, now visible, now gone. Only the gold circle pin she wore at her breast had any substance at all. She was not wringing her hands today, nor clutching her elbows and swaying. No, instead she looked agitated, and she was moving her hands to and fro slowly. I stared at her. She had never done this before. I had the wild thought that far from wishing me harm, she was trying to help me, urging me to do something.

"What is it?" I whispered. "What should I do?"

As I spoke, I saw the tears begin to roll down her wasted face, her hands come together as if in prayer before they began their usual wringing motion. And then, as quickly as she had come, she was gone and there was only a teasing of lilac left in the air to remind me she had been there.

I went to the window to stare down at the gnarled, twisted trunks of the bushes beneath me. I would not be here in the spring when they bloomed, thank God. I would be at the Court, safe with Luke.

I joined Edwin and Brede Hawes for dinner promptly at three. They were both of them still up in the boughs, and buoyed by their good spirits, I began to feel better myself. Perhaps in only a week or two I would be free of Bryce House and its ghosts forever. I wondered when my brother would leave. Perhaps he was already making plans to set off on his journey. Perhaps he would be delighted my marriage would take place before Christmas, for it would free him of his last obligation, a spinster sister.

As the footman presented a dish of sole in a lobster sauce, Edwin said, "I say, Kate, why on earth did you change my orders to Mrs. Harper when you came home? I expressly wanted the bread-and-raisin pudding as one of the sweets for the party."

I stared at him. "But I didn't change the menu," I

assured him. "I barely looked at it before I approved it."

He was frowning now. "But you did. Mrs. Harper told me so herself, she was so agitated."

"There has to be some mistake," I said, beginning to feel uneasy. "She must have misunderstood something I said to her." I turned to Harper then, busy at the sideboard. "Please assure your wife we will have the pudding Mr. Whittingham requested, Harper, if you would be so good."

He bowed, but I noticed the glance he exchanged with the footman, and I did not care for it at all.

"That's all right then," Edwin said as he helped himself to the fish. "But this is not the first time you have countermanded my orders, Kate, or changed your mind about something. It does confuse the servants . . ."

I opened my mouth to deny the charge and just as thoughtfully closed it. I had been feeling unnerved ever since we arrived here. Who knew what I might have said and done? I could not remember doing what Edwin charged, but it was entirely possible it had happened and I had forgotten it.

The day of our dinner party dawned fair and cold. I was delighted with the huge bouquet Luke sent from his glasshouse and spent a happy hour making an arrangement for the table and one for the drawing room. I was looking forward to seeing him, even if it did have to be in company. A message from him had arrived the morning after I returned from the Court, saying he had to make a sudden trip to Southampton but would be sure to return in time for the party. And I was to contact his mother if I needed her for any reason. He had not explained that cryptic message, but I understood it well enough. It made me wish I had never told him anything about the ghosts.

They had been very quiet after my first day home. There was no tapping on the walls, no scent of lilac preceding another ghostly appearance, no dagger-wielding cavalier on the stairs, and no one whispering my name. It was almost restful, or it would have been if I had not been constantly on the fret, waiting for them to make some move.

The carriages began to arrive shortly before two. Thanks to the countess, I had learned something about each of the guests Edwin had included in the invitations. First to arrive was an elderly couple named Rogers. As a young man, Colonel Rogers had served in the American Revolution. The countess had told me he recalled every skirmish down to the last detail and would speak of it endlessly unless properly handled. She volunteered to see to him herself. His wife, or Harriet the Hero's Handmaiden, as the countess called her, was a nonentity.

Next came the Broughtens. Viscount Broughten had a reputation as a squeeze-penny. His wife was a pretty little woman. With them came their equally pretty daughters. I did not remember including them in the invitation, and caught Harper's eye to remind him to set two more places at the table. Mrs. Broughten informed me with a sunny smile they never went anywhere without their girls, and I almost forgave her. The girls were of marriageable age. It was obvious the newly wealthy Mr. Whittingham and his companion, Mr. Hawes of Southampton, had become prime prospects who had the added advantage of making an expensive London Season unnecessary if they could be brought up to scratch. The girls were charming, although I saw the elder one pout when Luke and the countess arrived.

There were two other couples as well, somewhat younger than the others, a Sir Reginald and Lady Haywood, and a Mr. and Mrs. Mannering. Everyone said they were delighted to meet me and thrilled to have the chance to visit Bryce House.

"It has been a mystery place for so long," Alicia Mannering confided. "Is there any chance we might see a ghost? I understand the house is riddled with them."

"Hardly riddled," Edwin said, smiling at her as the

footman served glasses of sherry. "But we do have ghosts, do we not, Kate? My sister can tell you all about them. She is almost able to summon them at will."

One of the Miss Broughtens squealed, then quickly covered her mouth with her gloved hand.

"There is no danger," I said, wondering why Edwin had put it quite that way. "The ghosts only appear at night, and not often. I doubt there will be any sightings tonight. We are too large a company."

Luke excused me, saying his mother wished a word. I wondered if anyone noticed he did not take me to her, but to the other side of the room where we could be alone.

"I have missed you so," he murmured, his gaze caressing every inch of my exposed skin. I was wearing one of my new gowns, a deep-blue silk cut low on the shoulders. "You look beautiful, but then you always do. And exciting. And very tempting. Have I told you how I adore you?"

"I adore you too, darling, but I must see to my guests," I made myself say. "And you must behave yourself. By the way, Miss Broughten seems a little miffed at you."

"Delphinium?" he drawled. "I am not surprised. Dear little Delphi thought she might like to be a countess, and even tried, after the usual methods failed, to compromise me. Needless to say, the attempt failed. Miserably."

"Delphinium?" I asked, my voice quivering.

"Her sister is named Heliotrope."

I fled to his mother's wheeled chair before I disgraced myself. As she had promised, she had the colonel firmly in hand while his wife fluttered about beside him, looking nervous. I could see that if the colonel did not have his moment in the sun, he became testy, and I took him away so that would not happen. It seemed an endless time before Harper announced dinner.

As the gentleman of the highest rank present, Luke

was placed at my right hand, his mother at Edwin's at the opposite end of the table. I was delighted at this turn of events even though private conversation was impossible. But Luke pressed his leg against mine under cover of the tablecloth, and by occasionally changing his position, kept me in a state of heady sensation.

It was not very much later that I saw Harper and the footman, as well as Lizzie, the maid who had been pressed into service for the party, intent on moving dinner smartly along. I hoped it was not too obvious to the guests when their plates were removed so crisply, the courses advancing at such a rapid pace. As a platter of fish and smoked eel was served, Harper poured a white wine for everyone.

"What on earth is this?" Edwin said loudly, lifting his glass to sniff it. He grimaced and held it away from him as Harper bent closer to whisper to him. Appearing startled, Edwin's gaze settled on my face, as did everyone else's at the table.

Miss Heliotrope Broughten leaned forward to sniff her own glass. "Oh, I say, this is vinegar, not wine, 'pon my soul it is, Mama, so you need not look at me like that."

"Vinegar?" Lady Haywood asked. "But why would we be served vinegar?"

"Miss Whittingham requested it, milady," Harper said at his most pompous.

I started up, but before I could speak and deny any such thing, Luke's hand came down on my thigh to press it warningly.

"I believe it is all a hoax, is it not, Miss Whittingham?" he asked lightly. "Yes, Lord Byron began the practice. When he was on a reducing diet he would eat nothing but mashed potatoes and drink nothing but vinegar."

He paused and sipped his glass. Making a face, he put it down and added, "It would certainly put me on a reducing diet! How very amusing."

His mother laughed, and the others smiled, and he took my hand in his and squeezed it.

"Please clear those glasses, Harper," I said. "You may serve the correct wine now."

I was furious but determined not to show it. Furious and confused and face to face with a solution I could not even bear to consider. For I had not ordered the vinegar, and Harper had not served it on his own. I did not dare look at my brother.

Chapter Eighteen

I do not remember much of the rest of dinner. I was very angry, and I was also confused. Fortunately, Luke took over the duties of hostess for me and conversed so winningly, I am sure my preoccupation went unnoticed.

Every so often I stole a look at the other end of the table, where Edwin sat deep in discussion with the Countess of Bryce. I thought he looked agitated. Once, Brede Hawes caught my eye. He shook his head a little and smiled at me, but I was not fooled. He had just been treated to yet another instance of my growing insanity, and in front of guests at that. But I knew I had not given the order that vinegar be served with the fish. I knew that as surely as I knew my name. Therefore, since I could not imagine Harper concocting such a scheme himself—why would he? what purpose would it serve?—I was forced to acknowledge that my brother was the culprit.

I managed to tell Sir Reginald Haywood I would not be coming out for opening day of the Lechton Hunt. "I enjoy a good ride, but have no interest in watching a poor animal get torn to pieces," I said.

This statement drew fire from the gentlemen present, and I was able to return to my musings while supposedly attending to a lecture on the destructive ways of the fox, its danger to the local farmers' poultry, and its unfortunate habit of producing large litters.

Was Edwin perhaps trying to show the Tremaines how unstable I was? I wondered as I toyed with my fish. Was this his way of making sure I did not marry

Luke Tremaine? But why would he be concerned about that? He might not care for the earl, but he would have to admit my marriage to him would be a real coup, especially since he planned on some extensive traveling. Was it merely selfishness? I knew Edwin was selfish. My love for him did not blind me to his faults. Perhaps he wanted me to go back to our aunt Sadie until his return so I would be ready to help plan his new mansion, furnish it, and run it for him.

"I will have to take your word for it that the winters near the coast are milder than they are inland, my lady," I said. "It has seemed very chilly here lately."

Luke smiled at me, and I felt better. Calmer, even. Whatever had caused that debacle with the vinegar, I would discover it, and in short order, too.

Later, Harper caught my eye and indicated with a nod that the time for the servants' departure had arrived. Edwin and I had discussed this and had decided to make as little of it as possible. Certainly the entire neighborhood knew of their habit of leaving the house at dusk and returning at dawn.

I nodded my permission, and the three servants were quick to leave the room. We were still eating our sweet course, and the port had not gone around, but Edwin had said he could handle that chore himself.

"As you can see, our servants leave us now," I said as lightly as I could manage.

"The ghosts," Mrs. Rogers said knowingly. "Oh, I could tell you a tale of them, Miss Whittingham!"

The colonel coughed loudly and glared at her, and she subsided. But later, after the ladies had left the gentlemen, I sought her out in the drawing room.

Away from her martinet of a husband, Mrs. Rogers relaxed. I judged her age to be about sixty. "I would love to hear your stories about our ghosts, ma'am. It has been difficult to find out anything about them, for our great-uncle wrote little of them. The one they call The Gentleman, now . . ."

Mrs. Rogers waved a thin, veined hand. "I have

never been sure there was a male ghost," she said. "He has only been seen once or twice, and then only by young servant girls. You know how impressionable they are."

"But what of his tapping?" I asked, confused. "We have heard it many times in the large front bedroom—yes, and his pacing as well."

She frowned. "I never heard of him doing such things, and my grandmother knew the house well. When we arrived tonight, I recognized everything about it from her stories. As for any tapping and pacing, well, I am sure I cannot explain it. Can it be another ghost has taken up haunting here?"

I shuddered. "Indeed, I hope not," I said. "Two are enough."

"Ah, the girl with the chestnut hair who weeps so and moans," my companion said knowingly. "Have you seen her?"

I explained her visits while the lady sat wide-eyed with interest. "Lilacs, you say?" she mused when I finished. "Yes, I do seem to remember my grandmother telling me of a lilac scent that trailed her. I had forgotten that part of it."

"Why is she so unhappy, do you think?" I asked quickly. I was afraid the men might arrive soon. They were such an oddly matched group, it seemed very possible they would not linger over their port.

"My grandmother refused to tell me, so I suppose we may safely assume it was because of some scandal involving a man. An unsuitable man, most likely. Legend has it she left Bryce House late one May evening with her mother and was never seen again. She just— disappeared."

"But obviously she did not," I argued. "She must have died here if she continues to haunt the place. And she is so miserable about her haunting, I wonder she would not be glad to go.

"My brother and Mr. Hawes have never seen her, by the way. They have only heard her moaning and shrieking."

"No, she would not bother with them," Mrs. Rogers said. "I have the feeling she would know from experience that men would not help her."

"I have tried and tried to think what I might do so her spirit can rest," I said, trying to ignore the men's voices I could hear coming. Mrs. Rogers had no suggestions, and on her husband's arrival at her side, reverted to the innocuous little woman she had been on arrival. I did not envy her her marriage.

The Misses Broughten honored us with a few musical selections, one playing the pianoforte, the other singing. It was pleasant for they had been well trained.

Not long afterwards, the Broughtens announced their departure. I could tell the girls were growing more and more uneasy with every passing minute, their mother as well, and there was no need to delay for obviously tea would not be served later. The decision caused everyone to begin to gather their things.

Mr. Hawes ran to the stables to summon the carriages, and Edwin fetched wraps, playing footman with a flourish. The two girls stood close together, staring up the dark stairway.

No doubt it was bad of me, but for a minute I wished we might see The Gentleman, masked and brandishing his dagger. It would make the perfect ending to our party.

"I will come tomorrow afternoon," Luke murmured, holding my hand for a moment. "Do not worry about the vinegar episode. No one thinks anything of it."

"Thanks to you," I said bitterly. "I did not order that vinegar, Luke. You must believe me."

"I am sure you did not. It is one of the things we will discuss tomorrow," he said. "Sleep well and rest easy. Remember, I love you and you will be leaving here soon."

The Tremaines were the last to go since the countess's wheeled chair had to be disassembled and stowed in the carriage. As soon as they were on their way, the three of us remaining sought the library as was our custom.

"A delightful party, Kate," Brede Hawes complimented me. "The food was excellent. And did you see the appetite Broughten brought with him? He acted as if he had not eaten for a week."

I nodded, but I was staring at my brother where he stooped before the coal fire to poke it to life. "Why did you contrive that episode with the vinegar, Edwin? Ask Harper to lie about it as well?" I asked, too perturbed to temper my words, or wait until we were alone.

"I?" he asked, as if astounded. Rising to his feet and dusting his hands, he came to grasp my arms and look me straight in the eye. "I did not do anything of the sort, Kate," he said quietly. "Can it be you really do not remember? Harper said you made the special request this morning, right after breakfast. When he tried to advise you, you would not listen, and you told him if he said anything to me, he would be discharged. I should be asking *you* why you did it, not the other way around."

Put on the defensive again, I said hotly, "But I did not say anything to Harper, I did not! Surely I would remember such a singular thing, don't you agree?"

"Perhaps, but why would Harper say you had if it were not true?" Hawes interrupted. "It made him the center of attention, and good butlers hate that. Come now, confess! We are both anxious to know if you were trying to emulate Byron, as the earl claimed."

I stared at him. Hawes had no right to question me. No right to interfere in a family discussion. He was a guest here, for all Edwin treated him like a brother.

"I did not order the vinegar served," I said slowly and carefully. "I did not discuss the wines with Harper for that is your province, Edwin, not mine. Whatever you may think of me, I am not guilty of this."

"But who else could it have been?" Hawes insisted. "Edwin did not do it, and Harper would have no reason to. Certainly *I* would not give an order here."

He stopped and the two men looked at me solemnly and, in the case of Hawes, with a pitying expression. There was silence in the library then, a heavy silence full of conjecture, accusation—doubt. But I would not back down and admit to something I had not done. The evening stretched long and longer before me as I took my usual seat and opened my book. The two men moved away to the window where they stood talking quietly. Every so often they glanced my way. Edwin looked perturbed, Hawes knowing. Eventually, they began to play cards for their usual high, imaginary stakes.

I excused myself very early. I found I could not bear to remain with them when I was so confused and with such an edge of bright anger lurking right beneath the placid exterior I was trying so hard to present. Edwin came to kiss me and hug me. To show he forgave me, I thought as I went up the stairs, my candle held high.

To my surprise, I fell asleep quickly and, wonder of wonders, slept undisturbed by any ghostly attention. I remember my last thought was of Brede Hawes, and his impudence in daring to take me to task.

I woke early, so early the maids had not even come in to make up the fire and bring hot water. Stretching, I tried to see past a crack in the draperies what kind of day it was going to be. Not that Luke would fail me, of course, I told myself as I swung my legs over the side of the bed and felt around for my slippers. I encountered something hard, and looking down, I gasped. My toes had connected with a large knife. I had never seen it before and had no idea how it had come to be there. The blade was stained, and as I bent closer, I saw it was covered with dried blood. I sat up so quickly, my head spun. What had happened? Why was this knife here, by my bed?

As I looked down at it again, almost as if I hoped it were just a delusion, I saw that the front of my nightdress was spattered with drops of blood, and my hand, as I reached for the bedpost to steady myself, was stained in like manner.

There was a soft knock, and the little maid who waited on me slipped in with a steaming pitcher of water. She stopped when she saw me, dropped the pitcher, and screamed. I was sure she would swoon. Instead, she turned and ran shrieking from the room.

"What on earth?" I heard Edwin ask sleepily from his doorway down the hall. "What's amiss?"

Quickly, I ran and closed the door. I had no plan in mind, I just felt I must hide whatever had happened from my brother. Because I might be guilty of something dreadful? I did not know for I was not thinking at all clearly. I stripped off the stained gown and pulled on a shift. As fast as I could manage it, I wrapped the knife in the stained gown and hid it in the bottom of the armoire before I washed my hands as thoroughly as I could in the cold water left over from last night. I was fastening my gown when I heard Edwin's knock.

"Kate? Are you all right? Please, let me in. The maid said she found you all bloodstained. Kate?"

I went to the door. I had to. There was no escape from this nightmare. Edwin stood there in his dressing gown. I have never seen him looking so ill, as if he dreaded what he was about to discover. He inspected me carefully before he took me in his arms to hug me tightly.

"Thank God," he said fervently. Then he held me at arm's length. "But what is this tale of being covered with blood?" he asked. "I see no blood."

"My nightdress," I said in defeat. "I do not understand it either, Edwin. When I woke I found a bloody knife beside my bed, and I had blood on the front of my gown and on my hands. I was so frightened. I—I hid the gown and the knife just now in the armoire."

He pulled me back into his arms again to hold me close and pat my back, all the while murmuring it was all right, all right, we would discover the problem together, and like sentiments that made me feel a great deal better. At least he was not accusing me this time.

"I say, what's the to-do?" I heard Brede Hawes ask, and turned to see him leaving his room. He was wearing only a shirt and breeches and it was obvious he had just awakened for he sported the beginning of a dark beard, and his hair was uncombed.

"It is Kate," Edwin said shortly. "She woke and discovered her nightclothes bloodstained, and a knife beside her bed.

"Sister! Are you hurt? I never thought to ask."

"No. I am all right," I managed to say. "Oh, do you think it was the ghosts?"

"Ghosts do not bleed," Edwin said, biting off his words again in the greatest distress.

"See here, I suppose there is no avoiding it . . ." Hawes began. We both stared at him as he held out his right hand. It was covered by a large, bloodstained bandage. I felt Edwin start, and I felt something else as well. His comforting grip loosened, and he moved away from me slightly.

"I was not going to say anything, but since even the servants know something is amiss, there is nothing for it but for me to tell you the truth," Hawes continued. Turning to look at me, he added, "I am so sorry, Kate."

I stared at him. I was numb with shock and disbelief. And dread. Dread of what he was going to say next.

"I woke last night to discover Kate standing beside my bed," Hawes went on. "I knew she was not herself for although she stared at me, she did not appear to see me. When I spoke to her, she ignored my question. Instead, she raised a large knife and tried to stab me. In the heart, I am afraid. I grabbed at her arm, and in the process managed to get my hand slashed.

"No, no, it was only a flesh wound," he went on, although both Edwin and I stood frozen, incapable of speech.

"How could you see her?" my brother asked after a long silence. "In the dark? At night?"

He sounded suspicious of Hawes's story, and that comforted me.

Hawes's face flushed. "There was a candle burning. I confess I have not been able to sleep easy here without one.

"She ran out of the room then," he went on, as if anxious to get past his cowardice as quickly as possible. "I admit I locked my door before I washed and bandaged the cut. There was a lot of blood, but as I said, it is not serious.

"Do not make too much of it, my friend," he added, for Edwin alone. "I am sure she was sleepwalking again and did not have the vaguest idea what she was doing. We must not censure her for it."

"It is very good of you to take it this way, Brede." Edwin sounded as if he were strangling. "If you would excuse us now. I would speak to Kate alone."

"Of course! No need to ask," Hawes said quickly. He did not look at me as he left us.

Edwin drew me inside my bedroom and led me to some chairs near the fireplace, carefully avoiding the large wet stain on the carpet where the hot water the maid had brought me had soaked into the rug.

I could not speak as he pushed me down gently. I could only stare at him helplessly.

"Do you remember any of this, Kate?" he asked. "Anything at all?"

I managed to shake my head.

He sighed and ran his hands through his blond hair before he leaned forward to take my hands in his. "I have never felt so reluctant to act, but act I must, Kate," he said. He sounded so full of despair, I wanted to tell him it was all right, just to comfort him. Strange, is it not, the stupid things we want to do in moments of crisis?

"I have to insist you see a doctor, as soon as I can summon one from Southampton. This has gone beyond a few strange incidents. It has become serious indeed if you would attack Brede."

"Why did I do that, Edwin?" I asked, past denying anything even if I could not remember it.

"Because he annoyed you last evening? I could see you were angry when he entered into a discussion that should have been a private family matter. Indeed, I took him to task for it later. But never, never did I think it would lead to—to attempted murder."

I gasped, my gaze never leaving his anguished face. "Murder?" I whispered. "Oh, surely not murder, Edwin!"

He nodded, his mouth grim. "You heard him just now. You were going for his heart with that knife. Only his quick reaction deflected the blow. Thank God he woke, or we might be waiting for the justice instead of a doctor. No, we cannot pretend any longer that all these things that have been happening are little, isolated events brought on by the stress of living in a haunted house. I fear the ghosts have brought you to madness, Kate."

I stared at him, horrified. He truly thought I was insane, and this time I was frightened that he might be right.

."It might not be permanent," he added quickly, squeezing my hands tightly. In my distress, I had forgotten he was holding them. "Perhaps there is some cure. Perhaps if you left here, went to some safe place where people understand such things, you would return to your rightful frame of mind. I shall never forgive myself, you know, for bringing you here. Never."

I did not hear what he said at the end for I had fastened on one sentence, and it was so terrifying, I felt I might die. Bedlam. He was suggesting I go to Bedlam, and I had heard enough about that madhouse to know I would kill myself before I consented to it. Consented? I thought. Idiot! You will not be consulted, nor will your wishes be honored. Madwomen are put away for their own good, and for everyone else's. No one *asks* them if they would *care* for it.

Edwin rose and patted my shoulder awkwardly. "I shall bring you some breakfast, Kate, and see to your fire. I think it best if you remain in seclusion. And I doubt any of the maids could be persuaded to wait on you. It is a shame when you are so docile now, but perfectly understandable, don't you agree?"

I nodded, although I had suddenly remembered that Luke was coming to see me this afternoon. When I told Edwin, he frowned.

"You must write and tell him you are ill," he said quickly. "After the doctor has examined you, we will be able to better decide what the future holds for you. You must face the fact that you may not be able to marry the earl. It would not be right, to bring madness into the family. What of the succession? Your children may well become mad, too."

"I know," I whispered, staring down at my muslin-covered knees as if I wanted to memorize the sprigged pattern of the fabric. "I know that, Edwin," I said, feeling as if my heart was breaking.

"So you will write to him now?" Edwin persisted. "I will have the groom take your letter to Bryce Court as soon as it is ready."

My throat ached so with misery, all I could do was nod.

Chapter Nineteen

Edwin took the knife away with him. I was glad to give it up, although I did wonder where I had got it. Had I gone down to the cellars late last night, walking in my sleep past that icy spot in the wall to fetch it from the kitchen? I must have done something like that, for I had certainly never seen it before. But whereas once I would have shuddered just thinking of such a dangerous expedition, now I was too miserable to care. I sat numbly when Edwin left me, but when he locked me in, I jumped up, startled. He thought me such a threat that it was necessary to keep me prisoner? But why? I was calm, reasonable, and I had accepted the blame for what had happened, even agreed to his plans. Why lock me in?

It made me angry, but the anger did not last. Of course Edwin must take precautions. Having attacked Brede Hawes, who knew what I might do next? And just because I was awake now and acting normally did not mean I might not attack someone else.

But do you know, deep down inside I was having the greatest difficulty believing I had done such a thing. Or do all mad people think they are sane?

When Edwin brought my breakfast tray and the coal for the fire, the letter to Luke was ready. I had made several attempts, but had settled at last for a stiff little note that only told him I was feeling poorly and could not receive him today. I could tell Edwin was not satisfied with it, but I said it was the best I could do while I was so depressed. I had cried when I wrote it. Perhaps my red eyes and the trace of tears on my cheeks convinced him, for he took the letter without protesting further.

I paced my room for most of the morning, pausing now and then to stare out the window. It was a beautiful day, more like October than November, the sky a deep blue, the wind brisk. I could tell it was cold for the gardener, putting a final application of mulch on some of the flower beds, was dressed warmly. Once he looked up as he stretched his stiff old back, and when he saw me, he made the sign of the cross before he hurried away, leaving his barrow behind him.

That made me cry. I felt like a leper with everyone so frightened of me.

I think I expected Luke to come anyway that afternoon for I listened expectantly for the sound of the front-door knocker, his voice demanding to see me at once, his authoritative steps as he took the stairs two at a time. But he did not come, and when Edwin brought me my dinner, he said there had been no response to my letter. He also told me the groom had gone to Southampton for a doctor Brede Hawes had recommended. The doctor would be with us in a few days.

I only toyed with my dinner, and drank sparingly of the wine provided. I tried to read but I could not concentrate. Edwin refused to bring me my needlework. When I asked why, he said he did not trust me not to harm myself with the embroidery scissors. I think that is when I gave up completely. Yes, it was weak, but I have discovered there is only so much a person can take before they break. I had reached the breaking point, and by accepting it had fallen into deep despair.

I managed to sleep for an hour or so, but I had terrible dreams. I had never spent so much time alone before. In my aunt's house with its noisy band of children, I was constantly in the center of one whirlwind or another. Even here I had had Edwin and Brede Hawes, Bethany and her husband, for company. And I had had Luke. Luke. I wondered if he had heard

what took place here last night, and that was why he
had not come.

Edwin had suggested I write down everything I
could remember that had happened to me since coming to Bryce House. He said it would serve as a guide
for the doctor when he arrived, and he urged me to
be as open and clear as I possibly could.

Obediently, I listed all the instances of haunting I
could remember, including finding myself by that evil
section of cellar wall, all the girl ghost's visitations,
The Gentleman's antics, and the hoarse voice that
whispered for me alone to hear. Reading it over I did
not see how anyone could think me anything but insane. It was a litany of one unbelievable episode after
another. It sounded like the ranting of a madwoman.

I wondered if there was some way to temper it
somehow before I showed it to the doctor. Some way
to make it sound just a logical description of some
strange events, one written by a normal, skeptical person. But I realized there was no way to do this. The
doctor would ask me if I believed in ghosts. Once I
would have been able to say no. Now I could not.

It seemed an endless time before dusk fell and the
house grew quiet. Edwin came to see if there was
anything I needed before he locked me in for the
night. He held me for a long moment before he left
me, and his eyes were wet as he did so. It was obvious
he was deeply affected by what had happened to me,
and I loved him for it. The two of us were family. The
only immediate family we had left was each other.

Much later, I heard him and Hawes pass by my
door on their way to bed. Did I only imagine they
paused for a moment before they hurried on? I drew
a deep breath. The whole long, endless night stretched
before me. I did not think I would be able to sleep,
so I did not bother to undress. I tried to pray, but I
felt my pleading for release from this nightmare went
unheard. I made up the fire again, lit another candle
against the shadows, and hoped that at least the ghosts
might leave me alone. I felt so fragile, so tenuous—

much like the girl who came to visit me here, in fact, all diaphanous wisps of being and lilac scent with no substance to her at all. I felt as if one more little thing would send me spinning down into a dark purgatory that I would never be able to escape. It frightened me to death, this feeling, but I could not put it aside or make light of it. Instead I tried not to think of it, tried to pretend it was not crouched at my feet, waiting.

It must have been an hour or more later when I heard someone at my door. I stared at it, bemused. I knew it was not a ghost. Ghosts had no need to scratch at a lock or turn a knob. Then the door opened to reveal Luke standing there, the finger at his lips cautioning me to silence. He need not have bothered. I was so stunned, I just stared at him. He closed the door softly and locked it again before he came to me. He did not speak as he lifted me from the chair into his arms. Then he put his cheek against my hair and said, "Do not worry anymore, Kate. I am here now, and we will see about getting you out of this fix you find yourself in. Come, let us sit down. You have a lot to tell me, and I am anxious to hear it."

As he spoke, he carried me over to the bed and sat down beside me on the edge of it. "We must talk softly," he said, smiling at me as only he could. "No one knows I am here, of course."

"How did you find out something was wrong?" I asked.

"First from the note you sent, so formal yet woebegone. Then I waited at one of the maids' cottages in the village until she returned there at dusk. Remember Lizzie? Her sister works at the Court and she would like to join her there. For the promise of employment, she told me quite a tale."

He paused for a moment before he added, "Come to think of it, I am not sure it was necessary to promise her anything. What happened here today has become the talk of the village."

"Then you know of my sleepwalking? The knife I used on Brede Hawes?"

"Not the true version. What I heard was that you had suddenly become violent and attacked both your brother and Hawes. And that this morning, you tried to stab the maid who came to wait on you. I heard you had been locked in your room until the doctor could confirm you were a candidate for Bedlam. Oh, and that you howled like a wild thing and threatened to kill anyone who came near you."

I lowered my eyes so he could not see the despair in them, but he was having none of that. Lifting my chin, he said clearly, "That will not happen, Kate. You are not mad, and no one, *no one,* is going to put you in a madhouse. Not even your brother."

"How can you be so sure?" I asked past the rising hope I felt just knowing he still had faith in me. Not waiting for his answer, I reached for him and kissed him, losing myself in his nearness and strength, happy to transfer the heavy burden of my troubles to his broad shoulders. He held me close, and when he lifted his head to smile at me several minutes later, he held my face between his hands as if it were some delicate, precious thing that, once broken, could never be replaced. And it was then I felt precious and loved. Hopeful, too, that with Luke's help it might be possible after all to escape this tangled, frightening web I was caught in.

"I also heard you are a witch. Well, I knew that," he said easily. "You have certainly cast a spell over me, woman."

"A *witch*?" I asked in confusion.

He nodded. "Indeed. The boy who used to work here in the gardens claims he saw you one afternoon in the beech wood, carrying on a wild dance and talking to your familiar. Perhaps some day you might explain to me exactly what this 'wild dance' was all about."

Only a moment's thought recalled the day I had felt so happy, I had skipped in the wood and called out to a chattering squirrel. I am sure I colored up just thinking of the boy watching me there, but at least now I knew why the gardener had made that sign of the cross this morning.

"Most of your actions seem known in the village," Luke continued. "I have to wonder why. Do you have any ideas about it?"

I shook my head. Why anyone would find me interesting enough to keep track of my movements was a mystery, I led such a prosaic life. Of course there was that morning the servants had found me at the foot of the main staircase. Perhaps that was what had set them to buzzing.

"Tell me exactly what has been going on here. It is the only way I can help you," Luke ordered, his voice stern. "That way we may be able to make some sense out of what has happened to bring you to this pass. It is obvious you have not been open with me, Kate. I want to know why you hid things from me."

For one mad moment, I almost begged him to just take me away from Bryce House, carry me back to the Court and marry me when he pleased. I did not want to tell him of the ghosts or speak of those un speakable things that I had endured, yes, and kept from him lest he think me mad. But of course that did not matter now, when the whole world was saying I was.

Obediently, I went to fetch the list I had made. I tried not to watch his face as he went over it, tried not to read something into every grimace, every raised brow, every shake of his head. I was not successful. At last, he looked up and stared at me.

"Do you now think me mad, too?" I asked. "I could hardly blame you if you did. But what I wrote there did happen to me. It is all true. I swear it is all true!"

"All right. Let us start there. Now, go back to the beginning, if you please. The Gentleman Ghost you mention. Both Hawes and your brother could see him too when he first appeared? Hear him when he paced over your heads and tapped the walls?"

I nodded, and he went on, "But later, they claimed he was not there when you saw him clearly?"

I could hear the doubt in his voice, the confusion, and I knew the struggle he was having, trying to be even-handed, trying to trust me. Because he loved me. I could have wept . . .

He asked me to describe the man and I did so right down to the dagger he brandished.

"Was it the one you found here this morning?"

I had not thought of that, and it was a moment before I told him that one was an ordinary kitchen knife.

"So, he was masked. I wonder why. What was he like physically? Can you describe him?"

I shrugged helplessly. "I suppose he was of normal height, neither tall nor short. Heavy set, though, and somehow I do not think he was a young man, although I do not know why."

"You never saw him when you were alone?" Luke persisted.

"There was that one night when neither Edwin nor Mr. Hawes saw him, although I did. Right at the top of the stairs," I said with a shiver. To be seeing things that others did not seemed a clear indication of madness.

Frustrated and confused, I added, "You do not believe me, do you? Not really. You do not think there are any ghosts at all. You think I am making all this up, don't you? Admit it!"

He put a gentle hand over my mouth. "I believe you saw things. I do not believe in ghosts. I never have. To have one described to me clearly, to hear of it tapping and pacing about, is difficult. But forget my disbelief. I may be able to discover something tomorrow that will explain all this, and why it is happening, too."

"Tomorrow?" I echoed, cast down because he was not going to take me away from here tonight.

"You must stay until this is settled, Kate. It is too serious to run from; forget. I will be here with you. You have nothing to fear."

"How can you stay with me? Edwin brings my food,

the coal; he even empties the slop jar. Were you planning on hiding under the bed?"

"No, I will be somewhere else in the house. Only at night, when it is late as it is now, can we be together.

"But to return. . . . Is there anything else you can remember about this 'gentleman'?"

I thought for a moment. "At our party, Mrs. Rogers told me she did not believe there was a gentleman because over the years he had never been seen except by a couple of young maids. I told her he does exist."

Something else occurred to me then, for I was still silently brooding over Luke's disbelief. "You have the key. I want to show you something, here in the house."

He looked wary, and I tugged his hand. "It will only take a few minutes, truly."

Once he had unlocked the door, the hall stretched long and dark ahead of us, and I was very glad Luke was with me. As quietly as we could we made our way down the servants' stairs to the cellars. There I paused, holding my candle high

"This way," I said in an ordinary voice now there was no chance we might be overheard. "We must go single file now."

He looked askance at me, but he fell in behind. When we reached the place I dreaded, I stopped and held my hand out to the opposite wall. Once again the obscene cold washed over my arm, tried to wrap around me to capture me. I jerked my arm away and pressed back against the wall behind me while Luke stared at me, his face a study in confusion. Grasping his coattail firmly, I said, "Hold your arm out as I did toward the far wall. Not too far! Now, tell me what you feel?"

"It is cold. Very cold. Why—why, what the devil?"

He pulled back with visible effort and cursed as he rubbed his hand and arm. "What is there, Kate?" he asked. "It felt as if something was trying to pull me to it."

"Yes, that is exactly what it does," I told him. "I

brought you here so you could discover that there are some things that cannot be explained. I do not know what is in that wall, or how long it has been there, but I do know that it is evil. And it does try to capture people. Once, long ago, a young maid died here, probably of fright. The servants avoid it like the plague. You should see them stop before they reach it and turn sideways to edge along this wall. It is the worst place in Bryce House. There are other cold spots, of course, but they are only cold, not malevolent."

Safely back in my room again upstairs, I was glad to see Luke looking shaken. Glad, because it meant he believed now as he had not done before.

He studied my list again before he said, "Tell me more of The Lady."

When I had described her, right down to the gold pin she wore at her breast, he smiled and said, "You seem to know her very well. Why, you almost sound fond of her."

"I suppose I feel sorry for her," I said slowly. "She is so miserable." I told him then what Harriet Rogers had said about a possible scandal.

"Ah. You do remember what I told you about the stern, straitlaced Whittinghams? If the girl was indeed up to something she should not have been—and yes, I quite agree it was probably a man—her parents might have reacted in ways we would deplore in this more enlightened age. That might be why she weeps and pleads."

"Edwin and Brede Hawes have not seen her," I remembered to tell him.

"What?" he asked, his face suddenly alert again. "Never? But that is unusual, don't you think?"

He did not seem to require an answer, for he began to pace, much as I had done all day. I was content to lean back in a chair and watch him. It was amazing how calm I felt, how peaceful. I knew it was because Luke was with me, because I knew he would be able to get me out of this dilemma. Somehow. My eyes

filled with sudden tears of gratitude. I was very tired,
or I would have despised the weakness.

"I never considered that ghosts might be selective
in their haunting," he mused, almost to himself.

"Mrs. Rogers thinks the girl obviously knows men;
how they would not be likely to help her, since they
are so self-involved."

I did not say this coyly. The situation was too serious for that. "She thinks I was chosen because I am
of the same sex and could sympathize with her problems. And so I would, if I knew what they were," I
added. "But although she sang a snatch of song once,
she does not seem able to speak."

We discussed this particular ghost for quite some
time. At last, Luke referred to the voices.

"You have heard them only in this one room?" he
asked. "Not on the stairs? In the library? And always
when you are alone? What direction do they seem to
come from?"

When I told him I could not be sure, for sometimes
it seemed the whispers came from one side of the
room, and other times the opposite, he frowned.

At last the casement clock in the lower hall struck
three as I was hiding a yawn. Luke saw me, for he
came to pull me to my feet and lead me to bed.

"It is very late," he said as he lifted me in and
pulled the covers up to tuck around me. "Time you
slept."

"Don't leave me," I whispered. "Please don't go."

He bent and kissed my nose. "I won't. Not for a
while, anyway. Go to sleep. I will be right here in a
chair near the fire. And tomorrow, when you are alone
again, I will come back."

Half asleep already, I said, "Luke? How did you
get the key to this room? I thought Edwin had it."

He chuckled as he smoothed the hair back from my
brow. "I had only to take one from another door. The
maid, Lizzie, told me all the rooms on this floor open
with a single key. Why anyone of any intelligence
would have it so, I have no idea, but it does make me

glad you are only distantly related to your Whittingham relatives."

I think I fell asleep in mid-chuckle, and I know I did not wake until I heard Edwin unlocking my door much later that day.

Chapter Twenty

I opened my eyes when Edwin came in with my breakfast tray. He peered down at me, his face doleful and strained, and all the horror of my situation came flooding back.

"I hope you slept well, Kate," he said. "And did not hear any voices?"

I shook my head, ignoring the whispering I could hear in the hall. How exciting it must be for the maids, I thought wryly, to be so close to a madwoman. Edwin must have heard them as well, for he shouted an order and they scurried in to deal with the fire, the chamber pot and slop jar. I concentrated on the chair beside the fireplace. The dented cushion gave proof that Luke had been here and it gave me courage. At last they all left me. Edwin locked the door behind him as he had before and I was left to seesaw between wild hope and desperate conjecture.

It was the longest day I have ever endured. I was more than half afraid the doctor might arrive and take me away without Luke knowing a thing about it, so I spent most of the time listening for carriage wheels or a knock on the front door. I wondered what Luke was doing today, and what he would have to tell me when he returned. He had said there were things he had to do, and information he was waiting for to arrive from Southampton. He had sounded determined when he said it, too, but when I questioned him, he would not explain.

Edwin came back many times that day. He seemed awkward and nervous somehow. And he looked dreadful, as if he had slept even less than I had. Several times I thought he wanted to say something, but then his lips would thin and he would turn aside. Once Brede Hawes knocked on the door and called him away. I thought to ask how Hawes's wound was and was told it was healing well and that he held me no ill will. That was a relief. It still bothered me to think I had actually tried to hurt him.

Eventually night came, and with it another wait until it was late enough for the two men to come up to bed and leave me free of possible interruption until morning. Only then would Luke be able to join me. I felt taut and on edge, and I could not seem to sit still.

Luke brought a bundle and a bottle of brandy when he came. He set them both down carefully before he put his arms around me to hold me close. Gratefully, I closed my eyes and felt myself relaxing.

"Enough, woman," he said finally as he put me away from him. "We have things to do."

"What things?" I asked, remembering to speak softly. I thought Luke looked very stern and wondered at it. Pray God he did not have such bad news that he could not save me.

"I have discovered some things that are going to hurt you, Kate," he told me. "I wish I did not have to tell you of them, but I must. They are true. You must accept them."

"You are frightening me, you are so serious," I tried to say lightly.

We took seats across from each other before the fire. I hoped we might sit just this way years from now when we were old, Luke nodding off in the warmth of the fire, and I rubbing my eyes because I could not see my sewing clearly anymore. Like Darby and Joan in the old song, I thought.

"Tell me, Kate, when did you learn of your great-uncle's death?" he asked, and I made myself return to present business.

"I remember exactly. It was my cousin Mary's eighth birthday. We were all delighted when Edwin arrived from London so unexpectedly. It gave us two occasions to celebrate."

"The date, if you please."

"Why, September nineteenth."

"That confirms what I thought. You must have left your aunt's house shortly thereafter."

"Yes, we did. You know we had to be here by the first of October because of the stipulation in Great-Uncle's will."

Luke did not say anything for a long time, and for some reason I did not ask why. I only waited, holding my breath.

At last, his face set like stone, Luke undid the bundle he had brought with him, still without saying a word. I gasped as a white suit was revealed, then a broad-brimmed plumed hat, white gloves, hose, and shoes, and a full white mask. The suit had thin streamers of various pale grays sewn to it in many places, but I did not need to see them to know what it was.

"You recognize this, of course," Luke said as he laid everything out on the floor between us.

I stared down at it, both fascinated and repelled. "Yes, I do. It is The Gentleman's costume."

"Costume is the correct word for it. You see how these ribbons would float when the man who wore it moved? How they would make him appear ghostly?"

He reached into a pocket of the suit and pulled out a large piece of gossamer cloth. "And how if this material was held before the man as he backed away, it would make it seem he was disappearing right before your eyes? Of course you would have to be prepared for the illusion, and the light would have to be uncertain."

"It was. He only appeared at night, in the dark at the top of the stairs. And I was prepared," I managed to say. No, I told myself. No, it is not so. He had nothing to do with this. There has to be some other explanation.

"Where did you find it?" I asked. My fingernails

were digging into the palms of my hands, and I struggled to relax the fists I had made so inadvertently.

"In the attics. No one has used them for years. I had only to follow the footsteps so plainly marked in the dust to a chest in one of the box rooms."

I barely heard him, I was thinking so hard. I felt better immediately when I realized that Edwin had had nothing to do with this charade. He had been right beside me every time The Gentleman had been either seen or heard. He had not tricked me.

"No, it was not your brother or Brede Hawes who created this illusion," Luke said, as if he had read my mind. "It was the butler."

"Harper?" I asked, stunned. "But he and Mrs. Harper always left the house at dusk."

"Nothing to stop him from coming back, was there? It would be simplicity itself to creep up to the attics, don his costume, then wait at the top of the stairs for the three of you to come up to bed."

"He could have been the one doing the whispering, then."

"Yes, I believe he was. I have inspected the rooms on either side of this one. Someone has recently made two holes in the wall there. Come and see."

I followed him over to the bed. He moved the curtains behind the headboard aside, and I could see a hole plainly, just above where my head would lie on the pillow. On the other side of the room, there was a hole behind a mirror. They were both small. I had looked around the room earlier, the morning after the whispers started, but I had not spotted them.

"It was easy enough to go into either room and whisper your name," Luke said as we took our seats again. I had begun to tremble and I clasped my hands together hard and tried to concentrate only on the surface of this thing he was telling me. No, I thought again. No.

"What about the pacing? The tapping we heard?" I asked.

"I had to wait until everyone was busy elsewhere

before I could get into that room over the library. As I suspected, the fitted carpet had been cleverly cut so a path on the wooden floor could be exposed and just as quickly covered up again. The pattern concealed the edges of the cuts except to someone looking for it on their hands and knees."

"I see," I said bleakly. "It was all a—a hoax."

"The Gentleman was, certainly."

"I do not believe the other ghost was contrived, however," I said, still talking more to stave off the inevitable confrontation with the truth I knew was coming than to learn more. "No, I am sure she is a real, live ghost."

Luke did not smile. "She may be. But I do not think she was the one who shrieked and moaned from the cellars. I think Mrs. Harper did that. Like her husband, she has often trod the boards. In the provinces, at least. I could find no record of their having done so in London, but they have been players for years. Well able to act the perfect butler and housekeeper, as well as ghosts, you see."

I looked down at my hands as he fell silent. For a long time no one spoke. At last, telling myself I must not be a coward, I said, "It *was* Edwin? Edwin who was behind all this? But *why*?"

My tears began to fall when he nodded, although I did not realize it.

"Daniel Whittingham died in early July, not in September," he told me. "Do you remember me telling you the Whittinghams sometimes left everything to their daughters? That is what happened here. I suspect the old man had you both investigated since he knew so little of either of you, and not liking what his agent discovered about your brother, resolved to leave Bryce House to you."

"What did he find out?" I forced myself to ask, determined to see this through. There would be time to mourn later. A lifetime, in fact.

"Your brother is addicted to gambling. He is not lucky at it. Gamblers seldom are. They just think they will be, and that hope sends them back to the tables again and again. Edwin has been borrowing from his friend Hawes for years. I suspected something must be wrong when I first met you. The upstairs maid would have scorned to take your castoffs, they were so shabby, faded, and old-fashioned. Edwin kept you on a very short leash, didn't he?"

When I nodded, he went on, "You probably are not aware that your brother inherited an excellent fortune from your parents, but he squandered it all. He could not touch your portion from your grandmother, but he controlled everything else. That is why he left you with your aunt, so he would be free to pursue his addiction."

Luke went to pour two glasses of brandy then from the bottle he had brought with him. He wrapped my hands around one of them, but he did not touch me otherwise. I was glad. I think I would have lost all control of myself if he had tried to hold me, comfort me.

"Drink it, Kate," he said softly as he moved away. "This is a terrible shock to you. I wish I could save you from it, but alas, it is not possible. For what it is worth, I think Hawes was in on the scheme from the beginning, if indeed he was not the first to see the possibilities. In July, when your brother was notified of Whittingham's death, he posted down here with Hawes. They found what must have seemed a perfect situation, a haunted house, an eccentric recluse who had shunned the neighborhood, and an elderly lawyer who could be easily hoaxed, for of course, as elder brother, Edwin would handle all the details of the will for you. Men usually do that sort of thing. And so he and Hawes set about making their arrangements. They hired the Harpers for a large sum after they pensioned off the former butler and his wife. You never suspected they were not your great-uncle's servants. Why should you? By September, all was in train, and Edwin went to fetch you. The scheme almost succeeded."

"Yes, it did," I said. "I did indeed."

"In a way, I am to blame for that," Luke said, looking grim again. "If I had not fallen in love with you and insisted on marrying you, Edwin might not have been forced to act as he did. Because, of course, he knew I would discover the truth of who inherited when the marriage contracts were drawn up. And he could not let that happen.

"Tell me, did he ever ask you to sign any papers? Papers that he did not bother to explain?"

I remembered that time in the library, Edwin's eyes glowing with happiness, and I nodded. "He said he had a surprise for me. My dowry," I said dully.

Luke gestured, and obediently I sipped the brandy. It slid down my throat like liquid fire, but it did not warm me.

"No doubt you signed a release, giving him the power to control the money. I will see that is negated.

"But to resume: our coming marriage meant the plan they had made had to be enlarged. It was no longer enough just to let everyone, servants and gentry, think you were short a sheet. Lizzie said the servants here had been told you were highly nervous and given to spells, and that it was important they not upset you in any way. She said they were all frightened of what you might do."

I remembered the little maid who waited on me, how her hands had trembled doing my hair, how she could barely speak to me. Poor child, to be so terrified. I also remembered Edwin alluding to my "weakened mental condition" and how he had claimed I could almost conjure up the ghosts when he spoke to the Beasleys and our dinner guests. But Luke was speaking again, and I put all this aside.

"That scene at your dinner party when the vinegar was served—that was to reinforce the idea of your increasing madness. I guess they thought if you seemed balmy enough, I would not marry you. Since I showed no signs of crying off, they were forced to go further. They had to drive you insane. That or kill you."

"Edwin would never have done that!" I cried, lashing out at him. "Never!"

"Perhaps not. But Hawes would," came the quick retort.

I sank back in my chair as he went on, "He was as desperate for money as your brother, and he knew Edwin would never win enough to repay his debt. By the way, that business of Edwin having to sleep here for thirty-one nights was concocted to keep you here so they could work their wiles on you. That condition in the will confused me right from the beginning. It seemed so quixotic."

I had been thinking. "They must have drugged me," I said slowly. "They must have put something in my wine or my food. How else could I have slept so soundly that they could carry me down to the basement without waking me, or place that knife at my bedside? Why, they even spattered the front of my nightrobe with blood and stained my right hand with it."

"Yes, this was all most carefully thought out, and there was no reason for it to fail as long as you remained a spinster. There, I am afraid, your brother did fail miserably. You are beautiful and spirited and good, full of intelligence and life. How on earth did he hope to keep you unmarried, Kate?"

"Perhaps because he knew no one would want a madwoman for a wife," I told him. Unbidden, I took another sip of my brandy.

"Yes, that bloody knife and gown were the final piece of business. It is entirely possible your brother fought against using them, but Hawes must have convinced him there was no other way. And I don't think Edwin meant to put you in Bedlam. No, he probably intended to hire a nurse and install you both in some little rural cottage."

"You do not have to try to make me feel better, Luke," I said. "It would be impossible to anyway. What Edwin is guilty of trying to do is . . ."

I stopped, took a deep breath, and changed the subject. "What do we do now?" I asked.

"I will confront the two of them tomorrow, threaten them if necessary with the law. I except they will be off like a shot, both of them, the Harpers as well. And then we will close Bryce House for good and retire to the Court. We can be married next week."

"I do not want Edwin to suffer," I found myself saying. "I could not live with myself if I thought he was in want, or imprisoned in Newgate for debt."

I was remembering his looks of despair, his obvious reluctance today for what he was doing. More important, he was my brother.

"I will see he has enough money to pay his debts and make a fresh start somewhere else," Luke said. He sounded almost bored. I suspect it was because he did not want me to thank him, or fall weeping on his neck.

"Do you want to see him?" he added.

I thought about it, biting my lower lip. At last I looked at him straight. "No. I do not want to see him ever again," I said.

"And so you shall not," he told me, just as serious.

"Time for you to go to bed, Kate," he said then. "I will stay with you tonight. Tomorrow this will all be over. Finish your brandy and get ready for bed, there's a good girl."

I did as I was told. Luke tucked me into bed. He had removed his coat and cravat and boots. Now he lay down next to me, carefully not touching me. We remained like that for a long time, neither of us asleep. I knew he was waiting for me to turn to him; that he would not touch me until I showed him I wanted him to, and I wondered such an arrogant man could be so understanding. But I knew that if I let him hold me, comfort me, I would dissolve. And that would never do, for I must stay strong and resolute until all this was resolved. And I must not think of happier days when Edwin was my shining big brother, or love that did not last, or the comfort I could find in Luke's arms, just by opening my own.

It was then I smelled once more the scent of lilacs. I knew Luke smelled it too, for he stirred beside me.

"Yes, she is here," I whispered as I looked toward the door. Luke had left a candle burning on the mantelpiece. It was light enough for me to see her there. She stood quietly, neither weeping nor wringing her hands, and I knew she was giving me a gift, that she had come here tonight only to convince Luke I had not been imagining things, to prove that she did indeed exist and there were such things as ghosts.

"She is standing before the door to the hall," I said on a gentle exhale. "Do not move suddenly."

I heard his sharp intake of breath, and I knew he was seeing May Whittingham, if that was who she was. She seemed even paler, very weak and fragile, but even though she was barely there, I thought she was trying to smile. Because I at least would have a happy ending? I cried for her a little then.

There was a stronger scent of lilacs for a moment, and then she was gone, disappearing like ribbons of fog do when there is a wind shift. I knew I would never see her again.

Chapter Twenty-One

I was awake before Luke the next morning, and I turned my head to observe him. He was sleeping on his stomach, one arm around his pillow, one around me. With his eyes closed and his rugged face relaxed, he looked much younger. I slid away from him, careful not to wake him, and went to the dressing room. There was some cold water left. I made do, leaving some for Luke.

As I was struggling with my gown, he woke and stretched. I could see his reflection in the mirror above my dressing table.

"You look a pirate, sir," I told him, eyeing the impressive beginnings of a black beard.

"And will continue to do so," he said as he swung his legs over the side of the bed. "I have no liking for shaving in cold water."

"Since there is no razor, the decision does not arise."

He nodded, and before he went to the dressing room, he helped me fasten the back of my gown. It was not the moment to comment on his expertise, but it was duly noted.

As he used my comb, he said, "I did not dream that ghost last night, did I?"

"No, she was there."

"It is amazing," he said softly. "And here I was so sure ghosts were only figments of the imagination, conjured up by slightly hysterical, rabbity females."

"Thank you."

He grinned at me then, that white slash that did

such devastating things to my insides. "Time we set about concluding this adventure, love," he said as he bundled up the white costume. "Shall we go down to the library? We can have breakfast at the Court later."

There was no one stirring in the upper hall. I could hear servants' voices somewhere in the distance, but the maids had not progressed to this floor as yet. It was very early.

We saw no one at all as we went down the stairs and across the hall to the library.

"I think some coffee might be in order," Luke said as he rang the bell.

Harper was quick to respond. I watched his face pale when he saw me, then turn positively gray when Luke held out The Gentleman's costume.

"I believe this is yours, Harper," he said. "Dispose of it. We will have coffee, and perhaps some scones, Kate? And immediately."

Harper managed to collect the bundle of clothes, although he dropped the hat once on his way to the door. He was shaking badly. After a few minutes, I moved to the window.

"What are you looking at?" Luke asked.

"I am waiting for the Harpers to appear on their way to the gatehouse and escape," I said. "It is a lovely morning for traveling, don't you agree? Ah, here they come now. I do not think it can be good for them to run like that at their age and the size they are, do you?"

"I gather we will have to make do without coffee," Luke observed. But there he was wrong, for a beaming Lizzie, nodding and smiling at me as if she at least had never doubted my sanity, came in with a large tray.

I could tell she was eager to linger, hear our conversation. How disappointed she must have been when all Luke said before he dismissed her was to ask Mr. Whittingham to be good enough to step down to the library.

We drank our coffee, and Luke enjoyed a plate of

muffins hot from the oven. Idly, I wondered where Mrs. Harper had learned to cook so well. It must have been difficult, when she was on the stage. I myself had no appetite. My breath was coming quickly, and my heart beating erratically just thinking of the coming confrontation.

"Best you leave now, Kate," Luke told me. "Your brother should be here soon."

There was a small reception room next to the library. It had been built originally as a place for guests to wait to be received, and we had never used it.

I had left the door of it slightly ajar. It seemed an age before I heard Edwin coming down the stairs. He was hurrying, and I knew he had looked into my room and discovered it empty. I turned my back so I would not be tempted to look at him. I had meant what I told Luke last night. I did not care to see Edwin again.

Luke must have met him at the library door, for I could hear them plainly. I did not want to, but I found myself listening in some sort of perverted fascination.

"Where is she?" Edwin began, blustering and sounding concerned. "You do not understand, my lord! You were wrong to rescue her! No matter what she has told you, Kate is dangerous, although I agree she seems sane enough. I had no intention of having this known, but now I see I must tell you or you will not know what your life would be like if you married her, or what would happen to the succession if you got children of her.

"Only two nights ago she tried to kill Brede Hawes. He bears the wound in his hand even now. We can only be thankful he woke when he did to see her clutching a knife. She tried to stab him in the heart. He was able to deflect the blow. Since that time I have had to keep her locked in her room. I have no idea how she contacted you—some romantic maid, I suppose—but a doctor from Southampton is on his way here now. No doubt he will insist she be committed to an insane asylum. She is mad, my lord, mad!"

He stopped suddenly, as if conscious that Luke had

not said a word. I could not tell how the earl looked, of course, but when he did speak, I shuddered.

"You are despicable. This is your sister you are speaking of, and you have been trying to drive her mad for the money she inherited. And why? To feed a gambling habit. Do not bother to deny it. I know all about the contents of Daniel Whittingham's will. I had a most interesting letter from your attorney, sir, in answer to a query of mine; Mr. Gardner has done some trifling work for me. It was not difficult to discover the contents of the will. Do not bother to tell me how Kate signed away the estate to you. You gulled her, talking of dowries. If you attempt to fight this, I will bring you down so hard, you will never see the other side of a prison wall in your lifetime. I trust we understand each other?

"Good. Kate does not care to see you in want. She has some feelings still for the brother she once loved, in spite of my misgivings. Come in here and we will discuss what you will need to settle your debts and start over.

"I will make arrangements for you to take the next ship sailing for foreign parts from Southampton. In return for this largesse, you are never to return to England, never write to Kate or try to see her."

I did not hear what, if anything, Edwin had to say for I shut the door then. I waited for it to be over by a window, staring out at nothing and trying to think of something, *anything* else lest I lose my composure.

It seemed a very long time before Luke came to fetch me. The carriage was at the door, and as we went down the drive, I did not look back.

"It is all settled?" I asked. "Hawes, as well?"

"Yes, I spoke to him after I had seen your brother," Luke said. He was frowning, and with his unshaven face, he looked dangerous. "He tried to put all the blame on Edwin, of course, but I was having none of that. You may rest easy, my dear. You will never see either one of them again."

I leaned back against the leather squabs and closed my eyes.

For a while we rode in silence. I could feel the black waves of depression that threatened to overcome me, and I fought them back with as much energy as I could. Luke Tremaine deserved a wife who was not a poor, sniveling thing mired in the past and broken by sadness. It would not be easy for me, but I would try because he was worth any effort of mine.

"Dear me," I managed to say in what I hoped was a light voice. "I fear I am disgraced, sir. Why, you did not give me time to fetch my gloves or bonnet or even my reticule. Whatever will your mother think, to see such a hoyden coming to take her place at Bryce Court? And the servants, too, will no doubt be horrified that their new countess is so careless."

He looked down at me, a smile coming to his eyes. "It does not matter what any of them think," he said. "I find you perfection, ma'am. Absolute perfection, in fact."

And then I was in his arms, and then it all came right at last.

We were married a week later, and a week later still the dowager countess left for Plymouth and a ship sailing for Bermuda. She was attended by her maid and two footmen, and a dear friend who had family there. I am afraid Luke and I did not miss her as we should.

Luke attended to the closing of Bryce House, since neither of us cared to sell it. The servants were either pensioned off or found new positions. Lizzie did not come to the Court, to my relief. Instead Luke got her and her sister placed with a friend of his near Salisbury. I had told him I would prefer not to employ the servants who had been at Bryce House, and as with all my requests, he was careful to carry them out. I had only to ask.

*   *   *

It was on a beautiful May morning that Bryce
House burned to the ground. We could smell the
smoke of it all the way to the Court, and Luke rode
over with a group of men to see if it could be saved.
Some of the stone walls were still standing, but the
interior was gone completely. It seemed strange that
such a thing could happen. No one lived there anymore, not even a caretaker in the gatehouse, and there
was no chance wandering vagrants would invade it. It
had too bad a reputation for that. Secretly, I suspected
Brede Hawes had come back and torched it, for I
knew Edwin had sailed to the United States, to a port
called Philadelphia. It seemed the kind of revenge
Hawes might exact. And to think at one time I had
thought him such a nice man, so kind and good, and
such a friend of my brother's. I was discovering people
often wore masks that had nothing to do with their
real selves.

Except Luke. Luke was just the man you thought
he was and I cannot tell you how I loved him for it.
I certainly had no idea love could be like this, so full
and rich and compelling. He had only to look at me
and I was lost—and, I am happy to say, so was he
when the tables were turned.

One day, shortly after the ruins had been inspected
and pulled down so any children playing there would
not be hurt, Luke asked me to ride over to what remained of Bryce House with him.

When I saw the blackened walls, the piles of broken
stone, I gasped, for the ruin of the house was so final
and complete.

"I am sorry now I did not think to take the family
journals from the library," I said as Luke lifted me
from Imp's back. "I never did get to read what old
Daniel had to say about the ghosts."

"I have them safe," Luke said, putting his arm
around me as we went around the foundation together. "I thought you might want to see them some
day, when all that happened here was not still a bad
taste in your mouth. Besides, even if you do not, our

children may well want to know more of their Whittingham relatives."

That reminded me of Edwin, and I shook my head. I had not put down in my journal what had happened. I had only said my brother had decided to seek his fortune in the New World and put a period to the page.

"Here we are," Luke said, indicating a box placed in the grass beside a pile of charred timbers and blackened stone. "I warn you, this will not be pleasant, Kate," he added, as he bent to open it.

I was startled to see that the box contained bones, discolored old brittle bones. There was a skull, too, and I put one hand to my throat and stepped back.

"Where were these found?" I asked.

"Near a wall in the cellar," Luke said evenly. "Just about at the place where we felt that icy, threatening cold."

"Someone was buried there? Wasn't that unusual?"

He grimaced. "There is another skull, too. A very small one."

He held it out to me. In his big hand it looked as if it had belonged to a doll.

"A baby was buried there, too?" I asked in wonder.

Luke put the little skull back in the box carefully and rose, dusting his gloved hands. "I think these bones belonged to your lady ghost, Kate. And I think the baby was hers."

I could only stare at him as he led me away to seat me on a marble bench that had graced the gardens. "What do you think happened?" I asked.

He stared at the place where Bryce House had been as he spoke. "I think your May Whittingham fell in love with a man her father would not allow her to marry. I think they were lovers, and she found herself with child. Perhaps she managed to hide her condition from her parents, but there was no hiding a new baby when it came, of course. And I think her father, stern, straitlaced Whittingham that he was, set it about that she had gone off on a journey with her mother in that carriage Mrs. Rogers told you of. In reality, I think he buried her and the child in the cellar wall. It would have been easy, especially if they were enlarging the cellars at that time."

"You mean she died in childbirth, the baby with her?" I asked, then bit my lip.

"No, Kate, I do not think so," he said as he took my hands in his. "If they had, they would have been buried in the graveyard. Remember, this all happened in the 1600's. I think he killed them and walled them up together because he could not bear the shame of having a daughter with a bastard child."

"So that is why she became a ghost for all those years. Why she could not rest," I said slowly. "That must be why she wept, and looked so sad."

The wind ruffled my hair, and I could feel Luke's hands holding mine tightly. I was lucky, and I knew it.

"Poor girl," I said. "That poor, poor girl.

"But Luke, how could any father do such a thing? How *could* he?"

He shrugged. "In anger, in disgust—because he was a monster?"

I looked back at the box. It seemed small to hide such a big sin.

"The men sifting through the ashes found something else," Luke said as he reached into his pocket. He held out the circle pin I had seen the ghost wear. Blackened and smeared with soot, it was the final proof.

"Yes, that is her pin," I said. "Put it back with the rest of her, please."

"We can give her and the baby a proper burial. Would you like to bring her back to the Court? There is a pleasant graveyard there."

I thought for a moment before I shook my head. "No, I would like to bury her here where she lived all her life. Not in the family plot. Never there. Perhaps down in the beech wood near the pool? She must have known the spot, even played there when she was a child."

"Of course. I will see to it, and a headstone as well," he promised me.

I smiled at him before I leaned forward and kissed him lightly, still holding his hands. "Thank you, my darling," I said. "I think I will plant a white lilac at the head of her grave. That way she will always have the scent of them when spring comes around each year."

I went into his arms then. "Hold me, Luke," I whispered. "Hold me tight! It does not seem fair that I have so much happiness when she had none, does it?"

He did not answer. Instead he kissed me until I forgot May Whittingham completely.

Do you know, somehow I am sure she would not have minded.